Author's Note:
The Northeast Blackout of 2003 as defined by Wikipedia: A widespread power outage throughout parts of the Northeastern and Midwestern United States and parts of the Canadian providence of Ontario on Thursday, August 14, 2003, beginning just after 4:10 pm EDT. A *Readers-Digest* version of the events is as follows:

The Midcontinent Independent System Operator (MISO) at the Dayton location suffered a failure of their emergency notification system. They had no knowledge that several major transmission lines became tangled in tree branches and snapped. FirstEnergy in Cleveland and Toledo were experiencing issues because of MISO's failure but had no clue where the problems originated. First Edison of Ohio was also completely blind. Its alarm and control systems had failed, and no one in the control room had grasped that their computer system had not been operating properly for over an hour.

What had been a local event, slowly brewing for two hours in the afternoon heat, suddenly reached a boiling point and pushed across Northeastern America and into Canada. As some circuits failed, power surged into others, overloading them, and tripping off circuit breakers in a cascading effect. Some of this sensitive hardware would be damaged beyond repair and need to be replaced. The overloaded lines and circuits in Cleveland had cut pathways toward the west and created a massive power surge flowing east to New York and Ontario in a counterclockwise sweep around Lake Erie.

The system failures in Dayton and Toledo essentially created a firewall that would not allow the rest of the grid to the south and the west to compensate for the imbalances created. The entire Northeastern United States and Ontario became a separate electrical island, with no input from the rest of the grid. Within that electrical island, power demand exceeded supply. With no way to draw in more power, the entire system became unstable and crashed. Once the power surge began in Cleveland, the system took a total of 90 seconds to implode.

Information surrounding the blackout was so disoriented that New York Mayor Michael Bloomberg and state Governor George Pataki made public statements that the event started in Canada. With the Twin Towers attack less than two years earlier, the politics of blame-finding were almost as important as solving the problem.

The immediate reports that the event was not terrorist-related had a major calming effect on the public. Even though the repairs took longer than promised on the radio, communities at least did not have to deal with fear. The date was also important. In mid-August, the major inconvenience was air conditioning, which most people could withstand. The commuters from the subways of Manhattan were shown on the news wearily walking home, the Brooklyn Bridge filled with pedestrians. There was also a light-hearted side, that grocery stores gave away ice cream before it melted and good Samaritans directing traffic through dark-stoplight intersections. It seemed that the absence of terror made the emergency easier to take.

An investigation was launched into the cause of the blackout and the solutions needed to keep it from happening again. However, the inherent reasons for its occurrence are still in place: A multitude of power companies control sections of the country and their systems do not communicate well with each other. When they do, it's through the internet, allowing incoming and outgoing data transfers. Transfers that can never be 100% protected. And these companies are trustee-owned and profit-oriented. New technology that promises dollar savings is courted, and although security may be a priority, it is not pursued with the same verve as solutions that help the bottom line.

What would happen if someone studied the scenario that occurred on August 14, 2003, finding a way to reproduce it in the computer systems and unleash it with some new twists? Terrifying twists. Maybe something as simple as instead of in the heat of summer…
a Cold Winter.

The Cold Winter. Original Publish Date: August 14, 2017—14th anniversary of the 2003 blackout. Second edition April 2, 2024.

The Cold Winter
By Chris A. Underwood

Contents

Chapter 1: The Boat...7

Chapter 2: The Awakening. 16

Chapter 3: The Neighbors...25

Chapter 4: The Five F's. 38

Chapter 5: The Purchase. 68

Chapter 6: Day 2..75

Chapter 7: The Walkers. 102

Chapter 8: Glory Be. 114

Chapter 9: Paying Charter. 135

Chapter 10: Get yourself to church, boy. 138

Chapter 11: The human animal. 165

Chapter 12: The railroad gets wheels.................................178

Chapter 13: Glowing Mudhens...186

Chapter 14: Boring Insects 193

Chapter 15: Doctor Dictator..210

Chapter 16: Bridge to Oblivion. 225

Chapter 17: Son of Satan...231

Chapter 18: Wolf Pack...256

Chapter 19: Doctor Who. 262

Chapter 1: The Boat.

The truck door closed with a reassuring thud. Thom Vesper looked over the marina and took a deep breath. It's the day. The day he'd been dreaming about. Everything was perfect; the seagulls were flying overhead, the smell of the sea in the air, a blue cloudless sky looking down upon him. And it's warm … so very warm. He paused to take in the heat and let the sun warm his skin. Yes, today was the day.

The marina was laid back, with not much trash lying around, but it wouldn't be considered clean either. Only a small section of the parking lot was paved, the rest was gravel. A section was designated for boat repair, many were on stilts, and a few looked neglected and forgotten. A partial fence had been erected to screen them off, but never completed. This was a fisherman's marina, not a country club, and it seemed that the owner took some pride in that fact. The harbormasters' building could have used some updating, but it was quaint and had some character. It had a high-pitched roof with some metal needing a little attention. There were about seventy boats in the harbor, and the piers looked to be in good repair. Thom stretched his neck to inspect the boats and the pier pilings, but it had to wait. He expected to get a better view later. First, he needed to chat with the harbormaster.

The entrance was nicely painted; there was no doubt that it was a door of significance. Buildings without a focal point door were always confusing. That's why Thom's house back home had an advantage back in the Storm, with multiple front doors. He smiled to himself just looking at the door. It was so hard to get the thoughts of the Storm out of his head, but he took it in stride. It was a great day. The day he'd been waiting many years for. As he walked in, he felt like he was walking into the set of an old movie. All exposed wood and rafters, with junk hanging on the walls. Mostly cool junk, but there were a few items that seemed to be on the last stop to the dumpster and they found their way onto a wall. Some light was coming in from the other side of the room. A double glass door and an array of windows looking out on the harbor filled the wall. A long stream of windows

7

was up high in the gable, bringing in lots of light. They seemed to be stained glass, with sparkles of color coming to the floor, but it was not stained glass. Years of neglect with smoke residue and grime had colored the windows creating the effect. Yes, this was the place he had hoped to find.

Three guys were sitting to his left around an unlit potbelly stove playing dominoes. One was smoking a cigar in the room, which surprised him. Thom walking in the door did not interrupt the fishing story being told. They didn't care. The harbormaster's desk was off to the right, and the old guy looked to be playing solitaire on his computer.

Thom approached the harbormaster.

"How are you doing?" he asked.

"Doing good today, yourself?" Thom could tell from his eye contact that he was not irritated by the interruption, but he seemed kind of indifferent.

"I'm Thom Vesper, and it's a great day," Thom said with a big smile as he extended his hand.

"Dave Marcus, I'm the Harbormaster of Sunset Harbor," Dave said as he shook Thom's hand firmly.

Thom hoped Dave was ready to talk business. This is the business that dreams are made of; at least that's what they say. Buying your first large boat is supposed to be a day you remember fondly, for a while anyway. He had owned a couple sailboats on a small reservoir back home, but nothing like the purchase he mapped out for today. The twenty-two-foot Catalina prepared him for the step up to the twenty-eight-foot O'Day, but today, today was the day.

"Randal Franks. What's he like?" Thom said, abruptly starting the conversation. It was a completely open question, giving him the freedom to say whatever came to mind about Randal. Add in the fact that he didn't know who Thom was. Maybe he was a bill collector or a relative or an old friend. Dave didn't know, and Thom put it out there, hoping he would get a nugget of information he didn't already have.

"He's a good kid. In slip K-12, with the Gemini Cat. His boat is for sale, you thinking about buying it?" The harbormaster was trying to feel Thom out before going any further about one of his tenants. It was a trait that Thom appreciated, especially considering that he planned to become a tenant himself.

"Yep, I'm here to take a look at it. Is he usually on time with his dock fees, and is he in good standing with the harbor?"

"Yes, he's never been late, and I don't think he's in a bad pinch. He's just not getting as many charters as he'd like with that boat," Dave replied.

Thom nodded his head, "The thirty-four footer would only be good for day charters, not for longer multiple day runs, I agree. Does he get along well with folks here at the harbor?"

"Oh, I haven't heard anything negative; I think he gets along with the other Live-Aboard's here at the marina. I've seen him kick in and help with repairs to other folk's boats. He's a good kid and seems to be a good captain."

The conversation had gotten back to where it started — with Randal being a good kid. "It's great that he helps out the neighbors, all of that sounds really good." Thom figured that he had probably mined all the data he was going to get here, and expected to say goodbye in the next minute. But the harbormaster wanted to be congenial and asked the question that Thom wanted to avoid.

"So where you from, Thom?"

"I'm from Ohio," Thom said with a firm lock on his eyes. Dave took a little unconscious step back. The guys telling fish stories became a little quieter. Maybe they now cared.

Searching for words a little, he asked, "Haven't seen many folks from Ohio. Were you there…?"

9

"Yes. Yes, I was, for the whole bit." Thom stepped away from the counter, adding: "And that's pretty much why I'm *here* now." His big smile returned, trying to make light of the subject, not wanting to elaborate any further.

Dave didn't deserve any further conversation in Thom's mind, especially on that subject. He didn't give Thom any information that he hadn't already gotten from Randal himself in emails. He didn't share anything of Randal Franks' character. There was no extra information other than his payment was never late and maybe he was a good captain. Still, it was a good conversation, and it confirmed the information he had gotten already, proving this was a great day. It was a really great day.

The conversation had caught the attention of the domino players at the potbelly stove. They watched Thom walk to the glass doors leading out to the harbor, and he called over to them.

"You boys have a good day now." A couple yelled back likewise and got back to their game.

He stepped out the door and was hit with the smell of sea air, the sunshine, and a wonderful view of the marina from a high point. The realization that directions to slip K-12 could have been a good question occurred to him as he started down the steps. It really didn't matter. There was no hurry to meet Randal Franks. The slip would probably be the end-cap of a pier, just because catamarans take up so much more space than a normal boat. He would find it eventually.

Thom was a person who would walk the marina's piers whenever on vacation at the ocean. Even if he didn't have a charter that day, it was always a joy in his life. The sea brought him tranquility, peace, and clarity. The harbor walk seemed to go on for eternity. The ocean-faring boats were more beautiful than the boats back home in Ohio. Their sleek lines drew him in and caused him to stand and stare. Time seemed to stop, or maybe continue without him.

He looked for familiar things, things that would settle him into a comfort zone. Markers that would connect him to this site and make it feel right. Things that would console him and confirm that this was the right place for his purchase.

That was when he saw it. Falling to his knees, he lowered his head. A pier post, much taller than the rest, stood right before him. A cross member had been attached to it, with a piece of gnarly nautical rope tied into a hoop and draped across the top, hanging off to the side. A cross, with a crown of thorns.

A quick prayer rumbled across his lips followed by a firm Amen. He crossed his chest and looked around to see if anyone noticed what he had just done. It was instinct; he just dropped. No questions. He didn't see anyone looking but decided to do something just in case. He acted like he was tying his shoe and slowly got up while inspecting the pier post. Someone had done this by design; the cross member had been hewn out where the posts crossed, with three rusty lag bolts tying them together. There was no reasonable function for the cross member to be there either. It was not an elaborate hitching post for a boat. And the tattered rope on top was nailed in place; it had all been done on purpose. He turned and smiled. 'Ask for a marker,' he said to himself as he continued his stroll down the pier.

"You look lost," the voice came from a beautiful forty-foot wooden schooner.

"Not everyone who wanders is lost," Thom replied to the gray-haired gentleman. He looked to be in his mid-60s, with a Tommy Bahama T-shirt on. He spoke to Thom from the boat deck, with a cold drink in his hand.

"Can I offer you an iced tea?" He said, as his wife stepped above deck with a pitcher and some cups.

"Well, that's an offer I can't refuse. May I come aboard?" Thom followed the boater's custom of always asking permission of the captain before boarding.

11

Upon their introductions, he found their names to be Dave and Judy Phillips, and this boat was where they lived. Compliments were given to their lovely boat; the woodwork was very nice and warm. They took Thom below deck, and he received a tour of the galley and living area. He was happy to see that there was plenty of headroom and space and he did not need to bow his six-foot height inside the boat. He enjoyed the coziness of it.

"I'm here today to meet Randal Franks." Thom began.

"Oh, Randal is a great guy, I like him a lot. I'll be sad to see him go when his boat sells," Dave said.

"I'm here to see the boat," Thom informed them. "But he doesn't have to leave once he sells the boat. I understand he wants to buy a larger one, so he could dock it here, right?"

"Oh, Randal has dreams," Dave said with a smile. Then Judy completed his thought for him.

"He wants a larger catamaran that he can use for longer charters, up to a week. He also thinks that he needs to step up to a nicer marina to set sail from with the richer clientele. I can see his logic, but we'll just hate to see him go," she said with a sigh while offering a seat in the galley.

"Do you talk with him very much?" Thom said while they sat down at the table.

"Oh, he comes by all the time and checks on us. He keeps the motor in good shape, and the plumbing. Because you know an old boat is like an old person, you must always keep the plumbing in check!" Judy laughed at her own statement with a little twinkle in her eye. She had a genuine sense of humor, and it was easy to see why Randal would go out of his way to be around them.

"So, what brings you to Naples, Florida?" Dave inquired.

"I'm trying to decide if you want the long version or the short one," Thom said.

"Give us the long one!" Judy replied enthusiastically.

He kept it short; "I'm a computer guy. I've come down here to do a project for a company called Whitehouse Clothes. Have you heard of them?"

After they shook their heads, he continued.

"Well, they are installing a new purchase order system that I've installed for five other companies, and it's something that will take about a year to complete. I've always wanted to live on a boat, so this is my perfect chance while working on the project."

"Sounds like a good plan to me, but hard to justify buying a boat for one year of living aboard," Dave said.

"Yep, you are right. But this might be my last project; I'm looking to retire after this one." Both Dave and Judy's faces brightened with the statement. It was obvious that they loved hearing stories of someone reaching for the brass ring and finding a way to actually get a grip on it. It seemed that they had done so themselves and wanted to share the experience, not hoard it.

"But you seem kind of young to be retiring, especially in this economy," offered Judy.

"Thank you, Judy, I'm fifty-five, but I'm told my baby face doesn't give it away. I work in a specialized field, and they pay me very well, so my family and I are okay. But I don't plan to totally retire; I have to keep busy, right? The charter boat business has some interest to me, and my wife will be joining me eventually to help get that going."

"That sounds like an interesting plan, Thom. Do you guys have any kids?" Judy said as she leaned forward into the conversation.

"Yes, we do, a daughter in college, and a son getting ready to go. He's a real momma's boy, so we will be looking at schools down here for him. We won't let him get too far from us, that's for sure," Thom replied with a warm smile.

13

"Where does your daughter go to school?" Judy inquired, knowing it would tell a lot about Thom. Ivy League? Community College? Some small college no one has ever heard of?

"She goes to the home school, the one where both my wife and I are alumni. Ohio State."

Thom waited for all the air to get sucked out of the room.

"My goodness," Judy spoke first.

"Were you there for the storm?" Dave asked.

It was weird how there was no official name for it. Calling it "The Storm" was actually a fitting title. In New Orleans they knew what to call it: Katrina. In New Jersey it was Sandy. In Manhattan it was Nine-Eleven. The War to End all Wars was the original moniker for World War I, a name that proved to be wishful thinking.

The Storm was just something really bad that kept on getting worse the longer it went on. Something so hard to give a name to, you would almost belittle it with a simple word. Some news sources called it The Outage, or The Christmas Blackout, but those terms didn't capture the event at all. A Storm pounds you and surrounds you, and it's relentless. It was "The Storm That Wouldn't Stop." The Cold Winter.

"Yes, we were there," Thom replied with a gaze into both their eyes, and then he had to look away. It was amazing what a chilling effect the subject had on him, even five years after the fact.

"They say that Ohio was hit the hardest," Judy said. There was so much feeling in her words; Thom imagined from her body language that she wanted to give a motherly hug to make it all go away.

"Yeah, we were the red-headed stepchild in their efforts. They sent all the help to New York and the New England states. We had to fend for ourselves pretty much," Thom was uncomfortable with the turn of the conversation and began to squirm in his seat. While Captain Dave searched his brain for a conversation segue to change the subject, Thom bailed him out.

14

"It is therapeutic for me to talk about it, and maybe I'll share some stories over a bottle of wine sometime. It's just that now is not the best time. I need to get my head straight for maybe buying a boat, you know?" The space filled with smiles again and the tension thankfully evaporated.

"I'd like to thank you for the tea, and again, I love this schooner. I am a woodworker in my spare time, and the warmth of wood does it all for me," Thom said as he prepared to exit, taking in the beautiful woodwork one more time.

A boat is a small space, and all the details of the woodwork are very close, almost in a person's face. If nice woodwork is going to be attempted, it must be done right, as it was in this schooner. Captain Dave and Thom spoke a little more about the specs of the vessel as they worked their way to the gangplank. Thom was completely captivated, and Captain Dave was thrilled to have someone interested in hearing the details. Of course, every captain's favorite subject is his boat. Upon stepping off the boat, the captain asked Thom the question he had been itching to ask since they first met.

"How often do you pause to tie your flip-flops?" He said it with a completely straight face, trying to catch Thom off guard.

"Three times a day, without fail. Some days it's many more," Thom shot back with an equally straight face. "You always nail some rope to a pier post?"

"It brings me luck," he said with a small smile.

"I'm sure it does."

Thom turned and walked down the pier, his smile slowly fading from his face. Darkness was falling around him, as if thick storm clouds had rolled in and blocked out the bright sunlight. Thoughts of Ohio came flooding in; they couldn't be stopped no matter how hard he tried.

Chapter 2: The Awakening.

The normal office chatter was going on. This was an IT department, and the nerd references were everywhere. The Star Wars pictures and the off-the-wall junk littering the cubes made it Nerd Central. Several were decorated with Christmas lights and ornaments, with the holiday being just three days away. A long table in the center area of the cubes had cookies and brownies set out in rows. The gluttonous scene was a common sight this time of year and a little ironic considering how scarce food was going to become very soon. The IT department was in the basement, just like so many other businesses. IT is used and abused, stuck in the dungeon, out of sight.

At 11:11 a.m., lights flickered once, twice, a third time, then gone. It was totally black for ten seconds, and then the emergency generator kicked in. The lights were just enough to get around, and while it was comforting to be able to see, the dimness of the lights gave an eerie effect. There was an uproar of complaints that people had just lost their work, and "Why now?" and all the normal reaction to a power spike. But this was different, and it became apparent very quickly.

"Hey man," someone called out. "Does anyone have a cell phone signal? Mine is out."

The panic started to ramp up for some people. The cell phones were not normally lost during a power spike, but none had service. The landlines were expected to be out, along with internet service, but cell phones were difficult to take. The woman in the cube next to Thom's simply stared at her phone in disbelief, waiting for the signal bars to respond. A portable radio was turned on. The radio station was normally a hard-rocking station, and seemed amateurish and bewildered as the DJ spoke on the air:

"We are broadcasting on emergency generators here at Q-FM, and we will get information to you as we receive it here at the station. All we can tell you now is that our sister stations in Cleveland and Cincinnati are both experiencing the power-outage as well. At this time, it appears the outage is statewide and possibly more. Please listen to this station for updates and information."

Thom Vesper began packing up his office stuff into a backpack. His buddy, Carl, stepped into the cube and put his hand on Thom's shoulder. "This is it, isn't it?" He looked fearful, but also a bit amused. "Do you think this is really bad?"

"It just might be the end of the world as we know it," Thom replied with a smirk. "Or a great opportunity for overtime to clean up the mess."

It was tough seeing Carl scared. Carl was a black man standing six-foot-three, and quite imposing with the full beard and shaved head look. He attended college twenty years ago on a rugby scholarship, not football, even though he had the build and ability. He would say that rugby was full of life lessons. 'There's only one referee on the field,' he once said. 'That one ref can't see everything. Rugby is about learning how to cheat and get away with it, just like life. Because all the players are doing it.'

They found their boss upstairs standing by a cubicle that had a battery powered radio playing. A different station was on, an affiliate of Clear Channel which owns stations across the nation. They were listing the affected areas of the blackout, and it was extensive. Indiana, Ohio, Michigan, Pennsylvania, New York, and the New England states were reporting no power. The radio station then confirmed that their stations in St. Louis and Lexington, Kentucky had experienced temporary issues but were expected to come back online.

The boss turned to Carl and Thom when the report was over and sarcastically told them that all their projects needed to be done by the end of the business today. The uncomfortable little chuckle was followed with confirmation that if things didn't come around in the next half hour, the workday was over. They were told that if the power did return tomorrow, it was all hands-on deck to clean up the mess that this outage caused. Christmas was three days away, but if the mess was big enough, they would be working through the holiday.

They were a retail clothing company, and the cash registers had to be polled each night to log sales numbers and inventory changes at the retail outlets. This outage would create havoc not only for the stores in the outage area, but all over the country. The stores with power would not be able to report the days' transactions to the home office and clear the log for the next day. When the power returned, there would be quite a mess indeed.

The radio announcer began going through his report again, and everyone moved closer to see if there was any new information. It was essentially the same, but a shocking tidbit had been added at the end. He stated that a rumor was circulating that the blackout was a cyber-attack. It was merely a rumor he reiterated, but there it was, nonetheless.

Carl looked at Thom shaking his head, and boss man Mike, a man normally in complete control was staring at the radio, dumbfounded.

"This is crazy," Thom finally said out loud. "Even if this is true, why would they tell us so soon? People might get a little nutso when they hear something like that."

"Maybe it just leaked out by mistake," Mike thoughtfully said.

"Could be," Thom said. "But I would think a news organization should feel obligated to not yell fire in a crowded theater. This will create panic."

"Yes," Mike rebutted. "But Clear Channel will be able to proudly say that they got the scoop on all the other stations."

Carl watched the conversation in silence, the tension slowly building. He and Thom returned downstairs and saw that the shadowy basement had gotten even scarier. It seems the rumor had made its way to other stations as well as Clear Channel.

Thom made his way to his cube and pulled out a stash of protein bars from a drawer. He then added them to the oatmeal stashed in another. With the office backpack full, it was time to get out of here; if he stayed much longer, he might get drawn into this frenzy as well. Looking up from his desk he saw Prakash, Ahmed, and Marsha in the cube doorway. This was his management team, and they were looking for answers. He shared Mike's instructions for work, but they wanted more.

"Go home, and stay home," he said. Don't try to travel; it's going to be crazy on the roads tonight."

"But there's power in Kentucky," Ahmed said. "I heard it on the radio."

"Forget it. There is a storm coming in too, remember? We were all expecting a short day today anyhow because of the weather. It's cold out there, and the traffic will be horrible. If you know someone with a fireplace, stay there. Otherwise camp out in your basement. Just don't do what everyone else is doing, like traveling... and freaking out," Thom said, raising his arms and looking to the others in the basement. "Don't do like they do, and hopefully we will be back in here in a couple days cleaning up the mess this caused."

Reluctantly the doorway cleared, and he noticed that Carl had been watching over the cube wall, listening in. As Thom tried to make an exit, Carl was right on his heels.

"This is really bad, ain't it?" he said over Thom's shoulder as they entered the stairwell. "You told me a while ago that you were a prepper guy. What hints do you got for a guy in the inner city if this thing goes longer than a couple days? What can I do?"

"Alright, come with me," They both hesitated before pushing the door release, because of the "fire alarm will sound" sign on the handle. Thom smiled at him outside, "I've always wanted to use that door, look how close we are to our cars!" Carl didn't smile.

"Come sit in my truck while it warms up. I'm not the prepper I used to be, Carl, you know that." The coldness of the truck was turning Thom's words into visible puffs of air.

19

"The preoccupation of prepping and researching consumed me. It made me crazy, and I had to leave it alone. And this event here, even if it is an attack of some sort, it might only last a day or two. We could be right back to normal in time for Christmas."

"But what if it goes longer? You've gotta pull something out for me, us brotha's don't prep." The light statement with a twinkle of a smile softened the tension in the truck.

"Ok, Carl. The rule of thumb is usually to bug out for your safe place within three hours of an event. You won't be able to do that though, so just cuddle up with the kids and camp out in the basement tonight. Literally put up a tent, even if it is makeshift and camp out. It will contain your body heat and be halfway comfortable for the night."

Carl's eyes lit up. "My kids! They will be going crazy waiting for me! I've got to go!"

"Calm down, Carl. It's a madhouse at the schools right now because *everyone* is doing that."

"Nobody is going to take your kids," Thom added. "Your son is a senior right? I bet he is taking charge and rounding up his sisters right now. The middle school and high school are on the same campus, right? They will be fine. Let's take this time to get organized."

Carl was calming down, breaths going in and out a little more slowly.

"What about your kids, Thom? What's going on with them?"

"Cool of you to think of us, Carl, but my wife and I discussed a vague plan if an event happened. Generally, she's in charge of getting the kids and getting home. She'll probably stop off to check on a family or two before heading home though, if I know her."

Carl was getting his head on straight, but he was still uneasy. "Man, ever since Deloris left me with the kids, I've become a worrying mom instead of a protective dad. Alright, back on course. What else?"

20

"If things are still sounding bad tomorrow, want to come and stay with us?"

"Thought you'd never ask."

Carl's face was expressionless; staring straight ahead as he absently said it. A woman was leaving the office building in her wool skirt and coat, carrying a box of belongings. It was so surreal, watching her walk to her car while carefully protecting her office goods. It looked like she was planning to finish her day's work at home.

"In your door pocket is a state map. Let me show you where I live. You won't be able to use GPS this time."

"Yeah, I don't remember much about the time I was there for the cookout. Deloris and I were having a bad day. I probably wouldn't even recognize your house."

"Well, it's got a green roof, but that will be covered in snow, so that's no help, and the number is hard to see really," Thom paused, but then a satisfying solution came to him. "We'll have an American flag out. We usually have one out anyway, even in bad weather. People say it's a disgrace to the flag, to fly it in the rain or snow. But I disagree. When you see the battle pictures and the dude is carrying the tattered and torn flag with holes in it – that's a flag! I think it shows real patriotism." Thom stopped and cleared his throat realizing the moment had gotten away from him.

"Sorry dude," was all he could muster with a little grin.

"No man, I got it. I'll look for a flag." He turned his shoulders square to Thom and said,

"Now. What do I need to do before I show up at your door?"

"That's tough man. Let's think this through." Thom reached into the glove box for a notepad.

"I'm a list guy." Thom continued. "You'll need clothes, but this is not a fashion show. Bring warm stuff that can be layered. And tell your

21

kids to bring all their socks and underwear. If it continues to be bad, doing laundry will be difficult."

Thom began writing on the pad. "Pillows and blankets … all the food in your cupboard, everything. Put your frozen stuff into a cooler, but do it right before you leave. We'll try to keep it frozen as long as possible. Dump your spice drawer in a bag … just bring it all. I've got a stockpile of canned soups and those are bland to begin with; it'll be nasty about the third or fourth time."

Carl followed along, nodding all the way.

"Now, as you are packing this stuff, put it in plastic bins, or boxes or even extra luggage. It will be easier to move that way. First aid. Just sweep all you got into a box. Don't try to sort it, just bring it all. Flashlights, batteries, oil lamps and candles should be a no-brainer, but they need to be on the list. Do you have any camping stuff?"

"My son used to be a boy scout, but he dropped out a few years ago. I'll have him pack whatever he has."

"Yes, anything, especially small stuff that doesn't take up room in the van. Do you have a gun?"

"No, I don't," he shrugged his shoulders.

"What? You're a black man living in a large city, and you don't have a gun?" The words were lighthearted, but still had a sting.

"Don't start profiling; you know how wrong that is," he gave some shit right back. "I went to college so I wouldn't have to own a gun…"

"Well now you do," Thom said.

The glove box opened again, and a 9-millimeter automatic was produced. "This is a 9-mil and it has no safety." Thom inserted the clip into the weapon and looked at Carl squarely, "Have you fired one of these before?"

"A dozen years ago." He took a deep breath, "Man, I don't need a gun. Really."

"It will be just in case. To quote the words of Tarantino: 'It's better to have a gun and not need it, than to need a gun and not have it.'"

There was a silence while the words sunk in. Finally, his hand came forward: "Alright. But I'm giving it back to you next time I see you."

Thom showed him how to cock the gun and put a bullet in the chamber. He then explained the importance of it. "The gun won't fire unless you cock it, alright?" Then he cocked back the cylinder and discharged the bullet in the chamber. When the bullet popped out and he caught it mid-air, Carl kind of smirked at him.

"You like doing that don't you?" he said.

"Do I like discharging bullets from guns? Yes. Discharging it this way seems most appropriate right now," Thom said as he flashed a smile.

"Do you have any silver?" Thom changed the subject.

"What do you mean?"

"Like a nice silverware set you got as a wedding gift, something small with value to barter with."

"No, not really. If there was anything good, she took it." He was getting grumpy again.

"How about an old coin collection or anything like that?" Thom still tried to stir something up.

"I do have a collection my dad gave me, and we might have some old sterling silver candlestick holders, now that I think about it." Thom added it to the list.

"Ok, we are covered in the kitchen, but if you have an old cast iron skillet," Carl was already interrupting with an "oh yeah," so Thom continued,

"You are a cooker, I remember that now. Yeah, bring that, and any other cast iron soup pots you've got. Toni will not be happy to put her

23

nice gourmet kitchen pots and pans over an open fire. You have to help me out there."

Carl liked that comment, anything to feel useful in this *please help me* situation. "How about my turkey fryer?" Carl queried.

"If you have the space. That will take up a lot of room, but definitely bring the propane tank. Do you have just one?"

"I may have two, I'll check."

Reviewing the list, Thom sat back and handed it to him. "I think we have it covered. You go get your kids, my friend. And one thing I want to make completely clear is that if you don't get going by 3 o'clock tomorrow then wait till the next day. Driving on strange roads at night isn't worth the risk. Plan on taking surface roads, not the freeways, just another rule of thumb."

"Ok, Ok. I'm on the job." He was overwhelmed. He took the pistol and the notepad and stepped out of the truck. Thom met him outside to shake hands and give a heartfelt man-hug.

"Good luck and God bless. The next time I see you will be in Galena, alright buddy?"

"Yes Thom, God bless. Be safe in your travel home." His eyes were a little shiny and Thom hesitated when he noticed it. A light snow was starting to come down and it helped to make the goodbye a short one.

Chapter 3: The Neighbors.

Not far away from Thom and Carl were Linda and Allen Lansbury, also residents of the small village of Galena. A nice athletic couple in their early thirties who had been married for a couple years and trying to start a family. At the moment though, they were trying to start the gas pump that wouldn't respond. The station attendant in his little room just raised his arms in a helpless fashion. The pump had stopped working about midway through their fill-up, and both Linda and Allen were poking the buttons in frustration.

Allen took his attention away from the pump and the reality of the situation started to sink in. The gas station was an offshoot of the Giant Eagle grocery store and shared the parking lot. The grocery store was in an odd general location, not so much in a big residential area, more of an office park, and close to the freeway. The big draw of the complex was their gas station and the restaurants surrounding its parking lot for the office lunchtimes. Allen saw that people were pouring out of the restaurants — all with the same dazed look on their faces. The stoplights were dark, the restaurant signs were dark, and so were the restaurants themselves. Finally, Allen motioned to Linda to get back in their SUV to talk to her.

"I think something bad happened."

"Oh come on!" Linda wasn't having any of it. "You're such an alarmist."

Allen turned on the radio just in time to hear the news report that Thom also had heard: "All we can tell you now is that our sister stations in Cleveland and Cincinnati are both experiencing the power outage as well. At this time, it appears the outage is state-wide and possibly more."

A few minutes had passed since the pump stopped and Allen's view of the gas station entrance showed about five cars waiting in line for the next available pump. "This doesn't look good."

"No, no it doesn't," Linda motioned to the small group of people huddled around the station attendant's window. They were asking about emergency generators that could power the pumps. The attendant was unprepared, but trying to do what he could.

"Do you have your gun?" Allen asked.

"Come on Allen. Just because we got our CCW does not mean that I carry it around everywhere. It's in my car back home."

"Well, I have mine, and in the glove box I have a .22 auto," Linda opened the glove box to find the tiny, chrome-plated weapon. Upon finding the clip she turned to her husband.

".22 hollow points? I didn't even know they made those. I hope I don't have to use this. People are going to laugh at me." She slid the magazine in and heard it click into place.

"Better you than me."

The news report repeated again, and this time it was followed with the rumor of possible cyber-attack. An additional ten cars were now waiting for the gas pumps, and the entrance to the complex was completely blocked off with cars in line.

"We are done getting gas, honey," Allen concluded. "We should get out of here while we still can."

Linda agreed, and they pulled away from the pump. Another car quickly claimed their spot, obviously thinking that it was something of value. Turning their SUV to find the best way out, they faced down the little hill to the grocery store. Allen hesitated and stared ahead.

"The grocery store looks pretty quiet, doesn't it?"

"Allen. What are you thinking?" It was a playful scolding tone that didn't give much away.

"I'm thinking about going shopping. I'll bet nobody is thinking about groceries right now. Maybe later, but not now."

"Yeah, right now it seems that gas is the important thing."

Linda looked over to see the situation around the attendant's window continuing to escalate.

The grocery store seemed to be quiet as they pulled up. No one was running to the door or running out. Allen backed the SUV into a spot to the side of the building, not wanting to be directly in front of the building at all. The situation at the door could change at any time; he felt that being at the side was safest. Outside the vehicle, he reached under the seat and pulled out a 9mm Glock. The slim leather holster fit inside his pants hem. The adrenalin of the moment started to rise as the armed couple walked away from their SUV.

"Alright, I was in a grocery store a couple years ago when we had a short outage, and they were orderly giving away all the frozen food before it melted all over their floor," Allen said. "Just be nice, and let's see what happens in here. Regardless, we need to be in and out quickly."

At the door he pulled out a cart for his wife and another for himself.

Just inside the store was the manager — an older guy, kind of heavy. Allen looked at him and realized the gentleman was exactly what he would expect a grocery store manager to look like. He had tried to have a career, but ended up here. He stood there blocking the fresh produce to the left and directing people to the frozen foods area at the right side of the store. Not many people were in the store on a Tuesday morning, just the folks who happened to be there when the power went out. Some were standing at the registers with a full cart of food – unpaid for – and wondering what to do. The cashiers were clueless too.

"Have you heard anything?" the manager asked Allen. "The radio is giving us nothing."

"The entire state is down. It looks like Pennsylvania and New York too. I heard something about a cyber-attack, so we might be down for

27

a while." The manager's face was crushed. "Not what you wanted to hear, huh?"

"The frozen foods are to the back, take what you want," he said in a helpful voice, but you could tell that his mind was a million miles away.

People were just standing around in the aisle, completely lost. Linda did her best to maneuver around them quickly, and Allen duplicated her efforts. In the frozen foods she passed by all the garlic bread and pizzas, and then found the vegetables.

"Nothing that needs to be baked. Only stovetop stuff; vegetables and stir-fry's ok?" Linda had analyzed the situation and knew the capabilities of a primitive kitchen. She focused in and took control. They grabbed out bags of broccoli and green beans along with Chicken Alfredo stir-frys. Allen soon lost interest though and was scoping out the area. The frozen food section looked sparse; a few people were starting up the aisle, but not many. He stepped beyond the end of the freezers and noticed that no one was hemming them into this area. Linda's cart was a little less than half full, and his was around a quarter. It was time to take it to the next level.

"Linda, come on, that's enough."

She looked up and saw that he was on the move. The frozen foods aisle was something she figured out and understood. She didn't want to leave yet. But there was a trust between them, and she quickstepped to follow.

As his cart rolled past the end caps of rows, he checked down the aisle to see if they were being noticed. So far, so good. Allen moved to the front of his cart and pulled it so that he could get the best view down the aisle without being seen. He passed the lunchmeat doors and the island coolers of that area. One held a pile of brats and hot dogs. In one smooth motion he reached into the cooler with both hands, bringing out a pile and dumping them into his cart. Linda attempted the same, although not nearly as smoothly. Her hands were smaller and lost a couple on the way.

Allen gave her a smile for the effort and then found the aisle he was looking for: the canned produce.

"If only we could just pick up this entire aisle and put it in my truck," he whispered to her, and quietly placed some of his frozen foods into her cart. "Let me make some room. Now, let's fill my cart first, then yours. We'll cover the cans with frozen food to get out the door."

Linda started working, but Allen could see the look on her face. She was concerned. Sure, she wanted to survive this disaster, but she didn't want to become a thief to do it. Allen feared that she might crack when it came time to walk out of there with the carts.

"Look. If the power is out for long, this place is going to be down to the bare walls in no time. It's going to be raided down to nothing by people who have no other resources, and probably still will not make it through this. We are getting ours *now,* and we are going *to make it.* If we feel that we owe them something after the lights come on, we can come in and pay them then." Their eyes met, and she got it. She would follow. He turned and grabbed a tall stack of tuna cans and quietly put them in the cart while whispering the word, "Protein!"

After the cart was loaded most of the way, they began putting the frozen food on top, clearing space for canned goods in the other cart. They found a treasure trove of Dinty Moore beef stew and started piling it in. The job wasn't quite done when Allen spotted the manager walking their way from the corner of his eye. He didn't look angry — he just looked tired. Allen didn't wait for him to say something; he figured that being nice always works best.

"Do you want us to put it back?" Allen said, stepping towards him. In doing so, he was physically blocking the manager from grabbing the cart. It really didn't matter what the manager was going to say, Allen was going to leave with that cart. His hand rested near the 9mm on his hip, the trump card that would get him out the door. He didn't want to play it though.

"No," the store manager said simply, a look of defeat on his face. "Take it and go. The news just announced that the power is expected to be out for a week. A week! I'm getting ready to lock down." He began to turn and head back to the door.

"Sir, are you loading up a couple of these for your family?" Linda stepped forward and tried to be as congenial to him as he had been to them.

His face had the look that everyone has when they must put their work first. It's a common look that everyone has, from decades of priorities being hammered into their psyche.

"I'd like to, but I'm still on the clock," he said.

Allen brought his arm up and looked at his watch. "That clock stopped about thirty-five minutes ago, and it won't restart for a month. A month," he repeated for clarity.

"If they are telling us it will be a week in the first hour of the emergency, you know it's going to be a whole lot longer. If it was really going to be a week, they would be saying two or three days right now."

Allen watched the managers face changing expressions as the words were sinking in.

"This place is insured, my friend, your family is not. It's time to rearrange some priorities," Allen said while nodding his head. The manager began nodding his head hypnotically in response.

The manager turned and started fast walking towards the door, leaving the couple behind. Allen's hand started a low sweep towards his wife and their hands met for the low five plus a peck on the cheek. The manager had gained a bunch of space on them, and Allen wasn't quite done. There was still some room left in the carts. He grabbed a stack of canned chicken meat and tossed it in Linda's cart, then grabbed a second as he continued to roll slowly. She stepped up between the carts, pushing one and pulling the other, while Allen pilfered a few more stacks into the carts. They were full to the top when they reached the door.

Surprisingly, there was not a mob of people at the entrance. About eight people were leaving with their carts, and only a few were entering. As they walked past the manager, he didn't wave or try to shake Allen's hand, he did a casual salute. Kind of odd, but Allen returned the motion.

Walking out of the door to the sunlight and some light snow coming down, they felt a rush of adrenalin. They just walked out with two full carts of stolen food and were feeling like they would be handcuffed at any moment. Allen looked over at Linda and knew she felt the same way, but probably even more so. As he looked out over the parking lot, he saw why no one was clamoring to get to the grocery store. The gas station was occupying everyone. There was a line of cars to the station that was never going to move, and it was clogging up the entire entrance to the plaza. Nobody could get to the grocery store if they wanted to.

The couple pushed their carts along the front of the store to the end where the SUV was backed in. Stealing another look at the gas station, Allen saw that a fistfight had broken out at the pumps. It had been less than an hour, he thought to himself.

Reaching the SUV seemed to take forever. If they could have lifted the carts into the Suburban, they would have. Instead, the slow route of unloading by hand would have to be taken. Relief was felt when they reached the vehicle, but the adrenalin was still pumping. They were not free and clear yet.

The SUV was backed in at the right side of the store, so the passenger door was facing out to the parking lot. One cart was placed behind the truck a little to hide it, and the tail door was raised to load the first one. Allen could see that some of the people at the gas station took notice of them walking along with those full carts. It was notice that

31

he did not want to have. Allen was standing squarely at the center of the SUV, and tossing food over the cart into the vehicle. Linda was on the driver's side of the SUV, grabbing handfuls and tossing them into the truck. From Linda's vantage point, she could see most of the parking lot, and had a great view of the gas station. Allen was more sideways to the lot, and even had his back to it while loading. He was focused on getting loaded as quickly as possible and from his position he was doing good work. Cans weren't being dented, but it wasn't far from it.

They finished the first cart and Linda pushed it out of the way. The second was in place quickly so that they could continue with the system they had developed. During the switch, both had lost track of the bystanders a little bit. There were a few people noticing what the couple were doing up at the station, but they were staying there. As they got the second cart into position, Linda saw a couple guys leaving their spot in line at the gas station and beeline to the SUV. They were still fifty yards away, but they were walking directly towards the couple and their groceries. Linda was facing them, but still somewhat hidden behind Allen.

"Allen, honey, you need to trust me here, and don't look up. Just keep loading alright?"

"What's going on Linda? Are we in trouble? Don't leave me hanging here."

"Don't worry baby, I've got you covered." Linda pulled the .22 out of her waistband and held it by her hip at the ready.

"You're scaring the shit out of me sweetheart." Allen kept tossing, never skipping a beat.

The guys were in their twenties, looking kind of rough. Both of them had really light jackets on. Considering the snow coming down, it painted an odd picture, but that's kids these days. They were cocky. Linda could see that in how they walked, and she figured it was something she could use against them.

The one with the baseball cap nonchalantly stepped up, closer to the truck than she expected, and raised his shirt. The exposed butt of a 9mm automatic sticking out of his pants was supposed to put him in charge.

"Put the groceries back in the cart. Those are mine," he said with a smirk on his face.

Linda drew her weapon without hesitation. Her left hand was cocking a bullet into the chamber as the gun was coming up. The kid didn't really get the word 'mine' out of his mouth. The cocking of the gun pretty much stopped everything. Their hands went up immediately. The whole event really scared the crap out of Allen though. Her raised weapon was only about twelve inches from his face when all was said and done.

Once Allen got over the shock, his own weapon was produced to make sure the situation was under control.

"Dang, baby, that was pretty good," Allen congratulated her and eyed the cocky boys down.

"Take a step back, honey," Linda motioned to her husband. "I'll take care of these boys. You just finish loading."

Allen stepped back out of the line of fire, and she walked closer to the attempted thieves. As soon as she was clear, Allen resumed tossing with vigor.

"What are you going to do with that little pea shooter?" The first kid wasn't giving up on his cockiness just yet.

"The bullets may be small flyboy, but I've got sixteen hollow points in here and all of them have your name on 'em, you peckerwood!"

"My 9 mil would only need one to take your ass out." The game was still being played.

"I guess I'd just get more fun squeezing off so many into your sorry ass. And by the way, it doesn't do much good in your pants pal." She was done with this battle of words, and he responded with that smirk again. She began to wonder if he had any other expressions.

"You know, actually, I think it needs to be out of your pants. Slowly, let's put the gun on the ground."

Allen's ears perked up on this one and his pace began to slow. One hand was holding his gun now while tossing with the other.

She saw a questioning look on the kid's face; he obviously didn't want to do it.

"Come on man, right now!" she said, pointing the gun at his face.

He reached in and, with two fingers just like he had seen on TV so many times, he pulled out the weapon. He looked her in the eyes as he put it on the ground, muttering something under his breath.

"Was that really necessary?" Allen called out when he went back to using both hands again.

"Yes it was dear," she called over her shoulder.

Allen mumbled to himself as he continued to work, "I'm gonna die in a friggin' grocery store parking lot. What a thing to have on a tombstone!" The clank of cans hitting each other followed.

"Step back cowboy," she said after the gun was down and he had stood back up. "How about you Festus?" she said to the other one. "You packin'?"

He shook his head, which looked kind of funny with his arms straight up. He was reaching for the sky as hard as he could. His ears rubbed his arms as he shook his head. He followed her command to pull up his shirt to expose his waistband, and then to turn around to see the back. He was clean.

"Alright, take a couple more steps back." They weren't happy, but they were following orders.

34

"Hey man, you ain't taking my gun, you can't take my gun!" he said to her as she stepped forward and bent down. She palmed the thief's weapon with her left and kept the boys under control with the right. She could see that people at the gas station were beginning to take notice of what was going on down there. They were standing around watching. No one was heading their way though, and she took comfort in that. She also took comfort in hearing cans clanking behind her.

"We about done, honey?"

"Almost there."

"Come on man, that's my gun," the punk continued to plead.

"You made a gamble, and you lost. You tried to take my food, and you lost. You have to lose something when you lose. I'm teaching you a lesson, kid. Next time you might lose your life."

The kid didn't get it — he didn't care. She didn't either, really. She just wanted his gun. There was also a chance that he would take pot shots at the truck as they drove away, so she had to keep that from happening.

She finally heard the door slam behind her, and spotted Allen's automatic leveled on the boys out of the corner of her eye.

"Linda, Let's get going. I've got the boys covered too."

The couple saw that people were starting to move towards them from the gas station, and some people were at the grocery store doors trying to get in. They were now locked. Linda and Allen got into the SUV, Linda in the passenger seat with the window down, her peashooter still pointed at the boys.

"I hope you've learned your lesson, boys. You may not get a second chance." The 9mm was tossed a good distance from the SUV.

"Go that way," she told Allen, pointing to the left. It was the direction away from the gas station, but also deeper into the shopping plaza.

People were starting to point, getting into their cars, and they needed to move.

"There's no exit over there, you know."

"I know there's no back door. But I reckon, where do they want one?" she said, quoting some old movie that she'd long ago forgotten the name of. It was just a great line. "We'll make our own exit."

Allen reached behind the steering wheel and pushed the 4-wheel drive button. The familiar grind was felt as the transmission kicked in. She directed him to an area between buildings that led to an open field. They were putting distance between themselves and the parking lot folks, but it looked like a couple cars were trying to follow now.

"Are you sure you want to do this?" Allen protested.

"Do it all baby! Do it all!"

Allen hit the curb at an angle, so that it was just one wheel at a time, and it came and went relatively smoothly. The field had a couple inches of snow, but the terrain was pretty even.

Suddenly there was some giddiness to Allen; being out of the parking lot did it for him.

"I've always wanted to jump a curb and go 4-wheeling."

The smile became even wider when he realized that the two followers called it quits at the curb.

Luckily the field did not have a fence at the road, but Allen would have been fine with busting it. Maybe it would have given him another thrill.

A couple miles down the road, Allen pulled into an empty office parking lot to clear his mind. Dramatically, he took a deep breath and the SUV was put in park. The two of them still held their weapons in their hands and she gripped the .22 so tight her knuckles were white. He held his gun up in the air and slowly placed it on the floor beside his leg. Linda followed suit and slowly uncurled her fingers from the weapon and laid it on the floor as well. When the weapons were released to the floor, a noticeable weight was lifted from their shoulders and separated them from the strife.

"Honey, come here." Allen's only words led to an embrace that lasted an exceptionally long time and might have caused bruising it was so tight. Tears streamed down both their faces.

"How are you? Are you ok?" Allen knew his wife was tough, but he saw a new side today.

"I'm good, but I've got a hell of a headache."

"It's probably Adrenalin Overload," Allen explained. "I was told that if you are in a standoff with someone like we just had, it must be resolved in ninety seconds. After ninety seconds of pointing a loaded weapon at someone, you could get delirious from the adrenalin and may not think straight."

"Well, I'm overloading on something, that's for sure."

"I bet you are feeling it, honey. I'm sure that a military person or a law officer can get a grip on this stuff after years of experiencing it. But I tell you what; my head is about ready to explode too." Allen looked over at her one more time to make sure she was OK.

"Are you ready to go back to Galena?"

"Yeah, baby. Home sweet home."

Chapter 4: The Five F's.

Thom Vesper's route home was simple. It was normally a forty-five-minute ride, all surface roads, and no highways. He was pleased to see that his gas gauge was between a half and three quarters full. A prepper's rule that he learned long ago was to never let your tank go below half full. It was a rule that became a habit, and he felt some satisfaction in it. Thom had visualized a ride home from the office after 'an event' back when prepping was a part of his life. He role-played in his mind the obstacles that might stand between him and home. Would the roads be clear of snow, fallen trees, stalled cars, and other debris? Would there be accidents to avoid because of freaked out drivers doing stupid things? Maybe there would be emergency vehicles going everywhere and a path needed to be cleared for them.

Thom saw none of these things. Everything appeared normal. The radio, however, told a different story. Where the scene outside gave the picture of nothing being wrong, and even caused a person to question their senses, the radio brought the harsh reality: The Niagara Falls power facility was down and may have even suffered physical damage caused by amperage safety thresholds that had somehow programmatically gotten out of whack. The result was that a section of the country on its grid was blacked out. The states out were Indiana, Ohio, Michigan, Pennsylvania, New York, and the New England states. The culprit was a cyber-attack, and they were already pointing at Iran, or North Korea, or both. Thom could hear the drums of war in their words. "Great," Thom spoke out loud to the dashboard. "We'll retaliate, and we'll bomb somebody, but how does that help me and my family? Stop with the politics!"

The distractions needed to be cleared of Thom's head, and he knew it. At the next stop sign, he took a few deep breaths to regain his focus. Back when he did the role-play of an event, he identified some people to visit if he had time. One thing he had was time, and he needed to build an arsenal. Sometimes the best arsenal is not necessarily firepower; it's friends. It was time to build.

38

The Tall Timbers housing development was the only gated community in the area. Relatively small, only about forty homes, but the layout was quite nice, and Thom loved rolling through it. Ed was a Rotary member with Thom and a prominent member of his church. The gate was open, which was good. The roads in their community hadn't been plowed either, and Thom mumbled to himself about the rich having to suffer right along with the rest of us.

He pulled into Ed's driveway, and noticed only one set of tire tracks, with their BMW still outside. Good, they were still home, he thought to himself. Thom saw lots of little footprints leading to the front door, and all three of the garage doors closed. It was probably odd to them, using the front door when they got home. They probably used the garage entrance every day since they moved in. But the garage door opener didn't work anymore, and for them, the oddities of entering through the front door would be just the beginning.

Ed's wife, Kara, answered the door when he knocked, and Thom was glad to see that she was in good spirits for the situation. He gave her a polite hug and asked how she was doing. Holding up well, Kara was a rock. She stood five foot nothing, compared to Ed at well over six feet, and tipping the scales at over 300. Ed had played Division I college football many moons ago at linebacker, and this odd couple seemed like a perfect fit. Kara was still the boss though, and there was never, ever a doubt about it.

When Thom stepped inside, he thought his senses were lying to him. The lights were on, and the room was relatively warm.

"You've got power. How's that?"

"I don't know," she said. "But it's only in the living room and the kitchen. No other rooms have power."

Thom found himself totally bewildered, and in a strange way, a little disappointed. Maybe the emergency wasn't as bad as he led himself to believe. After years of preparation, a person starts to *want* something to happen — maybe to validate their actions, maybe to prove all the dissenters to be wrong. One thing was for certain: he no longer had a grip on what was happening, and he didn't like it.

Right then Ed appeared at the door; neither had heard him pull up. Thom was closest to the door, so he shook his hand first. But he quickly gave way for him to greet his wife and make sure all was well in this time of turmoil. Once the hugs and greetings were out of the way, Thom splintered in at the first opportunity.

"Great to see you, Ed. Why do you have power?"

"Because of you, Thom, that's why. After you made your speech at the Rotary Club about becoming a prepper a couple years ago, I did a job swap with a generator guy. I haven't seen you at the Rotary meetings for a while, did you drop out?"

Thom's voice faltered at the question and tried to deflect it. "Yeah, I dropped out of a lot of things about a year ago. It was a rough stretch. But tell me more about this generator."

Ed hesitated to show he wasn't happy with Thom's answer, but moved on; "Well, my guys put a roof on his house, and he put in a natural gas generator maybe ten months ago. The opportunity came up and I jumped on it." Turning to his wife he said: "Sorry I didn't mention it to you, honey. I was kind of afraid you wouldn't approve, because the deal seemed like a real loser until right this second." She greeted his statement with an additional hug.

"Natural gas is still flowing then, that's a good thing to know." Thom felt better to understand why their lights were on, but the disappointment he first felt would be something he'd have to wrestle with eventually. "The generator only powers the kitchen and living room?"

"I'm not sure," he replied. "It only covers a few breakers, but the furnace and the water pump were the main ones. Everything else was considered gravy in my mind. It was all just pie in the sky talk when we put it in; I never thought we'd actually use it."

"Maybe we should have a look at the breaker box and see what we have," Kara added, trying to railroad the conversation and take control of her house again. She didn't like the surprise of this generator, although it was a quite pleasant one. She still needed to understand it, now that it was a part of her domain.

"Yes, I agree. You guys should do that," Thom responded. He held his ground, stopping them from heading to the basement. "Look, I just wanted to stop in and make sure you guys were okay, and it looks like you are. I am so glad to see it, and I need to be moving on."

They agreed and took a couple steps towards the door to see him out.

"Hey, is there someone here in the development that has a wood burning fireplace?" he said, offhandedly at the door, like Detective Colombo as he was interrogating a suspect.

Ed pointed out the glass door to the house across the street and said: "Dr. Cliff has one over there."

"*Doctor* Cliff, huh?" Thom said. "What kind of doctor is he?"

"Ear, nose, and throat. He took out Mindy's tonsils last year. Why do you ask?" Ed's patience was wearing thin. He needed to show Kara her new generator in the basement.

"Well Ed, you are set now, but you need a Plan B, in case the natural gas stops coming in. A friend with a fireplace is what you need, just in case. A friend who is also a doctor is someone that everyone needs right now. We need to make sure that Dr. Cliff stays home."

Thom was transfixed on Ed, and he seemed to show understanding. But his poker face wasn't giving many clues.

"Well, if the generator fails, we will just move on. We don't need to bother Dr. Cliff." Ed wasn't buying in.

"Let's put it this way, Ed. If you saw a freeway on your way home today, you saw what a mess they are already. Tonight, they will be worse. The roads are going to be jammed and the weather is going to

41

be cold. Let's go talk to Dr. Cliff and make sure he doesn't try to travel anywhere far tonight, and maybe save his life."

"Good argument, a little end-around route to the same spot. You really want to talk to this guy, don't you?" He was smiling and toying with Thom, but not giving in.

"I've only got ten minutes for this, Ed. I have more stops on my list before I get home. It would be real handy to know if we have a physician in the neighborhood, just in case this thing goes longer than expected. Have you got ten minutes for me?" His last argument. His last shot. He had nothing else.

Ed looked at Kara, and she was handing him his hat. "Let's go."

They climbed into Thom's truck and drove over to the house across the way. The light snow was still coming down, creating a new layer on everything. The small amount of snow gave the appearance of mild weather. All it took was to step outside and feel the bone chilling cold to realize the weather was anything but mild. Inside a car with a working heater, however, a person would feel comfortable and protected.

Dr. Cliff's house was just as big as Ed's, but the driveway brought them around to the back door. You could tell that they were used to traffic through that door, not the front. The neighbor's house had a driveway running parallel with a similar arrangement to the back door. There was a recent set of tracks in the snow between the homes. Ed pointed to the neighbor's home, mentioning his name was "Steve, the Day-Trader" as if those few words described the person entirely.

From the rear entrance, which was a sunroom of glass, the kitchen was open to view. Dr. Cliff and his wife, Michelle, were having a very heated discussion in the kitchen when they walked up. The volume was high enough that Ed and Thom looked at each other at the door and contemplated not knocking. But in the end, Thom shrugged his shoulders and knocked anyway. The yelling stopped, and Dr. Cliff walked through the sunroom to the door. His expression looked

42

distraught, but it brightened a little when he saw Ed, who seemed to have that effect on people.

"Sorry to catch you like this Dr. Cliff…" Ed started, but he was cut off.

"You know better than that Ed. You call me Cliff, or I'm going to punch you in the nose!"

The statement caused Thom to giggle just a little. Dr. Cliff stood about 5-foot-7 and Ed, at 6-foot-4, towered over him. Ed may have been in his 50s, but he still had the basic physique of an offensive tackle. The threat of violence brought a smile to both Ed and Cliff as well.

"Cliff, this is my friend Thom, a fellow Rotarian," Ed changed the subject.

"So it's Cliff then?" Thom said as he shook his hand. "I have a sensitive nose."

"Yes, it is," Cliff returned Thom's smile.

"Well Cliff," Ed began. "We are here to talk you into staying home, and not getting on the road today."

"Dammit!" Cliff responded. "That's what Michelle is saying too. My neighbor Steve is getting on the road soon, and we were going to follow him. Come on inside."

"How much firewood do you have?" Thom said, as he got inside and scoped out the fireplace in the living room from the kitchen.

"Oh, about a half cord's out in the garage. It's all pretty dry. Now you guys are going to start working on me, aren't you?"

"Yes we are Cliff." Ed firmly stated. "Have you seen the freeways?"

"Not really. Are they bad?"

Thom could tell he was going to go along with them — it was his easy out. He would give in to Ed's argument and not to his wife. Thom knew all about spousal arguments: it's not about being right or wrong, it's about winning. This was a way they could both win. Thom was counting it as a done deal just from the tone of Cliff's voice.

Just then, Dr. Cliff's wife walked into the room.

"Hi Michelle," Ed said with a smile, which was quickly returned.

"This is my friend Thom Vesper," he said, and Thom reached out his hand.

"Let's get some kindling, Michelle, and start a fire. You guys are staying," Thom proclaimed as they shook hands. She smiled endearingly and stole a quick look at Cliff. He confirmed the statement with a barely noticeable nod.

Michelle and Thom set to work on the fire while Ed and Cliff talked about the storm and the power reports. They could overhear Ed talking about how dangerous it would be out on the roads tonight. Ed had tried to get gas on his way home and gave up after a short while. This was all news to Cliff, and his concern began to grow. As they spoke, Steve the Day Trader walked in the back door.

"Why are you guys building a fire? We are leaving in fifteen minutes!" Steve exclaimed. You could clearly tell that Steve was a control freak, and not used to his game plan being changed for him. As he looked around the room, he could see that Ed and Thom were the culprits for the change in direction.

"We are staying here, Steve," Cliff gathered up the backbone to say, so that Michelle wouldn't beat him to it. "We have the fireplace, and it's the safer route."

"Well, I can't stay. You know that. I've got six million out there, and when the stock market opens, I could lose it all if I don't move it. That market is going to crash as soon as the bell rings. I need to be at a phone line or my life savings, my house, my everything will go down the tubes. I can't stay."

"I hear you, Steve; I'm not asking you to stay," Cliff chimed in, "I have a bunch in the market too, but I'll just have to let it ride. I wish you the best of luck on your travels."

Thom wanted to butt in and argue that Steve should stay, that he was putting his life and his family's lives in danger by leaving. But who was to say that they wouldn't make it? He could argue for Steve's safety but what exact value is that? There is a finite amount of money, millions of dollars, waiting in Kentucky. How could he tell him not to go? It wouldn't be beyond most people to attempt a difficult feat themselves, for millions of dollars. And if Thom were to talk him into staying, and he lost the millions, maybe Thom would be sued. It's one thing to be responsible for saving or losing a life, but there's a whole different argument about losing millions of dollars. This is what the world has become. Life or millions ... which is the higher value? And life after losing the millions, it seems like not much of a life...

Steve was hurried and wanted to go. It was obvious that he wanted to stay and argue his point until Cliff relented but just didn't have the time.

"Cliff, give me your latest account statement and your password. I'll attempt to save what I can for you too." It was an action Thom didn't expect from Steve, just in the few minutes he had gotten to know him. A self-absorbed person from the get-go, he didn't see that act of charity coming. That's when Thom realized there might be more charity in him, and an idea came to mind.

As Steve collected the paperwork and opened the door, his back was to the group. Thom looked directly at Ed and spoke to Steve.

"Do you have children you are taking with you, Steve?" Tension was building from the open-ended question, and the time constraint. Adding to all that, Steve didn't know him from Adam. Thom just hoped that Ed saw the direction he was taking.

"Yes, I do. Why do you ask?" The guttural voice gave warning that a line was being crossed.

"That's right, Elizabeth and Luke. Is that right?" Ed came to the rescue. "Hey Steve, I have a natural gas generator at my house. We are set up and safe, with heat. How about you leave the kids here with me and Kara?"

Steve was stunned; this was a thought that hadn't come to his mind. His 'end-goal' mentality hadn't let him see outside the box on this one, and seeing outside the box was always considered one of his boasted gifts. Thom took the opportunity to chime in and add more to the argument, in the way a Day Trader would understand.

"Yes, Steve, without the children you'll be able to take chances. Chances that you otherwise wouldn't take, and you would have more options to get where you need to go." The words were left to hang in the air, and the argument wasn't pushed any further. Steve was a guy that liked to have his choices be his own idea, not someone else's. However, if he liked this idea, when he spoke of it to his wife, he could become 'the owner' of the idea. It could be *his* idea then. Ed and Thom could see the wheels turning in his head, but nothing was certain.

"We'll see. Thanks for the offer, Ed. Good luck to you all, I've got to get going. The snow is still coming down."

As Steve walked out of view, Ed turned to Thom and did a little fist pump. "That worked nice, thanks for the hand-off," he said.

"It's great to hand it off to someone who will run with it." Their fists hit and simulated a little explosion with their hands. It would've looked really cool if they weren't in their forties.

"Look guys, I have to go too. I think I've done all the damage I can do around here," Thom said, even though he still had a couple more things to say. Detective Colombo's strategy was being used again, but it was necessary. Focus needed to be turned to survival.

46

"How long do you think this will last?" Cliff pressed; it might have been a while since he listened to a radio.

"Last I heard was seven days, but I think it could be much longer. And if the snow keeps up with minimal road crews, we will be stuck right here, whether we like it or not. Can I give you some advice for survival long term?"

It was a tough question. Long-term answers are usually disliked.

"Of course we do," jumped in Michelle. "Staying right here for as long as possible is exactly what I want to do."

"Well Cliff, I'll tell you right now that I'm glad we'll have a physician in the area. We may never need your expertise, but it's good to know it's here. You guys should also find out who else in the development is staying, and bond together. You may need to converge into combined homes as fuel and supplies need to be conserved." So far, every head was nodding, and it made sense. Thom turned to the back yard, pointing through the windows to Steve's patio, which was in plain sight.

"Over at Steve's, it looks like he has a half cord of wood stacked up for his fire pit, under a layer of snow. Is that right?" Thom nodded as everyone else did. "Now without even asking, you should feel perfectly fine to go over there and claim that wood if it will keep you and your family from freezing. Am I right?" The nodding continued.

"I think the same should be said for the food in the empty homes' pantries in the neighborhood as well." Frowns began to form on their faces. These were well-to-do God-fearing folk. This was out of their comfort zone. This was stealing.

"It is not looting. You are taking things that you need to survive, not their flat screen HDTV. Let's take this neighbor on the other side — it looks vacant already. Let's say they made it to electricity, and if so, they are not coming back until this event is over. They don't need the food. If you were able to call them up, and ask them if you could have the food they left behind, what do you think they'd say? They'd say

47

please take it and feed your family. They would probably go on to apologize for not having more for you. Am I right?"

"I can't see us getting to the point of breaking into our neighbors' homes to survive," Michelle spoke up. "It's not going to get that bad. There won't be any need."

"I truly hope so Michelle," Thom said. "But if this ordeal looks to last a while, some discussion between you guys is going to be necessary. Keep an ear to the radio and keep the long-term thought in mind. The real looters will be cleaning out the pantries anyway if this thing goes long enough."

 Their eyes were glazing over, and Michelle looked a little shocked at his statement and the tone of his voice. He had overstepped again. Crawling into a dark corner and blocking out the world started to sound like a good idea, but he had done that before.

Thankfully to break the tension, the kitchen door opened and Steve's kids, Luke and Elizabeth, along with their mother, Jen, walked in. Jen and Michelle embraced. It was clear that Jen was terrified of traveling with her children, and was more than glad to impose on her neighbors. Thom took this opportunity to pull Ed aside and see if he wanted a ride back home because it was time to leave.

But before they left, Ed wanted to take a moment to do something that Thom would not have thought of, or had the nerve to do if he had. He called the group together in the kitchen and told them all to hold hands — a man as large and imposing as Ed, they followed. Then Ed said a prayer, asking the Mother Mary to watch over them in this time of tribulation. It was short and sweet, and he followed it with a Hail Mary. At that point, he found out who the Catholics were in the room because they knew the prayer and recited it with him. It was invigorating to Thom, and he thanked Ed for stepping up. Thom decided right then that this ritual was going to become a staple for himself. He was a regular churchgoer, and a God-fearing man, but not one for praying. He just figured he needed all the help he could get.

48

****

The old farmhouse at the end of the long drive with farm fields on each side looked like many in Ohio. Fresh tire tracks in the snowy driveway proved that Thom was not the first to arrive, which was good. The monster sized barn behind the house had a fresh coat of paint, a new metal roof, and extra tall sliding doors made of metal siding. The owner of the property was George Jones — no relation to the singer. He had sold off some of the farm in five-acre lots during the housing boom, and decided to lease the rest to local farmers, and sell off his equipment. The plan was to enjoy his later years and travel the country in his motor home. So, he upgraded the barn for storage of the vehicle and enough space for some of his new motor home buddies to store theirs for the winter as well, for a fee of course. It turned out to be a pretty profitable move for George to go into the motor home storage business; he had lots of takers for the open spots.

Thom pulled up to the barn beside Jonathan's little blue Saturn. As he got out of the truck, he saw that the entire car was packed to the ceiling with plastic totes filled with canned goods, even the passenger seat. In the back window, he spotted a couple cases of beer.

"That's Jonathan," he mumbled to himself, and he was certain there was more packed away somewhere. Jonathan was one of those guys that hosted everything. If there was a big football game, the best party was always at his house. When Thom decided to attend, claiming a couch was always necessary. He knew that driving home from one of Jonathan's parties was out of the question.

He followed Jonathan's tracks to the barn door and knocked while opening it. "Jonathan?" he called out.

The light inside the barn was remarkably good; there were several high windows with opaque fiberglass sheeting over them. It was surprising how well he could see once inside. From behind a green motor home, Jonathan stood at the bumper, pointing a revolver at Thom.

"What the hell are you doing with a gun drawn?" Thom scolded him, and he immediately put it down.

"Sorry dude, I'm just a little freaked out. Really man, I'm sorry." He walked forward and gave Thom a man hug. "Are you doing okay? You planning to join us here?"

"I'm fine, Jonathan, and no, I'll be setting up shop at home. How many people will be joining you here?" The two had discussed Jonathan's plans a while back over beers around a fire pit, but Thom didn't know the full deal. He just wanted to see how it all worked out, and since they were about eight miles from his home, add them to his group of allies.

"Oh man, the list has grown some buddy. My ex-wife will bring my son, Jonny, here. That should be a treat. I don't think the barn is big enough for the two of us together again, but you gotta do what you gotta do. Then my brother Toby and his kids, our parents, my buddy Kyle has the GMC next to mine for his wife and three kids, and of course the owner George and his wife in their camper," he rattled off the list on his fingers.

"You are running out of fingers there, Jonathan. You guys have a large motor home, but that's a ton of folks!" Thom threw his thumb over his shoulder and added: "Can I help you carry in stuff while we talk?"

He welcomed the help and they walked to the door. They each pulled a bin out of the car and walked into the barn with it. The canned goods bins had some weight and had to be held at the bottom.

"Yes, we have a full house for sure, Thom. But hey, we have eight other motor homes in here. If no one else shows up with the same idea, a few of us might upgrade!" They set their bins down on a folding table Jonathan had set up in front of his motor home. It was a thirty-five-foot beauty with Ohio State fathead magnetic emblems on the side. Jonathan hit all the OSU home games with this unit and many of the away games as well. An open can of beer was on the table, and he stopped to take a swig while talking. Thom gave him a little sideways look while he did that and decided to address the subject.

"Hey man, I know that you've never done anything around this motor home without alcohol being involved. I get that, and I'm not trying to be a downer, okay?" Thom started in on him while trying to keep it light. Thom had gone too far sometimes with his drinking too; it's never what a person wants to hear. He wanted to say more but Jonathan interrupted.

"Yeah, I hear you; this is life and death stuff going on here. My liquid stress medication is needed once in a while though. I'll keep it under control, I will." He looked Thom in the eye, and he took it for what it was: not much, really.

"That's cool, Jonathan, whatever," he still tried to keep it light. "But promise me one thing; keep that pistol in your pocket today. Nobody is going to be coming to this barn today that you want to shoot. Capeesh? A week or two from now might be a different story, but today everyone that pulls up to this barn is your friend. There might be a stranger with the same idea wanting to stay in their RV and you'll be living with them for however long this lasts. You don't want to meet them like you met me. Got it?"

"Yep, I got it. As a matter of fact, with alcohol in my blood, I shouldn't be carrying it at all," he said as he stepped in the camper and put the gun in the sun visor of the driver's side. As he exited the camper, he continued his previous thought. "This really is life or death friend. Did you hear that it was a cyber-attack on the radio?"

"Yes, I did. Pretty crazy, huh?"

"You know what it *really is,* right? It's a false flag event, it has all the traits." He took another swig of his beer and continued. "The scale of it is so big you can't realistically point your finger and say the government would do this to itself, so they are clear of blame. And the attack is so technologically based that they could manufacture

51

whatever evidence they want. They can say whomever they want did this. It's actually quite brilliant."

"The government did this, huh?" Thom said, looking at this man holding a beer with everything figured out. He was a knowledgeable guy on this subject, but this train of thought didn't give him much credibility. CNN would tear him apart.

"Or a shadow division of the government. Don't count it out man, keep your mind open," he said, pointing his finger to add emphasis.

"I will, Jonathan. You have your ear to the ground more than me with these theories. Do you think their goal is to go to war, is that it?"

"War would be one motivation for sure, and they might want to cut some of the fat from the population," he said, not caring if his words were offensive. "If this goes on for a while, the elderly will be the first to go. Then next would be the poor, who live month to month and have nothing extra in the cupboards. Those are also the people living on the government's dime, through welfare and Social Security and Medicare. A large portion of the people who would perish in a long-term event would fall into that category, and that would be just fine with the government's checkbook."

"Damn. I hadn't seen it so black and white. Those are some cold thoughts my friend. Let's get another load," Thom said and turned to head outside. Thom saw some off-kilter merit in his theory, but if there was more, he didn't want to hear it. Time to change the subject.

"So how will your living quarters work here in this barn? Does the camper's generator run the heat, or does the engine do it?"

"The generator runs it, just like it would the air conditioner," he replied.

"So I guess you are not concerned about fumes in the building."

"No, not in this huge barn, the fumes will just rise. The sound of the generator and the vibrations off the barn walls may rattle our teeth after a while though. I guess we'll find out," Jonathan said with a grin.

"Will someone be bringing extra fuel? That has to be a worry," Thom said, still searching for holes in the plan.

"No way, man. We have eight other campers here, each with one-hundred-gallon tanks. I've got a siphon hand pump in my camper, and we'll relieve all the tanks in the building if need be." He was laughing a little.

"This one is diesel over here; you won't get much use from it." Thom walked over to the Greyhound bus upgraded machine.

"Oh yes, this is a beauty. If the owner doesn't come in to claim it in the next couple days, I'm moving in. This is a half-million-dollar machine. I hope George has the keys, because I'd hate to bust out a window!" He stood there shaking his head, looking up at it.

Thom walked around the corner of the huge diesel to see what was behind it and was almost knocked off his feet. He pulled in some air and let out a catcall whistle. Jonathan stepped around the corner to look but wasn't impressed.

"Yep, somebody put a boat in here too," he said, as if it had no right to be taking up this valuable space.

Thom pulled up the drop cover to get a peek at the vessel, and once he saw a little, he had to see it all.

"This is a 1950s Chris Craft mahogany motorboat. What a beauty!"

Thom climbed on the trailer rack and continued to roll back the cover. The wood finish had been beautifully restored, and the red upholstery looked like new. The chrome deck hardware sparkled as well as the instrumentation on the driver's side dash. He was completely captivated by the craft.

"This is like a '57 Chevy Bel Air made for the water. You have to respect it friend."

"You sure have a thing for boats Thom," Jonathan said. "They don't do much for me. Give me the open road, and I've got it all."

53

"A boat on the sea makes its own road," Thom replied as he rolled back the cover, Jonathan stepping over to help. Thom jumped off the trailer and walked past him, still admiring the boat until she was out of sight. "Let's get some more bins; I've got to get going."

Thom brought in one more load of canned goods and made a production of looking at his watch. "Yo buddy, I'm getting out of here. I wish you the best with this man."

"The same to you brother," he said, shaking Thom's hand. "Do you have everything you need?"

"Yep, I'm set. I wanted to pass on to you that I just spoke to a dude at Tall Timbers who is a physician, and he is staying home. There's only one road through the development, and his address is 442, if you need to call on him."

"Man, that's great info, Thom. Thanks for letting me know, gotta make note of that." He pulled out a pen from his jacket and wrote on a cardboard box sitting on the table: "DR. 442."

"Then my job is done. You know where I live, Jonathan." He turned to leave, but then stopped, and remembered the promise he made to himself. "Dude, there's something I need to do, give me your hands,"

He recited a shorter version of the prayer Ed had said an hour ago. It was uncomfortable at first, but he just pushed forward. It needed to be done — he promised he would. Jonathan just allowed him to lead; he just had to stand there. They embraced in a man-hug after saying "amen," and with that, Thom headed out the door.

Driving down the farm driveway, the reality of what was going on started to hit Thom. The first wave of snow clouds had finished up and the sun had reappeared. *This is not so bad,* Thom thought, as the wrinkles in his forehead faded away. The radio was repeating the same information, nothing new about what caused the situation or how long it would last. They were still standing firm with a seven-day power outage. The weather report called for just another inch of snow and near zero temperatures. There was some mention of chaos in New

54

York and Boston. Reports of looting were coming in already. Thom noticed that no helpful hints were being given to the listeners about how to deal with the power outage. No warnings about placing candles close to something flammable, or not to attempt to put gasoline in a kerosene heater. They were simply reading the Associated Press wire printout aloud over the air. Thom's wrinkles started to reappear on his forehead the more he thought about it.

Thom remembered the little fifteen-minute presentation he did at the Rotary breakfast a couple of years ago. Prepping was the popular buzzword with guns and ammo prices rising at the time, but everyday folks weren't sure what it really meant. Did prepping mean building a bunker in the backyard? Thom tried to normalize it a little for the diversified group of two dozen over their scrambled eggs. He called it the Five F's. To successfully prepare for an emergency, even a small one, this was the simple list: Food, Firewood, First Aid, Firearms, and Friends. It was as simple as that for his Rotary presentation. In the months after, it started getting complicated. Then it got dark. As Thom dug into all the collapse possibilities — the EMP, the nuclear strike, the economic crash and ever-discussed false flag — the darkness truly fell. Thinking about all the ways a person's world could be turned upside down all day long can have a serious effect. Thom knew a collapse was going to happen. He knew it to his core. The unknowns were the how and the when, and it tore his core apart. Thom's personal collapse occurred a few months later, when he was found curled up in a corner sobbing. Then a wall was built between him and prepping — doctor's orders.

Eventually Thom drove into the small village of Galena, with a population of 400. The village was located in the crotch where two rivers came together. Coming into the town square from the east, he crossed the Big Walnut River. From the west, he would cross the Little Walnut River. Both bridges land at the town square. The town was started a year before Ohio became a state, in 1802. The Big Walnut was on higher ground than the Little Walnut, by five feet. At the closest point of the two rivers, a water-powered lumber mill was

55

built, and the town grew upon its shoulders. It didn't grow much though in its two hundred years, and everyone liked it that way.

Crossing the Big Walnut, Thom looked down from a fifty-year-old bridge in much need of repair, to a river frozen solid below. A layer of ice had formed on both rivers surrounding the village, caused by the unusually cold weather in the previous couple of weeks. Thom was moved by the eeriness of seeing a blanket of snow covering everything, including the unmoving river.

He rolled past the restaurant on the square to see the owner, Janice, carrying boxes out to her car. She was cleaning out the freezers, it appeared. She waved Thom down, so he pulled into the next spot.

"Want some steaks? This stuff is going to go bad," she said with a box stretched out to him. She seemed to be a little out of breath from carrying the boxes. "I gave a bunch to the employees before they left, but I found a new stash in the basement."

Thom took the box and offered some information he'd heard on the radio, but she didn't have the time to talk. She was locking down and still had a twenty-mile drive home. Thom looked at his watch — it was 3 p.m. already. It would be dark in a couple of hours, and with the next wave of clouds coming, dusk would arrive early today.

Thom parked in front of his home, only three doors from the square. His was the first home. Toni was yet to arrive, which was expected. Being the mother hen she was, it was certain she was helping some friends prepare. They had discussed an emergency plan outline over a year ago, for situations like this. Toni hadn't taken the conversation seriously, but he hoped she would remember to be home before dark.

He set to work right away in the house, lighting a fire in the fireplace and making sure there was enough wood inside for the night. Being the list person he was, a task list was written while watching the fire build to the point where it was safe to be left unattended. No screen would be put in front of the fire; maximum output was needed now.

He found that the natural gas stovetop still worked, but the electric lighting spark had to be replaced with matches.

Fine, we can do that, he thought. He still had water too, which he was happy to see. He ventured into the basement and retrieved a couple of empty plastic bins and tossed in some candles and some big punch bowls he noticed on the shelf. The bins were for carrying the groceries from storage in the garage, and the bowls for saving water, while he still had it.

Next on the list was shoveling the now six inches of snow from the front steps to the truck, and also from the back deck, which connected the house to the garage. The detached garage was where all of his supplies were stored, and it all needed to come inside. He was preparing himself to be a pack mule for quite a while: might as well clear a path and make the job easier. While shoveling, he began mumbling to himself the things that needed to be added to the list. Lots of time to think there, and when he was done, he added all that he could remember. The list was getting big.

'I'm going to need a bigger piece of paper,' he said to himself.

After shoveling both the front and the back walking paths, Thom decided to move his truck away from the front of the house and parked it at the bank on the square. When he reached his home, he looked at the structure in quite a different way than he ever had. It was a three-story saltbox-style structure built in the mid 1800s and served as the telegraph office of the small burg way back when. The wraparound porch, which he helped build, was a distinguishing feature of the home. It was wrapped around to a rectangular three-season room that was surrounded with eight sliding glass doors, which he also helped build. This room had been his favorite, and where he felt most comfortable. The three-season room opened to the backyard deck and gave access to the garage. The porch and three-season room were quite high off the ground, six or seven steps, and it was somewhat imposing. He hoped it would never come to a point where he would need to defend his position from up there. He shook his head

57

to put that stuff out of his mind; he shouldn't need to worry about that now.

Back inside, he grabbed a toolbox from the garage and set himself to work while the light was still good. Some blankets were hung over the doorway to the family room, where the fireplace was. There was also a cathedral-ceiling window to the rest of the house that needed to be closed off so that the heat of the room could be contained. Another trip out to the garage, and the ladder came in. The job was difficult to do alone, but it had to get done. Daylight was burning. It was 4:30, and still, no family pulling up front. A light snow was starting to come down, and not a road crew truck in sight. Where was she?

The list came out, and it was time to be a pack mule. The garage was normally heated, but now the food would be vulnerable to the freezing temperatures. Everything there was already in bins, so at least there was no loading. The general plan a year ago was to have an option to load the truck quickly if there was a need to vacate, so preloaded bins were important. Some were too heavy to carry safely to the house, though, and had to be partially emptied. The shelving contained about a dozen bins of various foodstuffs. On a top shelf, he spotted an old microwave oven he had bought in a garage sale for ten bucks. It contained a laptop and some memory sticks of important documents and old photos. A hand-crank weather-band radio was stored in there as well, which he took out and added to a bin. An internet site touted that the oven's structure would protect the items from an EMP attack. Overkill? Probably. Thom's wife got a good laugh on that one. He hoped that the other preparations would prove to be more helpful, but it was anyone's guess.

The bins came in easy enough, but by the end of it, Thom was winded. It was a little more work than he was prepared for at this hour of the day. He was running out of steam for sure. It was at this time that he realized he hadn't eaten all day. He had been running on nervous energy all day, and here he was pushing 5 p.m. with no food. A saucepan came out and a can of beef stew was dumped in. It was bulked up with a can of corn as well. The gas stovetop was lit, and

Thom stepped back to watch it work. Natural gas is pushed through the lines at a mere three pounds of pressure. The gas could last for a while if there is no break in the lines. Thom stood there, watching the blue flames, half-expecting it to stop any second. The flame continued however, and he stepped away.

Toni's van pulled up at that time. Thom breathed a sigh of relief but underneath that sigh was a frown. He knew the real stress was going to start now. Toni is a quite attractive and athletic woman for being in her mid-forties. She projects herself very boldly, and, oh yes, she's a control freak.

Thom walked out to the van from the front door. The kids were tired, they did not run calling "daddy!" They rarely did that anymore. David was twelve, and Chloe was sixteen. They walked up the steps quietly passed their father as he came down. He asked if they were okay, and got a nod from the girl, and a weak yes from the boy. Life is the same, even in an emergency.

Toni was rip-roaring mad stepping out of the van door.

"You told me to go to the grocery store! Do you realize what the grocery store was like? It was a madhouse!" The finger-pointing and head bobbing were in full effect.

"When did you go?" Thom responded calmly.

"An hour ago. It was crazy. I was lucky to get out of the parking lot alive!" A foot stomp came with that one.

"Well, honey, if you remember when we talked about this over a year ago, I told you to only go to the store if it was early in the event." The calmness in Thom's tone wound her up even more.

"Well, I couldn't make it early. I had to pick up the kids, which took forever, and check how the Roselles were doing, and I couldn't make it there early. I made it as early as I could!" Arms were waving now, and her voice could be heard bouncing off the frozen empty streets.

"Hey, don't blame me. The instructions were to go early or not at all. I think we need to drop this right now." This was going to get heated; Thom was going to get drawn in if the battle went much longer. "Did you attempt to go inside?"

"Hell no, I saw a ton of cars out front and the police cruisers lighting up the area and called it quits. But I had a hell of a time getting out of there! Cars were running into each other and sliding into light poles on the ice, and just plain madness!" She was getting close to tears.

"Wow. So, the police were tied up with protecting the grocery store, and probably the gas station too. Doesn't sound like a good use of their time. Do you have anything in the van that needs to be carried in? If not, let's get inside out of this cold. The temperature is dropping fast." Thom got a half hug as she walked up the steps.

The front door was on the side of the house, and as Thom entered, he looked into the three-season room fifteen feet away. He started thinking about defense locations in the three-season room and weapon positions as he heard more anger coming from inside the house.

"Why is my kitchen table covered with cans of food? And why are there wet foot tracks through my kitchen?"

Thom rolled his eyes and changed his thought direction. Now was not the time to be thinking about defense, and certainly not the time to think about what he'd do with a weapon in his hand.

"I've been bringing in the food stored in the garage, sorry about that. We could stack most of it in the back room."

"There's food boiling over on the stove," Chloe said in a monotone voice, adding to the tension in the air.

"You're sixteen, you know what to do!" Her father fired at her as he walked by with a bin of food.

"I thought maybe you knew this was happening. Maybe this is how you cook stuff," she continued with her monotone, reluctantly reaching for the stovetop dial.

60

After the bins were cleared from the table, Thom noticed the flag standing in the corner by the door. Knowing he would forget it later, it was best to hang the flag outside now. The gamble was that he wouldn't have to discuss it until morning, but it was not in the cards.

"Feeling patriotic?" Toni was still in her antagonistic mode.

Thom shook his head, knowing this was not a battle he wanted to face right now. "Carl from work might be joining us tomorrow. The flag is to help him find the house."

"What? I hardly know this man. A flag to get him here proves the fact! He was here at the cookout and barely said hello to me. You can't just go and invite every needy person to our house when we are going to be sleeping on pull-out couches ourselves! This whole prepper thing must stop!"

"You know the prepper junk went out of my life a year ago. I've pushed it away for you and for me. Luckily I've still got most of the stores in the garage though," he said, trying to keep it calm. "Look, you know the reason Carl was cold at the picnic was because he and Deloris were going through a divorce at the time. He's a really good person, and he'll be a good one to have around if this thing drags on for any amount of time. He has family in Kentucky, and if the roads are good in a couple days, he'll probably head south."

"Well, he'd better. The lights will be back on in a few days; just like every other 'disaster' we've seen."

"Honey, you know I just couldn't turn them away. I'm sure you've also told people that they can come to us for help, right?"

There was a pause. "But no one really took me up on the offer. The house is a mess anyway. Now we are going to have guests. You can't just open up our house like this to people!"

"Well, the deal is done, and like you said, it will just be for a couple days." In a louder voice, he called out: "Who wants some beef stew?"

"Wait a minute. You said 'them.' Is there more than Carl?"

61

"Carl got custody of the three kids in the divorce." He looked around the room. "I didn't hear any takers on the stew." If there were some crickets in the house, they'd be chirping.

Toni stormed out of the room and up the steps. This fight was over, but Thom knew the battle would continue.

He turned the stove off and walked back to the family room. Both kids were huddled around the fireplace. Watching the fire was usually a fun time for the kids. This time was not. They stared into the fire as if it may have the answer to what was going on. It didn't.

"The fire looks a little low. Chloe, I want you to put some wood on the fire." He was calm but direct.

"You always put wood in, I've never done it." Thom was glad that she was not back talking this time; it was more of a statement.

"Well, you need to learn. I'm not always going to be here to load the fireplace. We'll need to share jobs for the next few days, OK? We'll do it the first few times with me or your mother watching."

She did a pretty good job, setting them in squarely, so that they wouldn't roll out of the grate. She kept her body further from the fire than needed, but as she got comfortable, she would learn that she could get closer.

"Pretty good job," he praised her, and then looking at David said: "What do you think David?"

Fear went into the twelve-year-old's eyes as he thought he might be expected to do this as well. David was slightly autistic and had many fears. Unlike most autistic kids, who are usually bouncing off the walls with energy and short attention spans, David was the other side of the spectrum. He was quiet and emotional, with jumbled thoughts that made it difficult to find words when telling a story. He found peace in doing puzzles and long projects that the ADHD kids would never be able to focus on long enough. Helping him to express his thoughts was their household challenge, and success usually occurred in the form of two steps forward and one step back. He looked at David and waited.

"It's not going to be my turn next." It was a statement. He spoke his mind and told his father he wasn't going to do that. Thom was ecstatic. He was always such a wishy-washy Charlie Brown sort of youngster. This was a time of emergency, of stepping up and he knew it, but he also knew his limitations. This was a tiny breakthrough moment.

"No, you'll have other jobs, David." He smiled, happy to see him so direct. "How about this? At night we always put the screen in front of the fireplace. Would you like to do that job? Let's practice now."

A smile came over his face to be included. It was still a difficult job for a smaller twelve-year-old, with a decent fear of the fireplace. But he sought approval at every turn, and he was eager to give it a shot. He picked up the screen by the handles, which had some weight to it. It had a front part with two hinged sides to keep it stable and give complete protection. He set it in place, off-center and not close enough to protect the corners. He received some direction to move it closer and was shown what to look for in the corners, so that sparks could not spray into the room while they were sleeping. It was a good moment for everyone. The children worked with their father to develop a skill and Thom did not get frustrated — as he normally did — while trying to teach.

"Beef stew?" All nods around the room. "Ok, let's get a bowl, and go through my supplies. We'll need a few things for tonight."

They were eager to go through the bins set in the sunroom, kind of like Christmas, Thom thought. It occurred to him just then that Christmas was still three days away. They had walked around the unlit Christmas tree in the family room several times without even noticing it. This was going to be a tough holiday.

The sunroom connected the family room to the three-season room, and ran along the back of the main house. It had two sets of French doors leading out to the deck, and was normally a bright and sunny room. Thom had stacked the bins from the garage in the sunroom, and the pile amounted to twelve bins. Two bins were non-food supplies that needed to be sorted.

First, Thom pulled out three old fashioned looking lanterns. He asked David to grab a Sharpie from the kitchen junk drawer and put a "D" on one, and "C" on another, and "MD" on another for Mommy/Daddy lantern. He explained that it was their responsibility to keep track of their lanterns, and to set them in the sunlight during the day to recharge the battery with the solar panel on the top. Next was the crank and solar-powered radio. Giving David the job of cranking it was an easy decision, but hopefully the solar panel would suffice for future use. A wind-up alarm clock was pulled out and set to the correct time. The rest of the supplies were not needed for the first night, they had plenty of candles, and the binoculars, buck knife, and such were shuffled aside.

The lamps worked okay, considering they hadn't been charged in a year, but all they really needed was twenty minutes to grab bedding and pillows from the bedrooms. Toni helped in gathering what was needed to settle in for the night around the fireplace. The two couches in the family room folded out. They were very handy for overnight guests, and for family movie nights, and it worked out just fine in this situation as well. The unnecessary furniture was cleared from the room and gave space to spread out and be comfortable in their new one-room home.

While making the beds, the radio was tuned in. More complete news had reached the airwaves, they found. It was about 7 p.m., roughly ten hours after the start of the outage. The cyber-attack on the Niagara Falls power grid came in through the internet, that much was certain. The report spoke about the power station's protective relays malfunctioning, probably caused by the cyber-bug. The power station and transformers were "violently" tripped off, possibly causing physical damage to delicate and critical hardware. The attack created a cascading fault throughout the Northeast SCADA grid. SCADA was quickly defined as the Supervisory Control and Data Acquisition computer system, and it seemed that the controlling system was turned against itself in the attack. The fault cascaded throughout the grid until every power station, substation, and transformer station controlled by the Northeast SCADA system had been overloaded in some form or fashion. The result was that a substantial chunk of the nation's total power grid had been carved off from the rest. The timeframe for reconnection to the grid was notably absent from the report. Also not mentioned was that the entire transmission to stations in the region were processed in less than fifteen seconds. The cascading progression of the bug flowing through miles of circuitry was not watched on monitors by horrified technicians while they tried to reverse it. In less than fifteen ticks, it was over.

There was more information in that news report than Thom had received all day. The monotone delivery of data seemed to bounce around in his head and stopped making sense about halfway through. Thom reached for the radio and lazily turned the dial. Maybe he could find some sort of local report, of what was going on in the area. In the back of his mind, a request for some mellow music came, just to make everything go away. What he found was certainly not mellow.

"This is Daimon Hellstrom, and I've taken over 95.4 with my ham radio." The voice was loud and brash. The first impulse was to continue turning the dial, but Thom let him continue. "It seems that nobody else is using this nice frequency, so it might as well be me. And no, Daimon Hellstrom is not my real name, but I want to make it as difficult as I can for the FCC to find me later on. I have hijacked this frequency to save lives, friends. If you are hearing my voice from your car radio, as you sit in the new parking lots that used to be our freeways, listen closely, friends. And don't ask me how I know that you are not going anywhere on that interstate. Other folks have these ham radios out there with generators to power them, so I've gotten some good intel. I'm just one of the few with the 'nads enough to pirate a frequency. So please take these nuggets I have for you, friends. Because no freeway in the range of my voice is moving right

65

now, and you might as well get used to it. All it took was a handful of cars with engine trouble or fender benders or cars running out of gas. Combine that with road crews that can't find the disabled car because there is no cell phone service to tell him where to go. This is a perfect storm people, you are in the middle of it, and I want to help you survive it." Thom looked at Toni's expressionless face and scooted closer to the radio.

"So there you are. You might be four or five miles from an exit ramp that normally is the safe haven. In the past when you had car trouble or ran out of gas, all you had to do was get to the next exit. That rule does not hold true tonight. Nothing is waiting for you at the exit. The gas pumps are not working, and McDonald's is not open. I know you are thinking that the gas station should have generators to pump the gas for us and maybe a week from now they will get organized enough to make that happen — but not tonight. The temperature is barely above zero right now, and with wind-chill, it's well below. Don't test it. Stay in your car. Turn on the engine every hour for only a short while to heat up the car. If there is someone in the car with you, bundle together and use your body heat. If there is a safe way to drive out of your spot and get home, take it. Get home if you can, because right now the freeways are parking lots. By morning I fear they will be graveyards."

Thom turned off the radio and turned around to see his family in shock.

"He's kidding, right?" Toni was not buying whatever he was selling. "It's not that bad out there."

"Sure, honey. I'm sure he's exaggerating." Thom was in no condition to battle. His family was safe and the room was warm. Sleep. Sleep was all he wanted.

The kids took comfort in the fact that their dad didn't argue their mother's point. She must be right. Sleep came quickly for all.

Thom awoke around midnight staring into the glow-in-the-dark face of the wind-up alarm clock. It reminded him that everything was real. The events of the day really happened. It was not a dream. He got up and put more wood on the fire, and putting his robe on to brace for the cold, he walked into the front room. It was eerily dark and silent as he sat down on the couch that backed up to the front window. The dark street before him barely looked like his own. A streetlamp usually lighted it, but the dim moonlight lit everything in a completely different way.

It was so dark and cold, and he wished that he was sunbaked and warm, sailing on his boat on the reservoir.

Chapter 5: The Purchase.

Thom found *The Mystic* at the end of a pier, as expected. She was a beautiful fiberglass catamaran, thirty-four feet long, with a nice above-deck seating area, perfect for entertaining. A bright green sail cover kept the sail protected at dock, and gave the boat a nice, rich feel. An inflated dinghy hung off the back of the boat, and the solar panels along the roofline and over the dinghy gave an aura of self-sufficiency. The mast reached up so incredibly high as he approached. As the sun beat down on his face, he felt its heat and smiled. His body felt completely and entirely warm. It was a good day.

Randal was clued to Thom's approach from the sound of his flip-flops on the deck. Thom enjoyed making the noise, and he wanted to wear flip-flops for the rest of his time on this earth. No more snow boots for him.

"Thom, I presume?" Randal Franks was in his mid-thirties, tanned and in reasonable shape. His hair was full, but cropped very short, and begging for a hat. He wore his sunglasses on a tether around his neck, over a green T-shirt as he extended his hand. He had a perfectly relaxed look about him, and it was helping him sell his boat. Thom wanted that look — that relaxed look. Everyone wanted that look, and to feel like that. Thom was on the brink of saying "Sold" before shaking his hand.

"May I come aboard?"

"You surely may, and please leave your shoes on the dock beside mine." Randal was quite the host, pointing out many features of the boat in the above deck area.

"I remember the mention of the Awlgrip deck paint on the boat survey. The footing is great on this boat." Thom was soaking it all in and referring to some documents in a folder at his hip.

The Bimini hardtop gave plenty of shade to the cockpit area, with seating for eight or more in that space, in addition to the captain's perch. Most of the seating was on lockers for all the above deck equipment, such as life jackets, snorkeling equipment, and fishing poles. As they walked forward above deck, the trampoline area between the two pontoons was equally impressive. From the forward area, Thom had a good view of the three large solar panels on the Bimini roof.

"Can those power the entire boat?" he asked, pointing at them.

"Yes, and I have eight batteries in the engine compartment that are charged by them, to power things at night. There is a battery gauge below that allows you to keep an eye on the charge level. When it drops to a certain point, we go dark. You must make sure there're enough amps to start the engines if you need them." Thom nodded in agreement.

Thom noticed the captains' station had three interesting gizmos, a GPS, a depth finder, and a Raymarine Autopilot. "From the official survey, these electronics are all about three years old, right?"

"Yes, and in great shape. All that you'd need for open water travel. Below deck at the chart desk is the Garmin Chart Plotter to take you wherever you want to go, along with the short-wave radio." Randal welcomed him inside the dining area of the boat.

Thom instantly found the radio at the chart desk and held the microphone for an uncomfortably long time. "A radio is an important thing. How old is this unit?" Thom was still trying to shake some thoughts out of his mind while Randal responded.

"I believe it's original to the boat. It really doesn't get much use in day sailing, and what I do. I imagine that an upgrade could be in order if longer trips were the norm, and you're sailing at night. These units are not terribly expensive, and Dave the Harbormaster can find some great deals if given enough time."

Thom's head had stopped swimming, and he nodded in response. He stepped back to the entrance door and looked at the interior from that vantage point.

The doorway gave a line of sight to a large portion of the boat. From that vantage point, one could see the dining area, down below to the galley on the starboard side, and also the port hallway and bathroom door. Looking straight ahead, there were two windows in the dining room wall into the captain's quarters, which were directly forward in amidships. The great advantage in Thom's mind was not only that these areas were visible to the front door, but also that the front door was visible *by* all these areas. From the captain's bed, the front door was always visible. That gave peace of mind to many people, like him.

All the walls had a rich wood panel surface, which gave it a warm homey effect. The Gemini brand is comparable to the Chevy brand of cars — a middle-of-the-road, very dependable entry-level boat. The marine-grade wood panels were an upgrade. Most Gemini's have some wood accents but most of the fiberglass walls were still visible and sterile white. The wood softened things.

Toni will like this, he thought.

The boat had two aft cabins in the pontoons, one starboard and one port, both with double beds. The engines were underneath these beds — probably not the place to try to sleep while motoring, but otherwise very roomy and comfortable with some reasonable storage. The boat had only one head, and it was in the forward port pontoon. The galley was starboard. The captain's quarters had a queen bed and a back door access to the head. The layout had a good flow and efficient use of space.

Randal and Thom inspected the engines although the survey gave them very high marks. They went over the age of the ropes, sails, electronics, and winches, how long since the boat was hauled out and the bottom painted. All answers were just what Thom wanted to hear. He liked everything about this boat and was starting to get giddy.

"What do you need?" Thom asked. As with everything in this world, it always comes down to money.

"It's listed at one seventy, but I could do one sixty-five," he responded calmly, careful to not give away too much.

"How much do you owe?" Thom wanted to dig a little before showing his hand in this poker game.

"I'm at about a hundred grand right now." He wasn't too nervous about giving up the information, and the transparency helped the comfort zone.

"So, you are looking at about sixty-five grand of cash equity to buy your next boat. Do you have other savings you are going to add to your down payment?"

"Uh, not really. I've got a junk truck out there too that needs upgraded, so I'll have less than the sixty-five to put down when all is said and done," he said, a little down. "But it should still get me there, especially if I grab something that needs a repair or two. Those are the ones you find in the foreclosure listings. Having cash in hand and being able to move quickly is the main key to those. With the sale of this boat, I should be in the spot I need to be."

"Have you considered taking on a partner in this venture?" Thom said offhandedly, while still wandering around the boat. He was going through the galley cupboards, looking around.

"Yeah, I've talked to a couple of investors, but they want to take too much of the profit, while not being a part of the business. They think that plopping down some cash should earn them a ton, while I'm doing all the work. It doesn't get it for me." Randal's hand gestures and expression on his face were going the extra mile to explain his point.

"Well, maybe you'll find a partner that's willing to be a true partner someday," Thom said, while locking in on his eyes. "You will probably need more liquid capital to get a top-of-the-line charter business off the ground right." He went back to looking in the cupboards. "Got any beer?"

71

"Check the fridge; I should have a couple bottles."

He pulled out a couple Heinekens and grabbed the bottle opener hanging on the magnetic strip on the wall. Several utensils were stuck there in plain view.

"Pretty handy magnet there," Thom said as he came up the steps with the beers. Randal had already taken a seat at the dining table and was looking a little withdrawn. Thom's dancing around the price and talking about his next purchase probably gave him the idea that this sale wasn't going to happen any time soon.

Thom handed him his beer and said "cheers" as they tapped the bottles and sat down.

"How many people have you shown this boat to?"

"Oh, too many, maybe a dozen. It's tough to get financing, and interest rates have gone up too much," he tried to explain. "This is another reason I want to make my next purchase happen, before rates go higher."

"So if you sold your home here, where would you stay? You got a lady friend or a buddy with an open couch?"

"No major ladies right now, yeah, I'd probably couch surf for a while till I got my stuff together."

Thom sat back in the dinette booth and took a swig from his beer. He looked around the space, trying to think of things he would change if he could. He noticed a flat screen TV hanging from the ceiling in the rear port corner. "Is that TV connected to a DVD player?"

"Yep, I even have some small surround-sound speakers over here to help with the effect. I enjoy my movies."

"Me too, I really do." He took another swig from the beer, taking in the moment. "Alright. Here's the deal if we make a deal. I need someone to teach me everything about this boat. I only have experience with single hull sailboats, so I need some expertise on how

72

to sail a catamaran correctly. And I need help to get my six-person charter captain's license." Randal was nodding his head as Thom continued. "We are talking about a two-to-four-month project here. You could live here on the boat for free, but I am going to kick you out of the captain's cabin. That comes with ownership. You can continue to charter this boat with me as the first mate, and we'll split the charters fifty-fifty. And the price you'll take is one sixty," Thom said firmly.

Randal sat still for a few moments, staring at him, and playing this high-stakes poker game. He was measuring all that was laid out for him. The price was friendly, but it came with a lot of work and perks benefiting the buyer. He expected to lose his bed when he sold the boat, but staying on the boat and being booted to a guest cabin was an uncomfortable twist he hadn't expected. He liked the captain's quarters.

Still sitting at the dinette, Thom stuck out a hand, "So is it a deal?"

"I don't even know you, man," Randal said offhandedly. Being bold, but not over the top. "You come in here looking to be a roommate on a 400-square-foot apartment, while I work to get your captain's certifications for the next few months. This is tight quarters here for two strangers. This is quite a deal indeed. I don't even know if you have that kind of scratch."

Thom took his hand back, putting on his best Eastwood look. Thom had misjudged him a little, thinking he was more desperate than he was putting on. Reaching into the larger hip pocket of his cargo shorts, Thom continued to stare down his negotiating opponent. The pocket had been altered to add a reinforced leather slot inside. His concealed-carry leather holster with a Glock 9mm small magazine was perfectly handy inside the top of the pocket. Comfort came from running his hand over the weapon, then continuing the reach to the money clip at the bottom of the pocket. Eyes still locked, he decided to respond.

73

"What we need here is to build some trust. Trust, I have found, is the most important commodity on this planet. Trust is earned, never given. I will earn your trust, and you will earn mine. It may become the most valuable possession we own." The money clip was put on the table, and slid to him, "So let's start now."

It was a good stack of cash, all $100 bills in a money clip of hammered copper, an old-time sailing schooner etched in the center. Randal flipped through the cash and smiled.

"There's two grand there, call it my non-refundable deposit. You can keep the money clip too, my gift. Are we getting closer to a deal?"

"I think so pal, I like how you work." It was his turn to stick out his hand. He was left hanging for a second, and then Thom finally shook it.

Thom stood up and walked to the doorway. "Great, then I'll be getting some sailing lessons. Let's have the first one today." He slapped both hands on his belly like he was getting ready to have a big meal. "No time like the present!"

Randal gave a surprised expression. "I don't know man; I wasn't really planning…"

"What, you weren't planning on taking a potential buyer out on the water to see the boat perform? Now that the deal is done, you're going to gyp me on the ride?"

"Since you put it that way, I'm in. How much time do you have? How far do you want to go?"

"I don't have to report to work for a few days, Randal, and I want to spend as much time on the water as I can. I don't know if you have a charter tomorrow, but sleeping under the stars tonight on this vessel sure would be cool."

Chapter 6: Day 2.

Thom woke first to the sight of the smoldering fire. It needed wood, and he slowly rose to the occasion. A fireplace is an inefficient furnace. It burns the wood quickly and sends much of the heat up the chimney. It was not best for their purpose here, but it had to do. Thom's prepper supplies had an alternate plan for heat if needed, but he didn't look forward to implementing it. A decision would be needed in a few days, along with some extra muscle to help make it happen.

No one stirred after the fire was rebuilt, so Thom headed to the kitchen. The water still worked, and so did the gas. So far, so good. A teakettle was put on to warm some water. The street was just as he left it at midnight, with no new tire tracks in the fresh snow, and certainly no snowplow. He reached into the kitchen cupboard that held the medicines and pulled out his morning pill bottle. The bottle felt light, and a feeling of dread blanketed him straight down to his toes. Looking in the bottle he saw one pill at the bottom.

"That's depressing," he said to the bottle of anti-depressants.

Thom set the lone pill on the kitchen counter and cut it in half with a steak knife from the drawer. He took the half pill and saved the other for tomorrow.

"Not the withdrawal that a doctor would recommend," he mumbled to himself.

Looking out the kitchen window, he wondered about how many other folks out there would be going off their medications cold turkey this week. People don't keep a reserve of their medications on hand, even though the pills might be instrumental in keeping them alive. They've always been available, and with the pull-up window, he didn't even have to get out of his car. It was never a big concern. With a shake of his head, he set the bottle back on the shelf and closed the door.

The instant coffee in Thom's supplies was supposed to be the worst-case scenario and the last choice. Sadly, it was the only choice with the brewing equipment available. Thom made a point to check for an old-fashioned coffee pot in the garage, but for now he filled two cups.

"That smells disgusting," she greeted her husband.

"It tastes as good as it smells. Good morning to you too, dear." She drank it anyway.

The morning moved slowly as they watched the fire and sipped the coffee. Chloe absentmindedly flipped the light switch in the room while roaming around. As expected, the lights didn't come on, but the kid couldn't be blamed for trying. The foldout couches weren't horrible; an extra layer of egg crate foam had been added on top for extra cushion. It would certainly get old after a while though.

They each had some cereal for breakfast to use up the milk before it went bad. With their bowls in hand around the fireplace, Thom broke out the checklist for the day. Bringing up firewood from the pile at the back of the property was the first order of business, and he enlisted David to help. He would also run the five-horse generator in the garage to power the freezer for an hour and get the temperature where it needed to be. They also needed to consolidate the kitchen freezer into it, so that there was only one unit to worry about. Using the second outlet of the generator to charge some batteries would be a good multi-task. He also talked about blocking off and insulating the sunroom from the rest of the main house. They would need to eventually open that room up to the family room and try to heat them both with the fireplace. The extra sleeping space would be needed when Carl and his family arrived.

Talk of people being invited to stay with them irritated Toni again. Thom tried to cut it off at the pass.

"When we were renovating this house, we blocked off sections to contain the sawdust. We even designed the rooms for the purpose of blocking off sections. The sunroom used to be the workshop while we worked on the main house. We will be able to just do that again and insulate with moving blankets I have in the garage."

76

She just shook her head, "That fireplace is not going to be able to heat both rooms, this is not going to work. We don't have enough space for another family."

"We'll just have to make it work, and it will. I also need you and Chloe to be on a mission to put aside water. We don't know when the water will stop flowing through those faucets. It must be because we have a gravity feed water tower down the street, but when water lines in houses start to freeze and break, we will run out of water as their basements start to fill up with water. We need to save all we can."

Both their heads were nodding, "So what do we do?"

"I want you to use the big punch bowls I got out of the basement and every other large container that we don't need and fill them with water. Cover them with saran wrap if you are concerned about spilling them. We will find places to put them, maybe in the pantry and the fridge as we empty them from food. I have some drinking water in the garage, but not nearly enough. Do you understand? Every container that we don't need should have water in it." Heads were nodding — everyone was on track. "Then I want you guys to clean out the two bathtubs upstairs and fill them. Duct tape the drain cap so that we don't have to worry about leakage. Okay?"

That's where it all came apart.

"There is no way that I'm going to drink water from a bathtub, no matter how much I clean it. That whole exercise is a waste of time." Toni's finger was wagging at Thom's face. She was on her soapbox and not coming down.

"Let me ask you one question. How do you flush a toilet when there is no water running to it?" Her finger dropped. She knew where this was going.

"You pour a gallon of water in the tank, and it flushes. So I'll give you a choice then. Either you clean the bathtubs or you dig an outhouse hole in the backyard. I'll leave it up to you."

77

"You could have told me why we were doing this," she soberly replied.

"You could give me a little credit too. I won't have the time to explain reasons why all the time and sometimes… sometimes it might be best that you *don't* know why. We need to treat this like a military situation, and there's only room for one commander. Now we can work like a team, and get some work done to get us through this thing, or we can complain to each other all day."

There was a silence while the words sank in. Chloe raised her right hand from her side to make a mock salute but thought better of it at the last second and brushed her hair back to try to cover it up. Thom looked right at her during the motion and fought giving her a reprimand about it.

Toni looked at Chloe and said: "Well, we have work to do. Lunch will be made from the stuff in the fridge, and we'll also try to clean out as much as we can today. It will go bad first, so we'll use it first."

"Good idea," Thom said as he started up the stairs. Extra clothing layers would be needed for gathering firewood.

Up in the master bedroom, he decided to take inventory of the home defense equipment while there. A full-sized Glock was under the bed with an extra magazine and 300 hollow point rounds. He remembered a conversation with the bearded *Duck Dynasty* impersonator at the gun shop, as he stated that "clips go in your hair; magazines go in your gun." Thom obviously had the terminology wrong when he asked questions about the weapon. It was good to become educated.

Next to that, he laid the three-inch barrel 9mm that was used for concealed carry. It had a single file magazine holding only nine bullets, instead of the zig-zagging effect of a full-sized mag, affording sixteen rounds in the weapon. The smaller size was so much easier to carry unnoticed though, and as the gun salesman said, "If you can't get it done in nine shots, you are the wrong person in the wrong situation."

Toni's five-shot Ruger .38 revolver was next. It was a nice small weapon that had the unique ability to accept .38, .357, and .357 Magnum ammunition. It gave her the opportunity to learn how to fire with weaker powder count bullets, and then work her way up to the serious ammo with the same weapon. The inventory included a box of each type of ammo, and a couple extra boxes of the .357 Magnum, now her favorite. She enjoyed the two gun classes they attended, but it didn't hold her interest enough after that. Going to the firing range to practice was not her thing, but at least she knew how to handle and fire her weapon. She was not afraid of what would happen when she pulled that trigger; she knew quite well how it would kick, and most importantly, she knew what would come out the other end.

Next to those, he laid his dad's old .22 squirrel rifle. It was a Remington and fired true. It was not a very powerful weapon, but it never left his possession after he inherited it a couple of years earlier. Two boxes of ammo came with the gun, and Thom had purchased a couple more new boxes. He now felt that the amount of ammo for his lone rifle was not enough, especially considering half was questionable. He had no idea of the age or storage conditions of the older ammo.

He scanned the array in front of him on the bed. This was it. This was the extent of his weapons collection — three pistols and a small caliber rifle, plus the Glock that Carl had if he showed up today. He knew of several people who had accumulated an expansive weapons depository. This was as far as Thom would allow himself to venture down the rabbit hole of weaponry. If he had gone further into the Prepper's Wonderland and had the funds, the story would be different. He would have a gun safe the size of a refrigerator in the basement with a couple of AK-47s and who knows what else. But this is where the chips landed. At least he had some protection; that was more than many could say.

The firewood pile was at the back of the lot. The home sat on an acre, and it sloped downhill. At the back line of the lot, Thom had planted a zigzag row of pine trees about fifteen years ago. They were twenty feet tall now, and completely blocked his view of the lot behind it. The purpose fifteen years ago was that the house behind him was poorly kept, and he didn't like the view. Since then, it has changed hands a couple times, and the current appearance didn't need to be blocked. He still liked the trees though and had some pride that he planted them.

Thom grabbed up the plastic two-man sled and carried it down to the woodpile. He had done this work many times in years past when there was snow on the ground. He loaded up the sled with wood and dragged it up to the house. David followed, trying to keep the stack steady, and they only lost one load out of about fifteen loads. The six or seven inches of accumulation gave the lawn a light and playful feel. It would have been considered beautiful and welcomed in normal times.

"No snow angels or playing in the snow today, David," Thom told him.

"Why not? This is the good, heavy sledding snow. Why not?" he pleaded.

Thom held back and thought about it a little. He questioned if the child could handle it. Thom told him anyway: "I don't want any extra footprints in the snow around the house. I want to be able to tell if someone else has been walking around our house." Some recognition came to David's face in what Thom was saying. "Maybe we can play in the snow somewhere else, but not here. It's too important to keep it clean."

David's mind was chewing on what he said for a while, as they continued to stack firewood in the three-season room. Thom deliberately stacked the wood in the corner of the room that faced the back yard, creating a bunker, a position to defend from. The furniture was rearranged, and some was taken to the garage to give room for

80

work. It was time-consuming, but Thom was happy with the arrangement when it was done. The center of the 22-by-14-foot room was open space, with a couple of wicker chairs remaining, along with a couple of captain's chairs from the dinner table they normally kept in the room. Bunkers were created in a front corner, and a rear corner, along with a large stack for actual burning.

"Should I be scared?" David finally mustered the confidence to say, as they were finishing up.

Thom paused and sat down in one of the wicker chairs.

"Sit down, son. We are going to be living here without power for a while. How long, I don't know. But your mother and I and some friends are going to work together and pull through this. What you can be is alert. I want you to be aware of what's happening around you, but you do not need to be afraid. Does that sound okay? Aware, not afraid?"

"Aware of what?"

"Aware of things going on inside the house, and outside. Like the gray minivan pulling up out front. It looks like my friend Carl has finally arrived."

Thom stepped inside and yelled upstairs that Carl was there, only to find that Toni was five feet away in the kitchen. He apologized and stepped back into the three-season room so that he could go out its door to the porch. Greetings were extended to his friend on the porch, and he shook his eighteen-year-old son Erich's hand. Erich looked to be a good, clean-cut kid. He was a senior in high school, standing about 5-foot-10 with a good amount of muscle on his thin frame. He was in every sport imaginable, as Thom could tell from his varsity coat's sewn-on patches. Thom knew from the stories Carl told though, that Rugby ran in the family, and it was his favorite. Behind him came Carl's daughters, Sasha and Jacquelyn, ages eight and ten. Both girls were active in gymnastics and very energetic. A little too energetic for Thom's taste, but he got over it. Carl had several pet names for his

81

Baby Girls, and it was hard to keep track. Thom soon found that the younger would answer to Baby, and the middle child would answer to Sissy. To keep things simple for his attention-span-challenged mind, Thom latched onto that information and never permanently filed away their actual names in his brain. Sad, but true.

Toni was warm, as she is to all guests of her home. The van was packed to the ceiling with stuff, and the group unloaded it to the sunroom as a staging area. Thom noticed boxes of Christmas presents as being almost a third of the load in the van.

"I don't remember Christmas presents being on the checklist, Carl." Thom was surrounded by brightly wrapped boxes, and not happy about it.

"I couldn't just leave these things behind to be stolen by the looters. They are brand new."

"I'm sure it was a dilemma that lots of people faced, but just tell me you didn't leave food behind to make room for this stuff."

"I brought what I had on the list, Thom. It's sad how little food I had in the cupboards. I hope it doesn't get to the point that I wish the new Xbox was food instead."

"We got a new Xbox?" Carl's son Erich chimed in but was quickly waved off to get another load.

"How were the roads, Carl?" Thom relented on the presents and spoke in a hushed tone.

"I took surface roads like you said, but to get out of the city I had to cross a couple freeways. They were packed, man. And there were a lot of people on foot. The radio stations were sending them to the school buildings for shelter. I think the kids are still a little shell-shocked."

"Did you see any snowplows?"

"I did see one, but that was it. There're abandoned cars every now and then that are half-on and half-off the road. Probably ran out of gas. I bet it's hard for a snowplow to do their job with stuff like that going on."

"Travel is going to be tough, Carl. Get comfortable." Thom put his arm around his shoulder and gave Carl a brotherly pat on the back. "I think you're going to be here a while. Let's put these presents under the tree."

"Do you guys wait till the last minute with your presents?" Carl said as he placed his presents under the empty Christmas tree.

"Yeah, man, Santa brings them all." A little head tick motioned towards David, and Carl caught the hint.

When they were in the sunroom again getting another load, Thom came clean. "This was to be David's last year for the illusion of Santa, but we might have to bust the bubble a little early. It's a real shame, but just like your kids' ride-in this morning, some harsh realities are going to be faced."

"I just hope this thing doesn't go on for a long time."

"You and me both."

The food was organized, and most was stored neatly in the basement. Thom stored some reserves in two bins marked "xmas decorations," and hid them in the corner. He read that this was a good idea. So, if your main supplies were stolen, you'd have a reserve unnoticed. Hopefully this would be another overkill preparation that he would laugh about later. Carl certainly got a chuckle. Mattresses were brought down from the kids' rooms and thrown on the floor in the sunroom, which was blocked off. Toni was right, it didn't stay very warm.

As dusk began to fall, Thom asked for Toni's van keys and told Carl he needed to move his van too. "Everything should be parked at the bank parking lot down the street."

"That's not necessary; I'd like to keep my van where I can see it," she said flatly. "They are not going to get plowed in, there's no plows running."

"It's not about them being plowed in. I want a clear vision of the street in front of our house. It's a comfort level measure." Looking around the room, Thom could see that Chloe was eavesdropping, and so was Carl's son Erich. He still wanted to win this battle without being too alarming to the kids.

"What if it gets broken into down there? I want to protect my vehicle!" Her tone was getting louder, and the two young adults were openly paying attention now.

"Remember our discussion about what kind of operation this is?" Thom paused, but she did not back down. She wanted an explanation and wouldn't stop till she got one. "I need a clear line of sight from our location. Not only do the vehicles block my view, but they also become a location for a combatant to hide behind and attack us from. Do you understand what I'm saying? We have enemy bunkers twenty yards from our front windows, and I would like to remove them right now if you would please give me your keys." His eyes locked on hers and held out a hand.

Luckily, only the older kids heard that statement, but it was an eye-opener for them. They stood quietly, unmoving. Thom dared not glance at them as he took her keys.

"It's a little early for that kind of thinking — "

"Yes, it is," Thom interrupted her. "But now is the best time to take care of this. More snow is expected, and a snowplow actually might come through. We should move them while we can."

On the walk back from the bank, Carl asked if Thom really thought that they would be attacked.

"Last night, in your house, Carl. Did you hear any gunshots?"

"Of course I did. They were far away, not right out front. But yes, I heard some shots," he quietly answered.

"No shots here, Carl. But it's coming this way. We are off the beaten path, almost hidden, but we will have traffic. I am certain. Let's do the watch tonight together and work out what to look for."

"Sounds like a plan. I don't think we have enough beds for all of us to sleep at once anyway. It looks like we will have to sleep in shifts."

They came inside to the welcome aroma of food cooking on the gas burners of the kitchen stove.

"Oh, that smells good!" Thom said while taking off his boots. "And you know what it means when we have natural gas and still have running water?" Thom looked at Carl while saying it loud enough for everyone to hear.

"No, I don't know what that means," Carl said loudly also, playing along.

"The water heater is natural gas, no electricity needed… It means we have hot water!"

"Really? I had no idea, and boy do I need one!"

"Well Carl, I didn't want to say it in front of everyone…"

"But you thought so too, huh? Well, then I'm first! Point me to the shower!"

The downstairs bathroom had a full shower stall, and it was on the warmer side of the house. Everyone clamored to get their showers in, even if by candlelight. Thom announced that he would shower upstairs in the master bath, even though it would be colder. The warm water would make the difference he figured. The shower was the greatest moment of the day for probably everyone in the house, but especially so for Thom. He was able to drift away and leave this crazy world behind. The pain, the confusion, the stress, all rolled off his body and down the drain. As the steam rose to the ceiling, so did he. He let it all go just for a few minutes in the heat of the spraying water.

Getting out of the shower, Thom realized that the whole cold room and hot shower idea had its downside. He quickly dried and put on a thick robe. As he brushed his hair, he saw a candle come around the corner, held by Toni.

"How was the shower?" She greeted him with a smile.

"It was wonderful, but when it's over, it's over," he laughed.

"I'm sorry for questioning you, Thom," she solemnly said. Apologies didn't come often from Toni.

"No, a lot of this is on me, honey. I get all worked up trying to get ready for the long haul and it gets the better of me."

"And that's where we collide Thom. Because I don't want to believe that there will be a long haul. I am fighting the thought of a long haul. I'm not fighting you. I'm fighting that thought. And I don't want it to happen. Maybe if we prepare for it, then it will be more likely to happen."

"We are past that now honey. If it's going to happen, it's going to happen. Better to be ready than to be caught with our pants down."

Toni smiled at the comment of her husband while in a bathrobe. "I'll try to work with you more, but I will not give energy to the universe to help this thing last longer." She then put her hand on his side and gave him a kiss.

"I can work with that," Thom nodded in approval.

Toni's hand then moved to his robe belt and slowly began to pull as a sly smile formed on her face.

"Now what was that comment about being caught with your pants down?"

86

It was what they both needed — an escape, a return to normalcy, if only for a little while. And it was just for a little while, because it was dang cold up in that room!

Downstairs everyone was huddled around the fireplace, and the adults were glad to see the kids playing cards on one of the folded-out couches. No TV, no problem. To see that transition happening smoothly gave comfort, at least for the time being. They soon gave up and went to sleep at an early hour, with Carl tucking in his children. Thom grabbed the radio and let Toni know that he and Carl would be in the front room listening to the news reports. She gave him a heartfelt kiss before turning in with the kids.

The front window of the house was mesmerizing in the darkness. Snow was falling out there; they both knew it had been snowing for a couple hours. However, the dense cloud cover blocked out the moon and even the white falling snow found very little light to reflect back to their retinas. Just when the hypnosis seemed complete, Carl spotted something out of the corner of his eye on the coffee table and spoke.

"How about turning on the radio?"

It hadn't been turned on all day. Thom looked at the box with some trepidation but reached for the button anyway. The dial had not been changed, so the brash voice of the night before filled the room.

"We need to take the news reported today with a grain of salt, friends. They have found proof that Iran is behind the cyber-attack, and that's great. Did Russia help them? Maybe another country? What should we do in retaliation? I listened to one central Ohio radio station speculate for a full twenty-seven minutes on these possibilities. Does anyone in central Ohio really care? If the retaliation would melt the snow and bring spring weather tomorrow, I would be all into it. I guess it's all about perspective. The airwaves were full of this so-called news, but there was not one mention of when the power would be restored. I don't know about you people out there who are listening to me rant, but I'm pissed."

"Who is this guy?" Carl was not expecting Daimon Hellstrom when the radio was turned on.

"Just listen. He's a local ham radio operator." Thom kept his answer short to continue listening.

"It's true that the Columbus stations directed those stranded on the freeways to the local schools and municipal buildings. I imagine that many lives were saved from the frigid temperatures today, although I also heard that they arrived at empty buildings with food and supplies still en route to the locations. If you are lucky enough to be in your home, my best advice is to stay in and buckle down. And if a freeway refugee ends up on your doorstep, show him the same hospitality you would hope to see in his shoes."

"So, the traffic to be concerned with will be on foot." Thom tuned down the radio and used the ham radio guy's rant to lead into the conversation.

"Sounds right," Carl replied. "If they are driving, they are trying to shortcut around a road blockage, and they are going somewhere. This is not their destination, and they will continue their travel. The walkers are our real concern."

"The smoke coming from the chimney will draw them right to the house. If they are looking for shelter, friend or foe, it will be impossible to hide. I remember hearing about the prepper types that survived Katrina having the same problem. The bad guys would just listen for the sound of a gas-powered generator; the sound would carry for a good distance on the floodwaters. And that noise brought them right to the prepared people with food and water."

"But not everyone drawn to your door by the smoke will be a bad guy, though. You can't make that assumption."

"You are right, Carl, I can't. But we should protect our families by assuming they are bad until they prove otherwise. Once we meet them we must learn about them and decide if they can be trusted. If not, they must be shown the door."

"I see where you are going with this, Thom. I can also see that we will need a few more trusted adults in the house to cover watch times like we are doing right now. That's what we are doing right, standing watch?"

"Yes, Carl, we are. Let's talk about what to do when we first spot a walker. Let's say I see a group of people on foot to the south of the town square. The first thing I would do is call it out, but I'm also keeping them in my sight. I do not look away. I let someone else sound the alarm and tell the others. It's kind of like a man overboard drill on a boat. Someone must always keep an eye on the swimmer so that he is kept track of, and the captain and crew can do their jobs to save him. So, I am the spotter and I also call out the number of walkers in the group. I verify the count multiple times, and I also try to determine any weapons, how many men, women, stuff like that."

"Sounds like an awful lot of stress when they are far away. We'll soon find out when they get to the house, right?"

"Well, the count of walkers is crucial, because as the group gets closer, they may send off a flanker when they pinpoint which house is putting the smoke into the air. So, if we originally spot five and only four show up out front to talk, we've got a flanker trying to find a weakness in the fortress."

"Damn," Carl motioned to the large front window he was staring out of, "sounds like we need to work on the fortress."

"I guess so. I've got some left-over lumber in the garage from the house renovation. We could build a bunker here facing the front door. It's a French door, and the glass can be used against us too easily."

"Maybe we should block it off completely with a 2-by-10 across the middle so it can't be opened."

"Good idea, Carl. We'll use the three-season room as our main entrance and staging area to vet a refugee before letting them in the house. I made a couple bunkers in there with firewood, but we might need further protection. A room made of glass will take some effort to fortify."

"How are we going to build all this without power? I know they did it in the old days, but they had special tools to use."

"Well, Carl, I've got a little five-horse generator I've been using to keep the freezer at the minimum. We can charge up the cordless drill batteries at the same time and maybe run the miter saw to cut some lengths. I've only got about ten gallons of gas, but we should be able to get the job done. At least we are starting early. We shouldn't see aggressive people yet."

"Yeah, but how long do you think we have? I mean we have this bone-chilling weather and now the snow is really coming down. I mean, no fuel and food is one thing, but these news reports have to be putting everyone on edge."

Thom looked over at the radio. Daimon Hellstrom was ranting about the local government being caught without a plan for a large-scale power-down event. He felt the people in charge were scrambling for answers and not finding many. Some people were going to die because of their own unpreparedness, but countless more would die because their government failed them, according to Daimon.

"I don't know how long we've got till things get crazy, Carl. I really don't know."

Christmas Eve went well with projects and getting the house ready. The radio played throughout the day, but nothing material was reported. The weather was not warming up and the possibility of snow would be with them every day for a while. The kids were put to work gathering firewood and everyone was hungry when dinner was served around the fireplace. It was risky to turn on Hellstrom with children in the room, but the monotone of the day's newscasters had worn the adults down. They needed something with some entertainment value, and Hellstrom usually delivered. This evening was surprisingly so.

"Well, friends, it is certain that we will have a white Christmas this year, no doubt about that. Over the years we have had some special Christmases in this country, and some were celebrated on the airwaves. On December 24, 1968, the crew of Apollo 8 read in turn from the Book of Genesis as they orbited the moon. Bill Anders, Jim Lovell, and Frank Borman recited Genesis chapter one, verses one through ten — for which they were promptly sued by the American Atheist Association, which is probably why we don't hear of anything like this anymore. I would like to play the one-minute broadcast for you in its entirety. This was back when America was pure and excited about discoveries. Where she is now is anyone's guess."

The crackling recording came on the air, and the familiar first words of the Bible immediately gave comfort to everyone in the room. Smiling faces with tears streaming down the sides looked at each other and the words continued to come. Toni reached out to her children's hands, and the rest quickly followed suit.

Bill Anders

> "We are now approaching lunar sunrise, and for all the people back on Earth, the crew of Apollo 8 has a message that we would like to send to you:
>
> 'In the beginning God created the heaven and the earth.
> And the earth was without form, and void; and darkness was upon the face of the deep.
> And the Spirit of God moved upon the face of the waters. And God said, Let there be light: and there was light.
> And God saw the light, that it was good: and God divided the light from the darkness.' "

Jim Lovell

> "And God called the light Day, and the darkness he called Night. And the evening and the morning were the first day. And God said, Let there be a firmament in the midst of the waters, and let it divide the waters from the waters.

And God made the firmament, and divided the waters which were under the firmament from the waters which were above the firmament: and it was so.

And God called the firmament Heaven. And the evening and the morning were the second day.' "

Frank Borman

"And God said, Let the waters under the heaven be gathered together unto one place, and let the dry land appear: and it was so.
And God called the dry land Earth; and the gathering together of the waters he called Seas: and God saw that it was good."
"And from the crew of Apollo 8, we close with good night, good luck, a Merry Christmas – and God bless all of you, all of you on the good Earth."

The recording was over too soon, and thankfully followed with a moment of silence from Hellstrom's brash voice. It seemed that everyone searched for answers in each other's eyes, but in the end, found none.

The next morning, Toni brought the gifts up from the basement and tried to wrap some, but it was too much with all that was going on. Most were just in shopping bags with nametags on them. The kids were still excited; it really didn't matter. They were still able to escape and feel like it was any other Christmas morning as they opened their gifts. Only if they blocked out the temperature of the house, no lights on the tree, and the TV noticeably black beside it. At least Vince Guaraldi's Peanuts Christmas album played in the background from a battery-powered CD player. There was an uncomfortable silence when an electronic toy was opened. The newest generation Xbox should have brought much delight, but it awkwardly did not on this day.

David's expression through the morning was distant sometimes; Thom and Toni tried to keep him engaged. He selected a couple gifts and focused on them like he always did on Christmas morning. But occasionally he would look around or just stare at the floor in a sad sort of way.

Thom called him into the kitchen when all the gifts had been opened.

"You alright, buddy?" Thom kneeled on one knee so he could look him in the eye.

"Yeah, I'm alright, Dad. I'm okay." He wasn't covering up his down mood very well, though.

"Realizing there's no Santa is a tough one, huh?" It was finally coming home. They had kept the charade on for too long, but for him, it was easier than telling the truth.

"If there was one, he would take us back to the North Pole. He would help us. But there isn't one."

"Well, look outside. We've got our own North Pole right here," Thom said with a smile, but the weak joke didn't get very far. "I'm planning to take a walk around town today and see who's still at home. I'm going to wish everyone a Merry Christmas. Do you want to go with me?"

It was a great subject change, and it put a smile on his face to be a part of something so nice. Of course, there was more to it than being nice, Thom needed to scope out the territory around his fortress. Having a child along made him a less imposing character. If the neighbors didn't recognize him right away, their response should be a little more measured with a child in the mix. Besides, Christmas Day was the best day to go visiting. You'd at least hope that people wouldn't be trigger-happy on that one day of the year.

The pair suited up, and surprisingly, Toni was on board with the project – if she could join them. Thom fought the request, it would only leave one true adult at the house, and she could handle a weapon better than Carl. Toni knew many of the village residents and strongly felt she could help with the introductions. She ended up winning the battle because of Candice. Candice Donovan lived at the other end of their street and was suffering from terminal cancer. Toni wanted to check on her friend, and Thom gave her a pass. Much like she gave him one a couple of nights before.

The village had about fifty homes. The first few door approaches were nerve-wracking. Banging on someone's door in this situation was certainly a stressful event. The first couple of homes had no response, probably no one home, but the Vespers were recognized and welcomed into the third. The Johnson family had emotions that were all over the board. They were inquisitive and scared, but mostly angry. The Vespers' visit was used as an opportunity to vent all their problems and concerns on someone as if the Vespers had the power to fix them. Thom and Toni soon saw that their time was not being well spent in this situation and worked their way to the door. Some helpful advice about saving water was given, and they promised to be back when they could help more.

Once outside, Thom and Toni regrouped and devised a plan to speed up the process. Their objective was to find out which homes were occupied, and they even had a crude map to mark the homes and names on. They also wanted to define any special needs that a home may have and attempt to help. The itinerary of goals for the visit helped to keep them focused and also might get them home before dark.

A particular house in the neighborhood had smoke pouring from a chimney sticking out of the pole barn in the back yard. Thom was familiar with the family and walked towards the barn calling out Mr. Dennison's name. The only reply was the sliding load of a 12-gauge shotgun.

"It's me, Denny, Thom Vesper. I'm just checking on the neighbors to see if everyone is okay." Thom dared not to go to the door. He yelled from the yard, and the rest of his family stayed even further back.

"We're okay. You don't need to worry about us. Just go on and check somewhere else," he called through the door.

"Alright, Denny, I'll move on. I may stop back in a couple days to check on you if that's okay. I just want to know one thing, how many people do you have in there?"

"There're four. Now git!"

Thom loudly quick-stepped away from the barn as he caught up to his family.

"Didn't know he could count that high," Toni whispered into Thom's ear on the way to the next home.

About forty percent of the homes were occupied, and after a few empties, the Vesper's found the door of Linda and Allen Lansbury.

"What do you want?" Allen stopped them before they could knock.

"We are the Vespers from down the street," Toni took this one, with her friendly voice. "We are going around the neighborhood to check on folks to see if they need anything. Make sure they're okay."

"We're okay, don't need anything." Allen wasn't giving an inch.

"Allen, honey, do you recognize that boy? He rides his bike past here all the time to the park." Linda held her husband's arm.

"Yes, I do." He turned to look her in the eye. "I guess they really are neighbors."

"Let's let them in. I bet they are cold."

The door was unbolted and opened. "Come on inside, you must be freezing." It was Linda's voice this time.

"We can only stay for a few minutes," Thom said as he entered. "We have several more stops to make."

"What's your name, young man?" Linda asked when the family was inside, and the door closed.

"David," he shyly responded, and much to his parents' surprise, he stuck out his hand to shake.

The greetings ensued, and Thom helped himself to warm his hands by the fireplace. He noticed that the room had been blocked off from the rest of the house, and blankets were hanging over each doorway and window. In the corner, behind a chair, he spotted a few plastic bins with what appeared to be canned food inside — a lot of canned food. Thom didn't notice that some were dented from the unorthodox loading at the grocery store.

"Looks like you folks are set up just fine with no needs here," Thom couldn't resist saying something.

Allen picked up on where Thom's eyes had been, and it concerned him.

"Yeah, we went shopping." He stood a little straighter and put his hands on his hips. The movement brushed open his jacket to show the butt of the 9mm in his waistband.

Thom noticed, but then Linda noticed, and she placed a light elbow into his kidney.

"I don't think there's any need for muscle flexing, is there?" The elbow put her husband in check, but the words were pointed directly at Thom. There was no mistaking that her words meant business. Maybe even more than the weapon he was shown.

"Absolutely not. What's yours is yours. No worries there. This thing shouldn't last long enough for us to start talking about rationing and all that," Thom used his best diplomacy voice.

"What kind of timeframe do you believe this will have?" Allen was still standing firm with some sharpness to his words while rubbing his kidney a little.

Thom glanced over to his son.

"Not too much longer."

The motion essentially defused the conversation. There was a child present, and the answer for the child's benefit was given. It also showed that Thom believed the actual answer was far different.

"We've been giving advice about filling bathtubs with water," Toni stepped in to change the subject. A slight motion towards the door was passed to her husband as she spoke.

"We hadn't thought about that," Linda responded. "It could be used for many things. Maybe after boiling, I could even drink it." Toni smiled at her husband with the comment.

"We've also found a ham radio operator that has pirated the FM frequency 94.5. He's not for the faint of heart, but it's good to have different points of view." The Lansburys were the first family Thom had shared this tidbit with, but from the looks of them, they could handle it.

Toni then gave Thom a look that assured him it was time to go. Mention of Mr. Hellstrom sealed it for her. Pleasantries were exchanged quickly and the move out the door was made. Linda gave special attention to David in her goodbyes and again surprising his parents, he seemed to like it.

Candice and her husband, Jeffery, lived at the edge of town, and their home sat back from the street. The 1960s-era brick home turned out to be the last occupied home on this side of town. The shrubbery and trees in the large front yard had a beautiful look with the six inches of snow crafted to them over the last few days. The long driveway gave time for the mood to step down several notches, at least in Thom's mind. He knew what was coming. A woman he had known for several years who was always full of life and energy, now dying of breast cancer. The stress and dread of this moment brought about a pounding headache in his left temple and some difficulty keeping his balance by the time they reached the door.

Young Phillip Donovan answered the knock. Phillip was thirteen, and the disease that was stealing his mother's life was also stealing his adolescence. Phillip was jumping from childhood straight to adulthood — do not pass GO, do not collect $200. His eyes were firm and unwavering when he answered the door. Shaking everyone's hand, his greetings were polite and confident.

"Toni! Thom!" Jeffery entered the front room. "And how are you, David? It's so nice to see you guys."

"Great to see you too Jeffery." Toni hugged him. "How's Candice?"

"She's resting right now. She's doing okay; the blackout hasn't really hurt our situation much. We just have to pile on more blankets."

"That's surprising, Jeffery, what about her medications?" Toni continued to speak while Thom's headache seemed to take on a life of its own. The walls began to breathe in and out rhythmically in tune with the pulse throbbing in his left temple.

"We have a great supply here in the house. Our hospice nurse, Marie, stopped by the day of the blackout and gave us all she had in the car. I guess she lost one patient that day and they moved another, so we benefited by being her last stop of the day."

"Wow, even her insulin?"

"Amazing that she had extra from the patient she lost, she must have been diabetic also. The challenge has been keeping it at the proper temperature, but I've worked out a process using snow and a container in the basement. I've kept her sugar at a good level considering our obvious change in diet the last few days."

"I'd really like to say hi to her if she's not too tired."

"I just gave her some pain medication and she's out like a light," Jeffery stopped to smile at the unintentional pun. "Please come into her room anyway."

The group walked into the room and watched the dying woman peacefully sleep. Toni spoke encouraging words to her, hoping they would soak into her subconscious and give her strength. For Thom,

98

the walls slowly returned to their normal non-breathing mode, aided by Candice's tranquil appearance. His throbbing temple remained, regardless of how much he rubbed on it.

The group returned to the front room and Phillip tended to the fire. In classic 1960s design, the fireplace was situated between the living room and the kitchen and was open to both sides.

"The open design puts off a lot of heat to both sides, but it has a hard time heating both rooms," Jeffery explained while Phillip worked.

"Is there anything you need?" Thom finally jumped into the conversation, still rubbing his head.

Jeffery thoughtfully shook his head, but then came up with something when he looked at his son.

"Phillip left his boots at school in all the confusion, and they were the only boots he had. David is about the same size; does he have an extra pair of boots? It would really help with carrying in firewood."

"I think we have you covered, Jeffery," Toni assured him, "I have an extra pair for sure."

"I'll bring them to you tomorrow," Thom volunteered. "I'll also carry in a few loads for you tomorrow while I'm here." Getting out of the house had been good for Thom, and he wanted to get out again. He just hoped the headache would stay at home.

On the night shift, Thom decided to keep Carl company for some of his watch, even though it wasn't his turn.

"This coffee really is nasty," Carl informed him.

"That stuff is batting a thousand in this house. We need to find a true coffee brewer somewhere. Ever since Keurig came along, everyone has forgotten how to brew coffee." Thom took a sip of his cup anyway and twisted his face a little.

"The radio stations aren't giving us anything new. All they talk about is who they are going to attack. Should I give the crazy man a try?"

"I'd say it can't hurt, but some of the things he says, do. What the hell." Thom reached for the radio dial and was pleasantly surprised that the craziness was toned down this time.

"Well, friends, I've been scooping the rumor mill and came up with something interesting, especially for us Ohioans. Do you remember back in August 2003, we had a statewide power outage? It started in Ohio and cascaded all across the Northeast corner of the country, even taking out New York City. The news broadcasts made a big deal of subway passengers walking out of the subway tunnels, and civilians taking it upon themselves to direct traffic. This was two years after 9/11, so it was very calming that the news immediately stated that it was *not* an attack of any kind. It was caused by downed tree branches in Ohio and functional errors of what to do with the overloads. The overloads cascaded all the way back to the Niagara Falls power station. The outage lasted for only two or three days, depending on the location and it was back to normal. Well, friends, the latest story is that our outage was designed to duplicate the outage of 2003 by our attackers. Only worse. They analyzed it and reproduced it. Our outage started in Ohio just like the other, but ours packed more punch — overloading transformers and burning them out, instead of just tripping breakers in most places. We still don't know for sure who or why, but we do know the structure and design. I know this doesn't help any of us sitting around our woodstoves. But it's closer to home than hearing about a fleet of aircraft carriers headed to the Middle East. Stay safe out there, friends."

"Dang," Carl looked over at Thom. "Yes, I'm still talking about the coffee, hehe. That's an interesting rumor; it does make sense."

"It does at that. I guess it also explains why this section of the country is blacked out. It does mirror the blackout of 2003. The same area of the country and everything."

"Another difference from 2003 is that the cyber-attack news came out soon after the blackout. Chaos was created right off the bat," Carl added.

100

"I have to agree. That element ramped things up and helped to put all those people on the freeway, trying to escape. Maybe there would have been fewer travelers without that bit of news."

"So, the terrorists analyzed the error in the system from 2003 and recreated it?" Carl posed.

"Or maybe they didn't have to analyze the error of 2003, because *they* created it."

"What?"

"Maybe 2003 was the test run." Thom sat back and sipped the nasty coffee. "And now we are experiencing the perfected version of that test."

Chapter 7: The Walkers.

The first walkers appeared at about ten in the morning. Thom was napping by the fireplace to make up for his night watch shift and was awoken by Erich.

"We have some Walkers," he quietly said in a very measured tone. It was not an alarming tone, which Thom appreciated. A discussion was had around the fireplace one evening about how to wake someone up in emergency situations. People were able to sleep much more soundly knowing that they were not going to be woken by someone freaking out unless completely warranted.

"How many?" He said, reaching for his shoes.

"It looks like two adults with a small child," Erich replied, walking back to the front of the house.

He picked up the 9mm from the side table of the foldout couch and stood up only enough to sit back down. The dizziness caused by trying to get up too quickly made Thom sit there and hold his head for a couple of seconds. Looking into the crackling fire fueled his rage and frustration in having to deal with these headaches. The gun in his hand reminded him that now was not a good time to be angry. He stood slower this time and requested to anyone listening for some Excedrin.

He headed to the front of the house; Carl was there, waiting for him. He reported that the Walkers had come up from the square; no other Walkers were spotted with them. They were dragging a piece of luggage behind them and moving pretty slow. Right then, while Carl was talking about them, the adults stopped and pointed at the house. Their heads nodded, and then they continued forward. Game on.

"Okay. Erich you are on point with me. Time to put on your game faces, people. They look pretty safe, but I still want us to treat this like we drilled."

Thom took the Excedrin and walked back through the sunroom to the three-season room. The three-season room was the defense room, and staging area for new visitors. Three two-by-eight boards were

102

installed as the point man's protection, hanging straight down in front of the sliding glass door. The boards were removable when they wanted to actually use the door to let someone in. When the boards were in place, the point man had about a foot of clearance to talk through the open door and also to point a weapon. Once the protection boards were in place, they realized that one layer of wood two inches thick was not enough and doubled it. They were quite heavy, but manageable when taken down one at a time. Thom took his spot behind the boards, and Erich took his in the bunker protected by firewood. His first time firing a pistol was two days before, when he was taken to the river for shooting practice. He was nervous with the weapon, but it was hoped that he would get better over time.

The couple was young, thirty or so, with a three-year-old child. They were dragging luggage wrapped in a plastic bag in the snow. It was a sorry sight, and they looked like they were going to fall over at any moment. The steps to the front door had been shoveled and swept. The American flag was still proudly flying on the post. They left their luggage in the street and carried their child up the steps. On the porch, the father set the child down and both adults raised their hands to their sides. It really appeared that they didn't have the strength to raise them completely over their heads if they had to. They stared into the house through the front French doors waiting for something to happen.

"What do you want?" Thom called out. It surprised them, coming from the three-season room. And the husband turned quickly in the direction of his voice. To which Thom responded, "Slow down, pal. No sudden movements, okay?"

"Okay. Okay. A warm place — that's all we want. Our child…" his voice wandered off.

"Do you have any food?"

"We have some canned goods in the luggage, but not very much," he said sadly. Thom wondered how many other people would think to pack some food. Would they just drag around luggage full of

103

underwear, or had they thought about life sustaining things like… food.

"Where did you sleep last night?"

"In our car, on State Route 3. We slid off the road last night. We stopped at a couple houses this morning, but no one would take us in. You've got to help us, it's so cold and we're so tired."

"Do you have any weapons?"

"No. We have no weapons," his voice had a glimmer of hope. He hadn't been sent away, yet.

"None at all? Not even a knife or the tire iron from your car?"

"None," he said as he realized how good of an idea that was. But it hadn't occurred to him at all.

"Stand so that I can see both of you, and no sudden movements," Thom ordered them.

Thom motioned to Erich that it was okay, and he came over to remove the door blockades. Carl came back to the sunroom per the protocol. He was to stand in the doorway from the three-season room to the sunroom, and Erich on the other side of the room. With these positions the Walkers were surrounded in case they became aggressive. Carl had the old .22 rifle and Erich had one of the 9mm pistols. When everyone was in position, Thom invited the guests into the three-season room.

"My name is Thom; this is Carl, and his son, Erich," his tone was as pleasant as possible with a gun in his hand, not to mention the other two holding guns as well. At least they weren't pointing the weapons directly at them, but they were on the ready.

"I'm Brad, and this is my wife, Michelle. Our little one is Brad Junior. We are from Westerville," he added.

"Didn't get very far, did you? Where are you going?"

104

"My parents live in the country up in Loudonville. We were trying to get there," he said in a self-defeating tone. "I don't know what we will do now."

"Loudonville is at least an hour's drive from here, so I don't have any answers for you on that. Look, I know you guys are in a tough spot, and I think you realize that too. We want to help you, and we will help you. I hope you understand that. It's just that we cannot put our families in danger in the process of helping someone." Thom looked at Carl and got a nod of approval; they had passed the test as far as Carl was concerned, and Thom had to agree.

"What we are doing here is building trust in each other," Thom said as he turned his full attention back to the couple. "You stated that you do not have any weapons, and I do not believe that you are lying. However, I would like for both of you to press on your coat pockets to show they are empty, and pull up your coats to show the waistband of your trousers. I'm sorry for the imposition, but you can console yourself that other travelers will go through the same process. You will not have to worry that others in this house could have weapons to hurt your family either."

"Besides you," Brad spoke while pressing on his coat pockets, and his wife did the same.

"Yes." Thom used a consoling tone as the stress of the moment rushed blood to his skull and caused a piercing pain in his temples. "That is correct. Trusted individuals are allowed to have a weapon in the house. If that makes you uncomfortable, you are free to go at any time."

Brad looked at Michelle and saw the answer in her eyes. "We have the same concern for our family Thom." He raised his jacket and took his son so that Michelle could do the same.

Thom was very glad that the child was calm through the interview. Brad Junior had to be hungry and scared, but his easy-going nature was apparent in this time of stress. It was a blessing for the headache

Thom was trying to conceal. A crying child during their first walk-in could have been ugly.

"So, you guys stayed home the first few days in Westerville then?" Thom said.

"We have a generator. We powered a space heater for a while till we ran out of gas. Once we heard that the outage would last a long time, and that the freeways were closed, we knew that Loudonville was our only chance."

"Well look guys," Thom said, putting his weapon in his waistband. "You are welcome to stay here for two nights, and we may expect some work from you, but we will ask for nothing else in return. Your food is yours, and whatever else you are carrying. But two nights is it. More people will be coming, and we can't take in people long-term. Does that sound fair?"

The couple was reasonably surprised by the offer. It's uncertain what they expected, maybe a boarding fee of some sort, money, sexual favors, something. They had plenty of time to discuss what they may encounter while they were walking down the snowy roads. Being in their position must have been very scary indeed. One home that they approached fired a warning shot before they even got close, so they quickly moved on with Brad Jr. crying hysterically from the loud noise.

The new family was welcomed in, and some soup was warmed for them on the gas stove that miraculously still worked. The nervousness of the first house visitors put everyone on edge, but at least the smiling face of Brad Jr. put everyone at ease.

A short time later, Toni handed a pair of boots to Thom for his promised task. It was a welcome diversion from the house, and he suited up for the walk to the Donovan's house immediately. The walk was less than a mile, but in the cold, it seemed much further. It gave Thom time to clear his head, which he dearly needed.

Thom noticed that one of the vacant homes had the front door open. He slowed to evaluate the situation before him. Lots of tracks were in the snow at the doorstep, and further sight brought the tracks to the next-door neighbor's front door. That's when the neighbor appeared.

"Decided to take my advice, eh Dave?" Thom called out.

"Hey man, when the cupboard is empty, Humpty Dumpty gets busy," Dave called back.

"That was the little old lady in the shoe. You are getting your nursery rhymes mixed up."

"Do I look like a little old lady that lived in a shoe? I bet Humpty Dumpty didn't have much in his pantry either," Dave ducked into his neighbor's home for another load.

"See you, Dave," Thom continued down the street.

The homes on the Donovan's side of town were the most vulnerable. They were closest to the state route, and closest to the freeway, about ten miles away. Thom's side of town had access to the state route also, but it was not as direct.

The concern for the north end of town came to a boil when Thom reached the Donovan's driveway. A fresh set of footprints ran across the yard, and they came from outside of town — three adults, maybe four. He looked at the house and wondered if there was trouble inside. No signaling system had been devised, and he had no way of knowing what he was walking into. The Donovans may have been overpowered by these travelers and may not even be alive. Thom might be walking into a trap.

He walked up the drive, watching all windows and edges of the building for movement, but saw none. Thom slowed his pace to give them time to react; they certainly had to recognize his red-checkered coat. He nervously reached into his coat pocket to grip the short barrel 9mm as he slowly walked up the driveway. Finally, a head popped out the door and called for him to come to the door. When he got inside,

107

he found the family was distracted by their new visitors and the account of their travels they told.

The visitors were three adults and an eight-year-old child. They had stayed a couple nights at a farm a few miles away, and were traveling to Alexandria, easily fifty miles away to the southeast. It was going to be a long haul for this family — that was for sure. They were in good spirits, though, and enjoyed sharing the stories of their travel so far. The father of the child seemed to be talking the most.

First, he told his audience that the freeway was as horrible as your imagination could possibly make it. Entire families were frozen stiff in their cars, and this family almost found the same fate. They had been caught in the traffic jam of I-71, trying to head south. They knew that you were supposed to start your car every hour, to get the heat running and warm everyone up, and then turn it off to save fuel. Like so many others, they fell asleep. Before they knew it, four hours had passed before someone woke. In so many cars, no one woke up at all. Ever.

It was then that the family decided to make their move. They ran the car for a long time, getting themselves warm for their long walk. They accumulated every essential they could out of the trunk, and discarded things that were unnecessary. When they were properly packed and as warm as they could be, they struck out from the car and walked down the highway. It was about dawn on the second day of the event when they were put to walking at the mercy of the elements. The storm ravaged with fifteen-mile-per-hour winds and the temperature hovered right around zero. No mercy was found.

As they walked down the freeway, they saw more people doing the same. It was five miles to the next exit, and it took three hours to get there. The exit had two gas stations, a truck stop, and an adult bookstore. At that point Jeffery broke in, stating that these folks were twenty-five miles away, recognizing the exit description. They went on to tell that the adult bookstore was on fire when they walked up, and they were so glad to warm themselves by the flames. How it ignited, they did not know. Speculation was that someone was burning magazines to keep warm, and it got out of hand. It didn't matter, they were just glad about the heat.

There was a mass of people around the truck stop, and it did not look like a safe place to be. They spoke with some of the folks around the bookstore fire and found that a police officer had tried to create order out of the chaos there and was killed. They spent the entire day around the dwindling fire, waiting for the National Guard, or more police or somebody. No help came, but many more survivors did. As the fire went out, the mob decided that another fire needed to be lit. Somebody said it would be a beacon to the police that help is needed. A storage building particularly close to one of the gas stations became the choice, which was a reckless decision for certain. The family decided it was time to move again, for their own safety.

As the family walked down the road away from the exit, the sun was setting. They had not eaten in forty-eight hours, and their only water had been handfuls of snow when they found some that looked clean. The eight-year-old was well behaved, and she did not notice the scene when her father was trying to help a man sitting against a telephone pole. As her father shook his shoulder to see how he was, the man simply fell to his side, frozen in the same bent position. The wife started to scream at the sight, but the husband quickly covered her mouth. The third adult thankfully kept the child shielded from the entire event. Everyone agreed it was time to move on from this place. It would only get worse.

Walking away from the exit, the family noticed lots of unusual tire tracks in the unplowed road. There had been a traffic jam trying to get on the freeway, but it was already gridlocked. Cars waited hours, but all had given up, and turned around where they could. Lots of zigzagging to get turned around, and some failures were noticed in the ditch, abandoned. The wife came up with the idea to look for keys; maybe they could start one and keep warm until dawn. The plan was fruitful, and they did manage to keep warm for the night. She did pay a price for her idea though; a horrible nightmare of the car owner

109

coming back and beating on the window with a gun, and shooting at her as she ran away. It was a terrifying dream, and difficult for her to shake off for a couple days.

The next day they continued down the road, following many other footprints in the snow away from the exit. They attempted to approach a house that had a fireplace burning. But obviously many other survivors had made the same move, and the welcome had been worn out. As they first approached, all they heard was the cocking of a shotgun, and then they were told to move on. The mindset of people back at the exit was being analyzed over and over as they walked. Those people felt so deserving of help, and hateful for not receiving it. They lashed out at everything and everybody in retaliation. It was the human psyche in a dark state, and it was getting darker very quickly. The lack of food was driving the animalistic mood, with the lack of heat and shelter making it exaggerated. The homes closest to the freeway felt it the most, and they had to start protecting themselves right at the beginning.

The family decided to venture down a road less traveled, a county road branching off from the main one. After an hour or so of further walking they decided it was time to approach a home. Deciding which one became the next dilemma. The husband jokingly said out of earshot of the child,

"It feels like we are out trick or treating, and we are trying to figure out which house is giving out full candy bars and which might give apples with razorblades."

The residents were more hospitable this time and welcomed them into their home. When they were finally fed, they realized it had been almost seventy-two hours since their last meal. The residents took a liking to them, and when it was time for them to leave a couple of days later, they were directed to a friend about a day's walk away. When they arrived, they were welcomed easily because they said, 'so-and-so sent us.' They were in turn sent again to another residence the next day but couldn't find it. A home eventually took them in, but the

110

idea of sending refugees from location to location sounded interesting. They said that the residents were instructed to do this by their church pastor, who lived nearby. That made so much sense to Thom. Of course, the pastor would stay and tend to his flock. He would give them guidance to help those in need. A pastor would be the perfect hub to build a network around. The entire story became an epiphany of sorts for Thom, and divine intervention that he was present to hear the story in the first place.

Thom returned home with renewed energy and wanted to share everything with his household. However, he decided to wait until he got one more project out of the way. This was a good story for around the fire, and he had great ambitions about a new type of heat source.

There were a few hours before sunset, plenty of time to implement Thom's home heating alternative. It was becoming painfully obvious that the fireplace was not going to heat enough of the house, and the temperature outside was not getting above thirty-five degrees, even on partly sunny days. The storm had hung on for a week now, and the house was still quite frigid. They could see their breath in the front room, and pulling guard watch was not a pleasure at all. Now that there were four men in the house to help, the alternative needed to happen; it was time.

An old, wood-burning stove was stored in the garage, and it needed to come into the house. It was a heavy awkward bastard; Thom did not look forward to the task. It was a bear to get into the garage in the first place. Thom's father was a welder and had built it himself. It was used in his home until he passed a couple of years ago, and Thom put it aside as part of his preparation when he was gung-ho about prepping.

The main part of the house—the old part—had a chimney running up through the middle of the 25-by-25-foot structure. Originally, the house was heated by stoves — probably coal stoves. The stovepipe holes were still in the chimney and decoratively covered on the first and second floors. So, Thom had a wood-burning stove, some stovepipe, and some pipe tape to put it all together. None of this had

111

been tested, the chimney had not been cleaned in decades, and it was a complete shot in the dark. He hoped it would work, and not burn the house down.

They shoveled a pathway in the snow and dollied the stove from the garage to the front door. They then removed the barricades and set the stove on a pallet in the front room. The pallet was an attempt to protect the hardwood floor but also made it a nice height for loading. The stovepipe Thom had was only long enough to reach the chimney hole height. More pipe was needed after the elbow, so the exhaust pipe from the Reznor heater in the garage was dismantled and used to complete the run. The exhaust pipe fit perfectly after some minor adjustments. They taped all the connections and hoped to not fill the house with smoke on the maiden voyage.

The first fire was lit, and it worked beautifully. Everyone in the room was amazed that it worked at all, especially Toni. They discussed how to empty ashes from the stove while there is still a fire, and how to load it without overloading it. Thom was still a little concerned about the chimney, and how much coal dust and other debris was in there, but hoped it would get them through the winter. He believed in prepping enough to save the stove his father built, but not enough to pay for having the chimney swept.

The household sat around the wood stove that evening and Thom shared the story of the travelers. The story was entrancing, especially to Brad and Michelle, the new residents. The idea of creating a larger network was beginning to gel for Thom, and curiosity about the freeway was overwhelming him. He also spoke about needing more people in the house to cover all guard posts for eight-hour shifts. This led Carl to comment about the food supply and how adding another family to the mix would deplete the supply pretty quickly, not to mention the refugees that would show up at the door without food, and hungry. It was a depressing discussion, and no one had any answers. They finally called it to a halt before someone got heated and said something they would regret.

Thom said, "Let's give it to God," and took their hands. He said a short prayer thanking the Lord for the roof over their heads but also requesting help with their problems and called it good at that.

He had no idea they would get a response the next day with a knock on the door.

Chapter 8: Glory Be.

The wife and two children, ages ten and seven, stayed at the street while the husband came to the door. Erich had spotted them 100 yards away at the square and interrupted Thom's chess game with David. They were all in position and waiting patiently by the time the knock came.

"Hello," Thom said from the three-season room door.

"Oh, hi," he said, turning to the correct door.

Thom waited in silence, deciding not to ask the rude question, 'What do you want?' The man would say eventually anyway.

"Is there any way that we could warm our food at your fire and rest inside?"

"You have food?"

"Yes, we have several cans." They were pulling their belongings on a plastic sled, smart folks.

"Do you have any weapons?"

"Yes I do," he answered slowly. Out of the corner of his eye, Thom saw Erich shifting around in his bunker. He was getting nervous. "I have a pistol in my waistband."

His arms were raised up but not over his head, just enough to give everyone a comfort zone. He was waiting for instructions. Thom evaluated whom he was dealing with for a second. He looked to be in his thirties, and fit, maybe six feet tall. Work boots, a Carhartt jacket: he appeared to be a laborer, and Thom later found that he was correct.

"Okay. Let's take this real easy, and it will go smoothly. I treat my house like Dodge City in *Gunsmoke*. You leave your weapons at the sheriff's office while in town, and you get them back when you leave. Sound fair?" He nodded, without moving his arms. "I want you to put your weapon in the clear plastic bin there on the floor of the porch; you'll get it back when you leave."

114

He slowly pulled the automatic out of his waistband and placed it in the bin, then stepped back.

"Any other weapons? A knife or anything else?" Thom queried before moving to the next step.

He shook his head, "No sir, that's it."

"Any weapons on your wife?" He further asked, and received another "No."

"Okay, let's get you guys in out of the cold." Thom motioned over to Erich that it was time to remove the blockades. Thom was happy with how the blockade boards hung from the rustic beams in the three-season room and gave a good sense of protection. But they sure were heavy. Erich had to work at pulling each one off their mounting board over the doorway. With everything removed, the bitter cold poured into the room. It was only twenty-five degrees, and it was the warm part of the day.

Thom invited the rest of his family up to the porch and into the house. Everyone stayed clear of the plastic bin, as instructed. Once everyone was inside, Carl and Thom took their point positions around the refugees.

"Erich, I want you to bring in his weapon, and then bring in their belongings, okay?" Erich set to work.

The refugees' names were JP and Lisa, with their children, Sara and Max. Thom went through his statements about Trust being an important commodity to them, and the new couple was completely riveted. JP even answered with a 'Yes sir.' There was a hint of military experience about him in his stance and his words.

When it came time to check coat pockets, JP informed Thom that he had two extra clips of ammo in his coat pocket before going any further. His tone was calm and sincere. Considering that this was the first person to approach the house with a weapon, the interview was relaxed simply because of JP's demeanor.

115

When Erich came in with the luggage, he laughed about how heavy one medium-sized duffle bag was, and JP explained it immediately, "It's full of canned food."

"So, you planned it out before leaving home to bring food?" Thom was starting to get impressed with JP and Lisa. They had a weapon, were relaxed and confident, and brought food.

"Not so much," JP said. "We brought supplies for a few days, but we found that food this morning."

JP looked over at Lisa nervously, and she returned the look. He took a breath and looked Thom straight in the eye, "I don't know what you guys might think of how we got this food though. We slept last night in an abandoned house about three or four miles from here. The house was empty, no one was home, but there was plenty of food, lots of food, so we took some." He stood there sheepishly and looked at Thom and Carl for a reaction, but they gave none. They just stood there expressionless, letting him talk.

"We weren't stealing or looting. We just took some food, and they had so much," Lisa chimed in, agreeing with how much food there was.

"How much food was there?" Carl asked, still giving nothing away, but stepping a little closer.

"The pantry was stocked upstairs, but the prize was in the basement," Lisa was talking for him now, as Toni stepped into the room, curious about all the conversation. "There were two metal shelving units full of canned vegetables in old-time glass canning jars. Tomato sauce, whole tomatoes, green beans, and a bunch of jars that had a mixture of green beans, pinto beans, and corn, I believe," she said excitedly.

"Succotash," Thom said.

"That's what it's called?" She looked over at JP smiling. "We've been trying to figure it out, we had no clue."

"It's a hillbilly favorite. My aunt in the hills still makes it each year. It looks like you've stumbled across someone just like her. Strange that the house was empty like that. You'd think that an old-school person who cans food would stay home and try to tough it out."

"We thought so too," JP spoke up. "We've had time to banter this back and forth without much else to do. Based on the state of the house, that nothing was out of place, we figured that they did not leave in a hurry when the power went out. We think that they must have already been gone for the holidays before the outage happened."

"Huh. That makes sense. I bet there were lots of folks in that boat, already traveling before this happened. I didn't think much about that scenario." Thom was scratching his head and adjusting his baseball cap.

"So, you guys aren't upset about us taking the food? Food was all we took, but we weren't sure how people might react," he tentatively said.

"Well, I agree, you are taking what you need to survive. The people would give it to you willingly if you had a way to ask them. And I don't see any big screen TV in your back pocket, so it's not looting," Thom smiled. "Could you find the place again? If I were to show you a map of the area, could you give me an idea where it's at?"

"Oh yeah! You want to go back and clean it out, don't you! I am in!" JP was getting excited, "I would hate for the real looter types to get this stuff — you know what I mean?"

Thom looked down the line of JP's family and saw the sorrowful eyes of his two children looking at the new strangers peacefully, with their lips quivering from the cold.

"It's time to get inside. Toni, do we have some food on the stove?" She nodded, and everyone moved to the door.

They arranged themselves around the wood-burning stove in the front room and discussed the plan to get the food. Thom's truck was the

117

best option, and he knew the roads well enough to drive them unplowed. He figured that he could stay on the road, and if he did slide off, they were still within walking distance of home.

Bowls of chili were passed around to the new guests, and several hearts melted when the youngest offered to say grace. Toni whipped a tear away and whispered in Thom's ear, "We are doing the right thing."

Thom mapped out where they were going with JP and put together a plan for how to do the mission. Erich and JP were coming with him to the house. Erich as a lookout, and JP to make sure it was the right house and help with the loading. Carl needed to stay home and defend the house, and Toni could handle a gun too. Brad and his wife were still there, but they were an unknown. Thom didn't have any plans for them. They still had two hours of decent daylight, and that's all they needed. Thom started stacking empty bins in the sunroom for the group to take. Easy to load and easy to carry. While he was in there alone, Brad approached.

"I'd really like to be a part of this, Thom," Brad said earnestly. "I could go with you and be a lookout; you need to have more than one lookout on this."

"I don't know Brad —"

But Brad interrupted. He was an appliance salesman and knew the old salesman rule; never let the customer actually say no. Always interrupt when it looks like they are going to. Once they say no it's much harder to turn it into a yes.

"Thom, I hear what you say about trust being so important, and I don't know if you really trust me yet, but I can tell one thing, and that's that I trust *you*. I trust what you are doing with your home. I'd really like to be there for you. I can help on this job."

Thom stood up and stepped over to Brad. Reaching out his hand, he said, "Get some extra clothes on; it's going to be cold."

Carl had the ladies huddled around the wood burner discussing guard assignments as the group moved to the door. Toni grabbed Thom and told him to be careful, with a peck on the cheek. He tried not to make a big deal about this excursion, though. JP had been in this house a few hours ago, it should be a quick in and out without much fuss, as long as the travel went well.

In the three-season room, JP looked down at the clear plastic bin on the floor, "Can I take my gun?"

This was a tough one. Carl's weapon was the full-sized Glock 9mm. It had to stay with Carl to defend the house. Toni had her 5-shot .38 revolver, and the .22 rifle was staying home too. All they had left was the short barrel 9mm going with them on this mission. JP's gun would be good to have if there were problems.

"Do you mind if Erich carries the gun? We will need it at the lookout post," Thom said trying to be diplomatic.

"I understand what you are saying, Thom, and it's okay for him to carry it. But if we get into trouble, I'm the man you'll want to have that gun." He was so matter-of-fact and confident; Thom did not doubt that he spoke the truth.

"Hopefully that decision won't have to be made." Thom handed the gun to Eric but turned to JP with a sly smile. "You do still have those extra clips in your pocket though, right?"

They got in the truck and let it warm up for a few minutes while listening to the radio. They hadn't listened to the radio all day. The announcer spoke about all the lives lost already, which was estimated now in the thousands. All freeways of the area were blocked with abandoned cars. The National Guard was handicapped by the loss of mobility. Shoving the cars off the road with snowplow trucks was the plan in the East Coast cities where help was most needed. The winter storm was hampering all efforts as well and making all rescues more difficult. The thought of crushing these cars was being fought by some because many of the cars contained corpses. It was such a fine line to

119

walk in treating the dead with respect while trying to get aid to those who are still alive. Power was trying to be restored by utilizing the other power grids in Texas and out west to reroute energy to the northeast. The effort was having some success, but also found that during the initial shutdown, many substations and transformers were sent a power spike that overloaded them. Most were found to need repair or replacement before they could be used again.

Thom turned to Erich in the back seat.

"Remind me to unplug all of our major appliances when we get back home," he said. If they weren't fried already, they probably would be when the power did get restored.

The news report went on to talk about a bill that was signed into law back in 2009. This law allows the United States to consider any attack on the infrastructure, such as power grids, as an act of war. This law went on to say that not only would it be considered an act of war, but a nuclear-level act of war. This statement settled down the jabber in the truck immediately. Thom felt silly about his concern for the TV getting a power spike. The U.S. was going into nuclear war!

JP spoke up from the back seat; "No way are we dropping a nuclear bomb on anyone. Won't happen."

"What makes you so sure?" Thom said as he put the truck in gear and heard the 4-wheel drive kick in.

"The 'powers that be' want a good ten-year war like they had back in Iraq. For the military economy, for their political agendas, and whatever else, they need a long war. Dropping a bomb on them would be too quick. The war would be over in no time, and this whole creation of fear agenda that they have going on with Homeland Security and the TSA would grind to a halt. We, as Americans, wouldn't be so fearful because we just created a big hole in the middle of Iran or wherever. Besides, it will make America look like heroes for *not* dropping the bomb on them when we had the right to."

120

"I get the agenda of fear. I'm getting tired of the airport scanners at football games. But what's the use in having a nuclear bomb if we don't use it?" Brad argued.

"I'm with you man," JP responded. "If Iran did this, I say level the place. But I'm just saying it's not their agenda, not right now. It might invite an ally of theirs to send one back over here too."

"I could see a chain reaction occurring, yes I agree," Brad said. "Maybe we would still have the agenda of fear then, just a different kind of fear."

"No nukes in general sounds like a good idea to me, regardless of the logic," Thom spoke up, but his mind was clearly on the road.

The roads had about a foot of snow, and the drifts were nasty in spots. Thom searched for the part of the road with the least amount of snow, veering from side to side at times. He gave JP lots of advance warning before a turn, to make sure it was the correct intersection. Things were going well the first couple of turns. When they came to the point of crossing the state route, Thom's curiosity was piqued. Scoping out the area around Galena was just as important as the other goals of this mission in his mind. At the state route, he saw that an accident had occurred close to the intersection a while back, and the road was blocked. JP had answered his questions specifically that the roads they traveled today were all clear. He mentioned this accident, but also noted that the path would be clear for them, as it was. Thom wanted to check this specific accident out though. A roadblock on the state route could direct traffic into his town as a work-around. He stopped and examined the accident for a moment. His evaluation was that the road was totally blocked with a three-car pile-up and a handful of cars on each side that were either abandoned or went into the ditch to avoid making the pile-up bigger. Yes, this blockage could bring more traffic to Galena, and they would be coming into the south end of town, with Thom's house being one of the first stops. Good information, however, not good news at all.

The group continued south across the state route and soon JP started pointing to a one-story ranch on the right. They pulled up slowly, noting that the tire tracks in the area were old and drifted over. The footprints of JP and his family were noticeable coming down the driveway, and no other footprints looked to be in the snow. Thom made a daring move to back into the driveway, which was fifty yards long, and was successful. There was a clear view of the area from the house, and all looked good. All four men watched for movement around them and saw none. Stepping out of the truck, it was unsettlingly quiet.

"Twenty minutes guys, okay? JP, you lead the way, and let's go get us some succotash!" Thom cheered as they got out of the truck and grabbed some bins.

JP brought them around to the back door to the window he had broken out. Thom walked in with his gun drawn to the empty house. They checked the rooms to make sure there were no surprises. When all was clear, they set to work. Erich and Brad were positioned up front as lookouts in separate rooms with different views of the yard. If anything was spotted, the rule was to raise the alarm, not to take any other action. With their stack of bins, JP and Thom headed to the basement.

JP wasn't lying about the quantity of canning jars down there. It was like finding the Holy Grail; it almost glowed in the battery-powered lamplight. They set to work right away filling the bins and Thom soon wondered if the dozen bins they brought would be enough. JP and Thom divided the work into a loader and a carrier, so that they were not in each other's way. Thom started carrying the completed bins upstairs and staging them at the door. Erich caught his eye and motioned that they were still clear, and he returned for another load. The system continued until his legs began to burn and they switched. They did fill all the bins, and still needed more. This was a great spot to be in and they didn't want to waste it. They looked around the basement and spotted a stack of bins marked Christmas Lights and Halloween in a storage room. Out came the decorations, and they had

122

four more bins. A couple more were found in a back corner, and then Thom let out a little whistle. JP turned around to see him holding a Costco sized pack of toilet paper! Some high-fives ensued, and they began to feel a little giddy. They didn't really say much to each other, keeping quiet as if this was some major heist, and if they were to make noise, it might sound an alarm.

They continued filling the new bins and staging them upstairs until the job was done. Erich's face lit up when the toilet paper was brought upstairs, and Thom got another high-five on the find. Before leaving the basement, they made another circle around to see if any other treasurers were lurking around. A couple flashlights were spotted and a six-pack of paper towels. All essentials for survival they judged, and justified them for scavenging.

Upstairs JP began emptying the pantry, and Thom checked in with the lookouts. All looked good so far, but his wheels were turning from the non-food finds. *What else might this house have to help our survival?* Brad was stationed in a guest bedroom facing the northeast corner of the house, and Thom announced himself in the hallway as he approached.

"Coming your way, Brad." He was calm as Thom walked in the door, stating all was clear. "I want us to look around a bit for extra essentials before we go. Okay, Brad? Essentials only and what I'm thinking right now is weapons. If they are old school enough to use canning jars, they probably have a gun. Keep an eye on the window but look around too."

Thom looked in the master bedroom, and in the most obvious place he hit pay dirt. The bedside table drawer had a .357 revolver and two boxes of shells. A massive find! In the corner of the closet stood a 30-30 rifle. The real challenge was finding the boxes of shells, but they were in there. He also uncovered a couple of bins of sweaters and blankets. He dumped the sweaters and blankets, just wanting the bins for the pantry. He gave the bins to JP, who needed them, and received another high-five. Thom reconsidered those blankets and sweaters

123

though, and grabbed a couple trash bags while he was in the kitchen. Those blankets would certainly come in handy with all the new folks in the house. He brought the bedroom finds to the staging area by the door and stood back from the pile and smiled. Taking in the haul was quite satisfying, but then he realized they had already been there a half hour.

"Let's wind this up, guys, time to start loading. Are we still all clear, any movement out there at all?" Thom announced to the group.

"Nothing out front," Erich spoke up.

"We are completely clear," Brad called from the bedroom, and began down the hall.

"I've still got two shelves over here to load. I'm leaving no can behind!" JP bellowed from the kitchen.

The three others picked up a bin and headed out to the truck. Erich was stationed at the truck to be lookout at that location, and Brad and Thom served as pack mules. After five trips past the garage door to the truck, it dawned on Thom that they hadn't looked in the garage yet. JP was just finishing up in the kitchen and making his last circle of the room. Thom directed him to loading duty when he was done as he headed to the garage with the lantern.

One car spot was empty as expected, and the garage was just as eerie as the basement, when lit by a lantern. In the front corner was all the yard equipment, and he quickly found the item he was looking for, a gas can. He grabbed it and gave it a shake. Empty. But to his delight, a second can was further back. One more chance at the jackpot and this one paid out — a full five gallons. He picked it up and moved toward the door, not seeing anything else essential. At the doorway, leaning against the wall with all the other hand-rakes and shovels, stood a nice axe. He spotted it right away, with its yellow handle. Thom's was in bad shape but usable. All his firewood was already split, and he couldn't point to an immediate use for it, but it felt so good when he picked it up. He felt a little guilty because it wasn't absolutely needed like the toilet paper, but he got over it. It felt so good in his hand; it had to be his.

The guys cheered as he came out with the can of gas, realizing its exaggerated value right now. Brad made a little statement about 'the axe being used for chopping wood, right?'

"Hey, everybody needs one of these for home defense," Thom said, laughing as he slid it in between the bins.

The bins filled the truck bed almost completely — it was quite a haul. When it was all loaded, they circled the back of the truck and stood in awe. It was quite a sight, so much food and paper products.

Finally, Erich spoke up to break the silence. "We owe a lot to JP for finding this, but really, we owe so much to this family. This family really saved our ass."

This produced a giggle from all of them, with his choice of words. Brad then stepped forward and put his hand on the toilet paper and said, "Literally!"

They left the property without incident — everyone's head on a swivel to spot trouble but there was none. The excitement and adrenalin really hit all of them as they drove down the road away from the site. High fives ensued and the mood was great; but that changed at the intersection of the state route: new tire tracks were on the road. Their eyes followed them to the old crash scene 150 feet down the road. The red jeep wrangler was new to the scene and had plowed into a blue neon. The crash actually had a positive effect on the roadway in clearing a lane for traffic. Both cars ended up in the ditch as a result. The men sat there at the intersection, immobilized by the scene.

"They might be alive in there still," JP said from the passenger seat. "It must have just happened. I still see a little steam coming from the radiator."

"But we have all this food," Erich spoke up from the back seat. "We are taking such a risk; we could lose it all. We are vulnerable out in the open like this. The more time we spend out here…"

Thom turned the opposite way on the state route and then began backing down to the accident scene. "Complications, complications, complications," he mumbled to himself as he continued in reverse. "We'll have a quicker getaway this way."

JP couldn't wait; the truck was backing too slowly for him. He jumped out of the moving truck and ran to the jeep. Stopping beside the jeep, he swung open the door, and then just as quickly spun around in horror. By the time the rest of the group got to him he was on all fours on the ground, looking like he might heave. It was an awful sight. The airbag had not deployed, and the woman's head had hit the steering wheel sideways. Her neck and head were twisted back in an unnatural way much like something from the Exorcist. It left her looking directly out the door in a very ghastly, unnatural way. JP would have some sleepless nights after coming upon this woman. Thom put his hand on JP's shoulder to comfort him, but then he heard something that stopped him in his tracks — a sound that was like fingernails on a chalkboard to Thom. He wanted it to stop as soon as it started, but it continued and got louder with each second. It was a crying baby.

Profanities leapt from everyone's mouth except for JP. He was on his feet in a second, suddenly with new energy. The baby was on the driver's side back seat, but JP smartly went around to the passenger side. He was taking no chances at getting another glimpse of that driver again. Brad helped him unbuckle the baby carrier, and JP had it out in a flash. He carried the baby back to the truck and much to Thom's relief, the crying stopped.

Brad began pulling out the diaper bag and other items from the jeep. Thom merely stood in the middle of the street dumbfounded. Suddenly, they had a baby. He thought he was done with babies. When Thom's second child was out of diapers, he was so glad. They

126

stopped at that point for a reason. He was done. He even went to the doctor and went under the knife to make positive that he was done. There was nobody more done with raising babies than him. Watching this baby and the diaper bag being put into his truck was beyond surreal. All he could do was stand there and watch.

"What do we do with the mother?" Brad said after the jeep was unloaded.

"What do you mean? Like bury her?" Thom said, surprised.

"Yeah man, we can't just leave her like that," Erich chimed in.

"We can't bury her alongside the road, this is not a cemetery. They'll just have to dig her up and move her. Besides the ground is too frozen." Thom had to be making sense, but he was tired. It probably came out like he was whining.

"It just seems so wrong, man." Brad still went over and laid the car seat back for her and turned her head forward some. It was difficult to watch, so Thom and Erich didn't.

"Hey, make sure you get her purse and ID. We need to get this baby back to its family when this is all over," Thom called to Brad while he was adjusting the body. Then he turned and mumbled to himself, "Because I know Toni will want to keep it otherwise."

"The baby is a girl, not an *it*," JP corrected Thom's mumbles.

"Pink booties huh?" Thom said as he approached the child.

"And a pink hat. What's with you, man? You can handle the world coming to an end, but not finding a baby?" he said in a half-joking, half-finger-pointing way.

"I guess there are some tragedies in life that a person is better equipped to handle."

It was a good thing that the truck had a cap with all the new stuff being acquired. They managed to pack it all in, without any risk of losing it to the wind or weather.

127

They put the child in the back seat for safety, although it would be impossible for any harm to come to her. All eyes were on her, except Thom's. At least he kept his on the road. The closer they got to home, the more comfortable he got with the idea of the baby. It wouldn't be so bad, she wouldn't be his responsibility, and others would step up. Still, he needed some guidance. He needed to calm down and get his gyros in sync. An idea had been planted in his mind yesterday by the couple at the Donovan's home who told the story of how they were guided from one safe house to the next, and who directed them. He knew what he needed to do, and it put him at peace with absolutely everything that had happened that day. He needed to see his local church minister, and that's what he would do at the first chance.

By the time they pulled up in front of the house, Thom had joined in the happy conversation about the new addition to the family. They were all throwing out names for the little girl, and bantering them back and forth, while also shooting most of them down. Thom had to agree she did not look like a 'Rose.' He wasn't sure what a 'Rose' looked like, but she wasn't it. They had some laughs, and according to them, she laughed along also.

They pulled up to the house and rolled down the window, "All clear?" Thom called out.

"All clear! And we're ready for some good eats!" Carl called back.

"Well, you're not ready for what we got, I can tell you that!" Thom yelled out, with a chorus of laughter from the passengers.

They piled out of the truck with the carrier, the diaper bag, and other stuff from the jeep first. They could only imagine the expressions on everyone's faces inside of this sight. The ladies inside tried to show those expressions later that night as they sat around the wood stove retelling the days' stories, but it's doubtful they got the full effect. Telling stories around the wood stove was always an event the household looked forward to. It was a lost art with the invention of TV. Some of the stories got risqué too, when the kids were put down and a bottle of wine passed around.

128

"Glory be!" Toni yelled out as JP carried the new addition across the porch. Her arms were extended when the baby was still twenty feet away. It was certain that she was grabbing onto the baby first, and if someone made a move to get in front, they were getting an elbow.

"Gloria. Maybe we got a name," Thom said to the guys, looking around for approval.

"Maybe, maybe," Brad nodded to agree. "Let's get inside folks, don't block the door gawking at the youngin'."

They all pushed in and gave hugs all around to their families. It seemed as if a cloud lifted when they got home, the period felt much longer than the time they were gone. Much had happened. The women passed around the baby while JP told the story of finding her. Thom let him have the floor and talk; he was just taking everything in. Being a wallflower in the room was enjoyable sometimes, and this was one of those times. He looked around the room and saw all the smiling faces that this little girl created. She was a beautiful diversion from the deplorable situation.

When he finished with the recap of the day's events, Thom reminded them that they still needed to unload the truck and move it back to the bank. After the third or fourth load of food, the women were amazed that they were still carrying in stuff. They began to feel like the primal 'hunters and gatherers' that all humans are. There was real pride in how much they were providing to the household as if they had fought and killed it. Brad let the feeling get to him enough to jokingly put one foot up on a tote and began thumping his chest like an animal over his beaten prey. The pride continued as they opened the crates later in the evening and inventoried the haul.

Thom was glad to be the one who opened the crate with the .357 stashed in it. It wouldn't have been a good surprise for the unsuspecting. The inventory of the haul went on into the night over dinner; there was no rush, as they enjoyed it so much. Everything took longer with a baby being tended to anyway. They sat around the wood stove looking through the crates, one in front of each person, discussing the contents.

"Oh, I see that JP found the liquor cabinet in the kitchen," Thom said, pulling out a dusty bottle of Scotch. The entire bin was full of liquor.

"Yeah, I didn't know how you'd feel about that," JP said slowly. "It's not a necessity; it's kind of a gray area."

"Liquor is medicinal. It can be used to clean wounds," Toni spoke up, the only medically trained person in the room.

"Yeah, I know it *can* be used for medicinal purposes, but *will* it be used for medicinal purposes?" Brad added to the conversation. "Holy cow, Patron Tequila!"

That's when Erich took the floor. He had something to say, and he excitedly told it in dramatic flair. The household hadn't seen this side of him — he was usually so reserved. But that's how many dramatic actors are, especially when they have material that really means something to them. And this meant something to Erich, as the group found out.

"I want to share something with you that on the surface all of you will question at first, especially you Thom. But you must allow me to finish my story before you judge what I have done, and I think you will agree with my view. Does everyone promise not to judge or interrupt me until I am done?" he said, as he looked around the room. The fresh face of the eighteen-year-old was looking for approval, that was obvious, but he was sparingly looking at Thom or his father, Carl. There was some fear there for sure, but excitement too, the kid was wound up, and it was cool to see. It just concerned most of the group *what* wound him up.

"Give it to me, Erich," Brad said. "And give me that Patron too, while you are at it."

Erich took a deep breath, and then took control of the room from his chair, talking with his hands reaching out to everyone. "Let's go back

130

to the beginning of why we went to that house today. The food was there, and not needed by the owner. If we could have asked them wherever they are, they would certainly give us the food, and apologize for not having more. We have stated that before. We were also there because as this outage rages on, people are going to swarm out of the city like locusts and are going to chew up and spit out houses like that one. They will treat houses in the outskirts like pieces of chewing gum. They'll pull out all the flavor and anything of value and waste the rest. They'll destroy and burn and ravage out of lawlessness and frustration, and because they can. They'll accumulate and sell off the things of value at pennies on the dollar. Family heirlooms will be melted down to their base elements, destroying the workmanship along with the family history."

By this time Erich was on his feet, walking in front of the group and all around the wood-burning stove, his arms flailing about, emphasizing his points. Thom wasn't sure where he was going and was getting anxious for him to get to the point. The expression on his face must have given him away as Brad handed over the bottle of Tequila. "Chill," was all he said as he handed Thom the bottle. He obliged and took a swig. It helped more than he thought it would.

"I saw my father grab a couple of heirlooms off the shelf before we left the house, realizing that when we returned nothing may be there. So, as I stood watch in this beautiful living room today, surrounded by family treasures, I thought about how much this family is helping us. How much this food will mean to us, and to the next families that will come through our door. I decided that I wanted to repay this family in a small way. Now, you told me you wouldn't interrupt!" he said, pointing directly at Thom's open mouth, which was getting ready to speak. He raised the Tequila bottle to his lips instead and passed it back to Brad. He nodded his head and motioned for Erich to continue.

"Okay, I'll continue, but I'll use some props," speaking while he was moving, he walked over to the bunker built facing the front door. It was three layers thick of two-by-eights and stood four-feet tall, braced by the weight-bearing wall of the room. On the front of the bunker, facing the door, they had put coat hooks for all of the winter gear. Erich was going through the pockets of his coat, and pulled out some items, placing them on the arm of the couch.

"I looked around the room for things that were displayed right at eye level. These would be the things they were most proud of and treasured most. I found this monogrammed sterling silver cigarette case, and this sterling silver brush and mirror set, in the china cabinet, front and center. These were their prized possessions. I grabbed a piece of junk mail off the kitchen counter, so that I would have the name and address of the residents, and I'll keep all this together in a box for safekeeping. Then my plan is to return this box to the rightful owner when this is all over. I want to pay them back," he said as his eyes became glassy, imagining the scene as he spoke it. "I want to walk in that house after it's been chewed up, and greet them, whoever they may be. I want to tell them the story of the good their food created and thank them for it. Then I will present the box, and they will be grateful that these pieces of their family history had been preserved when all else was lost. That's when I will tell them that there is no need to thank me, I just apologize that I don't have more."

The room was silent as the dramatic production ended, and the last words finally faded away. The expressions on everyone's faces were approval, and they felt even better about it with every reassuring smile they saw. Thom just stared ahead, watching Erich, looking for a weakness. Looking for a flinch that might tell him that he had ulterior motives. There were none.

"I'm game," Thom said in a matter-of-fact tone. The agreeing words around him started gaining momentum to the point of some applause. Erich beamed with a grin and wiped the glassiness from his eyes. "But this is your responsibility now. You have to keep track of this stuff, and if this situation comes up again, you'll be the one in charge of that too. I'm a little concerned about what happens if the people don't come back home, how to get the stuff to the heirs, and what if there are no heirs. But we'll worry about those complications when they happen. Your heart seems to be in the right place, so I trust that you'll work hard to get the satisfaction that you're looking for. Good job, Erich."

They passed around the items Erich had borrowed and discussed the idea more until Thom decided to change the subject. "JP and Lisa, I want to ask you a question. How long has it been since you've had a hot shower?"

"You're kidding me, right? Since day one. We lost water on the first day. You've got hot water?"

"Hey, wait a minute!" Brad spoke up in a jokingly scorning tone. "You waited till the second day to tell us about hot water! They get it the first night?"

"Well, you didn't turn us on to a houseful of food the first day either!" he said jokingly back. "And give me that Tequila, we may need that later. Carl, you're in charge of the sentries, and I'll take these folks upstairs." Toni kissed Thom, kind of out of the blue, as he picked up the lantern to lead the couple to the master bathroom. The couple followed obediently, smiling from ear to ear.

Inside the bedroom he stopped and spoke directly to them. "Now, normally everyone uses the shower stall downstairs to bathe. But I figured you guys have been beaten up for so long that you are not feeling human anymore. You guys can take your time. Make it feel like you are getting ready for work on a regular morning, bumping into each other as you brush your teeth and shave. Take the time to become human again. Your kids are already in bed asleep, and we have the house under control."

They followed along to every word, not sure if they should laugh or cry for this wonderful gift. He walked them through the bathroom and put out a disposable razor and a new toothbrush. All of the bathroom products were theirs to use. He left the lantern with them, and walked away in the darkness, leaving them with one final statement spoken from the shadows, "and also, if you have the urge to become completely human, put a towel down on the bed." A giggle or two

133

emitted from the bathroom as the door clicked behind him. Toni gave him another kiss at the bottom of the steps.

"That was very nice of you," she said.

"Well, it's nice to share."

"At least they have heat from the stove now, their experience should be better."

"Not in my book darlin.' I can't see how it could possibly be better..."

And he pulled her tight.

Chapter 9: Paying Charter.

The catamaran pulled across the water with the mainsail and jib completely full and tight. The gauges displayed that the *Mystic* was cruising at 6.5 knots and handling the two-foot swells nicely. The charter passengers were nice enough. They had given their attention to Randal for the introductions and the normal safety walk-through before leaving the dock. Now they were settling into the sail and starting to move about the boat.

"So, you are the First Mate but also the owner? How does that happen?" The passenger in the plaid Bermudas asked in a point-blank way.

"Some things in life are not as simple as they seem friend," Thom was coy to the interruption in his prepping a fishing pole for a young passenger.

"So, you are a Captain in Training, huh?"

"I've passed sailing certification classes; I just don't have a license for captaining a boat with paying customers. It's at a different level."

"So, you bought a charter to gain that experience and certification? What's next then?" Randal's ears perked up at the captain's perch to the line of questioning, and if the answer would be the same he had heard.

"I'm selling everything back home and taking the leap before year's end. Getting blue water experience is my goal right now."

"So, where's back home?" The question Thom knew was coming.

"Most of my experience is in the fresh water of Lake Erie. I'm from Ohio."

"Damn, man. So, were you there for the blackout?"

"Yeah, yeah, yeah. The world got turned upside down and we held on to the edge." Thom handed the youngster the fishing pole.

"In the beginning, did you know it was going to be bad? They say that the ones who took it seriously in the beginning fared the best."

Thom recounted a couple points for the paying customer, which made a difference. A tourist asking questions like this from a barstool wouldn't have gotten this far in the conversation with Thom. They might have even gotten a threat and a peek at his holstered weapon to back it up. The stories told by Thom to Mr. Bermuda Shorts got close attention by Randal at the Captain's perch. It seemed that he was listening for differences, or exaggerations to bring doubt to the things he had been previously told.

That night Randal went out to a pub, and Thom just stayed behind with the boat. He returned to find Thom sleeping in a hammock on the forward deck. He crept up the steps to take a look at him in the hammock. Maybe he wanted to see *if* he could sneak up on Thom, after all he had heard. With the water rocking the boat, and the fiberglass creaking anyway, his movement might be masked, and hard to notice.

"Hi, Randal," Thom said, unmoving in the makeshift bunk.

"I can't believe you, man!" he said in a loud voice, kind of joking but serious in a way. "You tell me about how you can't trust people at all, but here you are, sleeping out in the open to the world! You say you always have a weapon, and you'll use it anytime. But here you are. Look at you!"

Thom said nothing. He did not move. He merely flipped the switch on the laser targeting for his short stock 9mm. It was pointed right at Randal's chest. The light beam on his shirt really freaked him out, and he tried to brush it off while letting loose some obscenities. Randal's legs were suddenly feeling untrustworthy, and he felt it best to take a seat on the fiberglass deck.

"Okay, I think I'm getting there, pal," Randal said wearily, still brushing the middle of his shirt.

"You okay? Sorry about that. Old habits die hard."

136

"I've got to ask you, man, have you actually killed someone?"

"Yes, but they all deserved it." Thom smiled to himself in the darkness, knowing that was a Schwarzenegger line from *True Lies*.

"Are you sure?" he said, still taking in what happened and getting his breath back.

"The first one, I'm sure. I can give you that much."

Chapter 10: Get yourself to church, boy.

Thom awakened early, just before sunrise. Sleeping in his own bed was great, but he never slept soundly. The addition of the wood-burning stove allowed them to use the whole house now. The heat worked its way up the stairs, and it heated the chimney all the way up as well. It wasn't really warm, they had four blankets on the bed, but it was livable. While getting ready, Thom focused more on what he wanted to accomplish today. He didn't know the full extent of it, but there was a seed of an idea growing inside. Today he would feed this seed. It all just felt right, except for that pounding headache. The Excedrin was running out, and that headache had made itself real comfy and wasn't going anywhere.

Thom made his way downstairs as the sun was breaking. Brad's wife was watching out the front window, and Brad was in the rear bunker of the three-season room. Thom checked in with her first, all was clear, no traffic at all. She was in good spirits too; her shift would be over soon. He found Brad shivering in the three-season room. It was a tough shift, the room was not heated, but it gave the best view of the back yard. Brad was hanging in there, and stealing glances at the sunrise towards the front of the house.

"Nice sunrise today, huh?" Thom greeted him, walking in the door.

"The cloud cover makes for some nice colors. My shift has been clear, no movement at all. Not even any vehicles passing through," he reported in.

"What has the radio been saying over night? Are we expecting snow today?" Winding the radio was one way to keep warm in the cold room, and listening to it out there didn't keep anybody else up.

"Some flurries are expected, like every day so far, but no major pelting. The temp is supposed to stay in the twenties. It's killing me that all the radio talks about is the east coast. They did release some news about the Ohio National Guard, though. The National Guard Unit stationed at Lake Erie had been deployed to Syria two weeks before all this happened. So the post at Lake Erie is understaffed and

138

the replacements are from other parts of the country and unfamiliar with the region. Ohio is being bitch-slapped, and I think its damn odd how that tidbit wasn't released till now." Brad was starting to get irate.

"I didn't think the National Guard went overseas! Don't they just stay and protect the U.S.?"

"Nope, not since nine-eleven," Brad said in a matter-of-fact tone. "I'm learning all kinds of things out here. There have been thousands of them sent abroad."

"I guess that means the National Guard won't be rolling in here anytime soon. The only people coming through here are by mistake."

"Yeah, but here's the kicker. I was listening to Hellstrom, and he had something to add to the report. He read an article from the Times about when Katrina hit New Orleans back in '05. The article mentioned one of the handicaps they had in the Katrina emergency was the same thing. Their local National Guard unit had just been deployed to Afghanistan and not many of the replacements knew the lay of the land. It slowed down the movement of the serious equipment and caused huge casualties that wouldn't have happened otherwise. He's also saying that the death toll they are saying on the radio is bullshit. He says take that number and quadruple it. And with this National Guard thing, the Jerry Lewis telethon number dials haven't finished spinning."

"Damn, man. It makes me want to see that freeway so bad. Just to see what it looks like. See it for myself. But I can't do that today. Instead, I'm going to check on a friend about five miles from here. I also wanted to thank you for your help yesterday — we worked well together. You have earned my trust."

Thom shook his hand and the look in his eye was so sincere, it gave him pause.

"We will need to make some arrangements as far as living quarters, though, Brad. It's been more than the normal two days, and some

139

decisions need to be thought about by you and Lisa. There are homes here in the village that could use a trustworthy watchman, and I would be happy to vouch for you and set you up in a home with your share of the food yesterday. You had also mentioned that you have family in Loudonville, and you were en route. That is sixty miles away, and I know of a barn where friends of mine are staying in motor homes that is eight miles in that direction. Maybe they could help on the next stop from there, if you want to continue your trip."

Brad was focused in and nodding his head through Thom's statements without much expression. "Again, Brad, you and your wife need to search your heart for what you'd like to do, and I'll help with either choice. We can discuss this later tonight as well and make a move tomorrow. Sound good?"

"It's been great getting to know you and your family, Thom. One thing I'm grateful for in all this damn mess is the good people I've met. I wouldn't trade any of that," he said, reaching for a hand to pull him up.

"Let's hope we feel the same way at the end of this thing." Thom turned and stepped inside to the smell of oatmeal on the stove.

"We still have natural gas. I'm amazed," Toni said to him. "I wonder what the gas bill will look like when we get it six months from now," laughing as she stirred the pan.

"I'll have a double dose. I'm going to drive to the church and talk to Father Michael." Her face turned quizzical, and he said, "It's something I need to do. I've had an idea bouncing in my head for a couple days, and today looks good."

"You just want to get away from the baby don't you!" she said, peeking around the corner at JP's wife rocking Gloria on the couch.

"Maybe so," he said, smiling. "No, this is for creating a network. We'll have a better chance at everything with a network."

"So, do you think this is a calling, to go see Father Michael?" she said, trying to pry.

"You mean like a calling to the priesthood? Honey, you know better than anyone that I could never be a priest," he said, kissing her on the cheek.

The house was waking up, the schedule had moved from sunrise to sunset, much like a farmer. It didn't matter that this was considered 6 a.m. It was just when everyone got up. Thom ate his oatmeal while listening to the radio and discussing the day's chores with Carl. He wanted to go, but there was still a house to run.

The truck started easily when he turned the key. The truck radio antenna was better than the one in the house, so Thom searched the dial for any station new and unfamiliar. He sat back while letting the truck warm up and mentally went down the map to the church. Thom's home was at the south end of Galena, and he needed to go north through town, and across the state route. He would then continue on towards the freeway on a county road until it intersected with another state route, number 36. At that intersection was the church. Going on another two or three miles on Route 36 would put him at Interstate 71. The curiosity of the freeway drew him, but he dared not. There was no reason, and there were too many unknowns and risks.

The news was the same, but talks of riots were beginning to run on the airwaves. Inner city Cleveland was having a rough time with lawlessness, it seemed.

The truck moved easily through the foot of snow. Nothing had been plowed, but Thom knew where the road was. Everything was quiet in town, and he saw a family walking on the State Route at the edge of town. They were walking away from him; they had already passed by the entrance to Galena. Maybe most people were doing that, he thought, and let them keep on walking.

The county road had not been plowed, and the tire tracks were old and drifted over. No one had driven on this road yesterday for sure, it seemed. He worked hard keeping between the ditches on the curves and hills and kept it slow. The gas gauge read half full, good enough for lots of little errands like this. The four-wheel drive was truly a Godsend.

It took a while, but Thom finally could see the State Route 36 intersection ahead. He soon realized that something looked wrong up there. An accident had occurred at the crossroads. He pulled up within a few car lengths and got the whole picture. A car pulling out from the county road was broadsided and the accident blocked his access to the road, along with one lane of the State Route. Snow was stacked high on the cars. It appeared to have happened on the first night, as it looked like cars could get around now. But it was probably a nightmare on that first night. Adding to the congestion of the interstate entrance ramps two miles down the road, this accident would have made the night horrible for many people. Looking down the road, there were six or eight cars that were either abandoned on the road or off on the ditch. The accident really complicated things as people tried to get out and travel that first night. In retrospect, the blockage may have saved many lives in the end. The accident blocking access to the freeway would have sent dozens of families back to their homes out of frustration. Being frustrated and still alive was better than the alternative.

The church was on the other side of Route 36, so Thom had no choice but to park the truck in an abandoned driveway. A sudden chill came over his body from head to toe when the ignition was turned off. The panic attack lasted for a good ten minutes as he sat rocking back and forth in his seat. The left arm still had feeling; he pinched it several times to reassure himself that this wasn't a heart attack. That consolation didn't do much for his spinning head. The blurring colors came into focus on the tree across the street. It was tall and leafless, with several squirrel nests made from leaves on one side. In his kaleidoscope vision, it looked like a palm tree swaying in the breeze.

He focused on this tree and let his mind drift, thinking warm thoughts about palm trees. After what seemed like a lifetime, Thom managed to pull it together enough to get out of the truck and brave the cold. The air helped to clear his head, but not much.

He pushed the lock button on the remote and set to walking. At the accident, he peered into the broadsided car. Some stains were on the seats, and the airbags were punctured. The other car was quite a mess too, an older vehicle with no airbags. A spider-web crack in the windshield was present on the passenger side of the car. The luggage was still in the backseat, but no bodies.

In front of the church across the street was a stark sight. Four graves had been dug at the corner facing the church, four wooden crosses stood over them. Two of the graves were noticeably smaller than the others and might have been children. Thom knelt down and wanted to say a prayer, but nothing came to mind. He crossed his chest and wondered to himself if this was Father Michael's handiwork.

Looking up at the church, Thom was still in awe. It had just been renovated, and the size of the cathedral had been doubled. He wasn't used to how it looked yet, so much bigger, it could hold a thousand people in the chapel. The ground was still torn up from all the construction equipment that had been on site for the last nine months. The church had grown so quickly in the area. The $2 million needed for the renovation was raised in less than six months. The church had been doing so well, and the parishioner count had forced a third mass every Sunday to get everyone in. Thom suddenly wondered how many of the parishioners were still alive today and would be alive when this was all over. It was a painful thought to have bouncing around in his brain, and he shook his head to get it out of there.

One of the glass doors to the church had been busted, and Thom became concerned. Looters that would steal from a church would have to be hard-core. Inside he saw that the chapel had been a place of refuge for many people at one time, but none remained. Maybe some had the first night, when there was so much confusion, and stopped

143

traffic out front. Maybe people came inside when they ran out of gas or were just looking for answers. Father Michael certainly took in all that were in need, and the church pews became resting places.

Thom saw that all the gold relics were gone — certainly they were in safekeeping. He walked up to the altar and said a prayer. A candle was lit on the pedestal where Mother Mary used to stand, and Thom warmed his hands by it. He then said a short prayer while struggling to keep focused on his vigil. As he prepared to leave, he grabbed a couple hymnals, which included the weekly scripture readings. Maybe the family could read those at home for their own church time, he thought. When he looked up the aisle he saw Father Michael standing there.

Father Michael was about 40 years old and had an athletic build. Much different than what Thom had expected for a parish priest when they first met six years ago. He often sprinkled his homilies with stories of sports, and rivers he had rafted, mountains he had climbed. He often took up parishioners on offers to go water skiing on their boats and on snow skiing trips. It seemed that no physical challenge was out of bounds for Father. Also very charismatic and a gifted speaker, he was unmistakably the reason why this church was doubling in size. After Thom attended the six-month course to convert to Catholicism, he found that he needed to have his first confession and confess all the sins of his thirty-nine years. Thom had turned to Father Michael and told him, "You'd better pack a lunch." Without missing a beat, he invited Thom to his home for a confession over dinner.

Looking at the hymnals in Thom's hand, he said, "Stealing from the church, are you, Thomas?"

"You'll hear about it in the confessional later, Father Michael."

"I'm sure I will," he said with a smile. He approached, shaking Thom's hand, and then pulling him in for a man-hug.

"So, what brings you to St. Joseph's? Is the family okay?" he said, while motioning Thom to a pew.

"Yes, they are fine, and we have been blessed with food supplies and heat. I've taken three families into my home, and that's great. But I'm coming to you because I want to do more. There has got to be a way to do more."

"I'm so glad to hear that, Thom, and I've heard that same statement from a few of our faithful. I've got about a dozen folks in my home behind the church, and a couple needing medical care."

"From the accident?"

"Yes, poor souls," he replied, "and I'll tell you right now that the hospital in Westerville is a madhouse. You would expect it on the first night of the emergency, but we went back a couple days ago, and now it's worse. The parking lot has become a tent-city of people with nowhere else to go. They practically attacked us when we pulled into the parking lot. And the hospital was so bogged down; they really couldn't help us at all. Both of my people have head injuries, and they couldn't give us pain medication, just antibiotics, and weak ones at that. I hope this situation turns around; there are many lives at stake."

"Yes, father, much is at stake. There are many who were traveling and are far from home or their destination. What I had in mind was a listing of 'safe houses' that are trying to help these people get home. That way, if a family is trying to travel north to meet relatives, I would have a list of sleep-over spots for the family to safely stop along the way."

Father sat back in his pew and crossed his arms thoughtfully. "Safe Houses, huh? That's got some legs to it. What if they have nowhere to go, though?"

"I'm still working on the plan; it has some glitches."

"I will tell you that the non-denominational church south of here has its doors open to people. They have a big fireplace in the lobby. For the holiday, they had collected a roomful of food for the homeless but hadn't delivered it to them yet. Now they are keeping it for those who need it here. I wonder how long it will last, with all the people showing up, but they are doing a great thing."

"That's exactly the kind of information we need: a listing of places where people are welcome and won't be shot when they knock on the door. You know what I mean?" He could see that Father was thinking, and the wheels were turning, so he continued; "My home is right at the square of Galena, and I've charted the homes that are occupied and friendly in the town. I also have a few charted outside of Galena in the southeast direction. What I need now is some on the country roads going in different directions." He handed Father a piece of paper mapping the village and out-skirting areas of concern.

"You've put some thought into this," Father said, looking at the sheet.

"It's been on my mind. It's a way that we can help more people. At this point, both your house and mine are filled pretty much to the max, and we're only helping a handful of people. A plan like this allows a much greater number to be helped. I don't have the entire plan, but with some input, maybe I could fill in the blanks."

Father sat back and looked at Thom, pausing for a second. It was then that Thom realized he was scratching his forearms incessantly without even knowing it. "You know Thom, I've put a lot of time in at the shelters and the soup kitchens. I know a detox when I see it," he said softly.

"Prozac," Thom confessed. "I ran out the day of the event. It's starting to hit me hard."

"Thom," he said as he came closer, putting his hand on Thom's shoulder. "The side effects of stopping antidepressants cold turkey can be devastating. It shouldn't be taken lightly. You've told Toni, right?"

"No, we've had our ups and downs with all this mess. I just thought it best to not add something else to the pile."

146

"Man up, Thom," he knew the real story, and he wasn't taking the cheap talk. "You are going to have some issues, and she needs to know why. She can help. Have you had thoughts of suicide?"

"No," he lied.

"You know who you are talking to right?" He broke out his priestly superpower: Guilt.

"I think we communicate perfectly, Father," Thom passed along the coded message. The message was: *Don't make me say it out loud; you'll just make it more real.*

Just then, the front doors of the church closed with a loud bang. A frantic man had crossed the floor of the lobby quickly and stood in the doorway to the cathedral holding both doors open. The light behind him created a silhouette similar to the savior on the cross as he held the doors open. His head hung down, but as it rose, the look of a madman came through his eyes. Those crazy eyes scanned the entire room as he fought to stand upright.

"Can anybody help me? My family won't be able to hold out much longer," he said breathlessly.

They both rose from the pew and rushed to the man. He looked to be in his forties, heavyset and was covered in snow and mud. He had fallen, and probably more than once, by how he looked.

"Slow down," Father Michael said. "Tell us where they are."

"On the freeway." His breathing was getting better, but not by much. "We had been driving on the berm beside the traffic jam, but I lost it into the ditch. I couldn't get the truck restarted, so they must be really cold now. You've got to help them!" His pleading was getting exaggerated, and to Thom, irritating. It was so over the top, and Thom's headache didn't help the situation.

"Calm down, we'll help," Thom said, coming closer. "Were you at the main exit when you got off, by the gas stations?"

"No, I was close to a bridge that didn't have an off-ramp. It was in the middle of nowhere, and my daughter is in a wheelchair. We would have never gotten her up that hill. They must be so cold, you must help!"

His pleading was driving Thom crazy, and he kept pointing towards the door. He wanted them outside in the worst way. It was the wild eyes, though, that were putting the Father and Thom on edge.

Thom pulled a map out of his coat pocket and laid it out on a table in the lobby.

"Here we are, did you turn off on this road here? It leads to an overpass," he said, pointing.

A dumbfounded look came over his face and he started to stutter a bit. "Must have been, look, we have to get going." He began to move to the door.

Thom looked over at Father, and he wasn't moving. Both stood their ground. Thom decided it was time to test things a bit. He opened a bottle of water from his backpack and handed it to the man. He thought it would help him settle down, while he ran his test.

"Look, buddy, trust is the most valuable thing we have right now, and I'm not getting there with you on this," Thom said while the man took a big swig of his water. "You might just want to get me out in the open and knock me out to take my possessions and move on. Maybe there's an ambush waiting for me out there. So, if you want my food, here's my backpack of power bars and some soup cans. And if you want my weapon, here's that too." Thom set the backpack on the table with the map and then reached into his pants waistband to pull out the 9 mm automatic. He set the gun within a stretching reach of the man and stepped back.

"What's mine is yours. Take it and go, no harm, no foul." Thom looked over at Father Michael, and he never saw his eyes as big as they were right then. Even during that dinner confession. Their detox discussion was undoubtedly going through Father's mind as he stared at the weapon on the table.

This was a classic Mexican standoff; *The Good, the Bad, and the Ugly* theme song could almost be heard in the background. All eyes were looking around at each other, trying to figure the other out. Finally, the man reached out towards the weapon, and Thom started to question his logic in this endeavor. He tried to remain with a relaxed stance, not revealing that in his coat pocket, he was gripping the butt of the short barrel auto. If the man did attempt to pick up that weapon, he would be dead before he hit the floor. Thom hadn't even realized that he put himself in the position of killing someone in a cathedral lobby. But the man's reach went to the side of the table, and he pushed the entire thing away from himself.

"I don't want your stuff. I want my family safe. Can we go now?" He was calmer now; maybe the reality of the moment had sunk in. Or maybe he had been dehydrated and the water helped, who knows.

"How many people total? How large of a vehicle will we need?" Father was talking now; he wanted full control of this situation after the wild direction Thom took it. He also watched Thom very carefully when the 9mm went back into his waistband.

"My wife and daughter. She's ten, but big for her age."

"Okay, I have an SUV here that we all should fit in. Let's get going." Father glanced at Thom once more while walking out the door.

At the SUV, Thom asked Father if he had a plastic child's sled, and he laughed a simple 'no' as he slid behind the steering wheel. So, Thom requested a trash can lid, and they stopped at the church dumpster shed in the parking lot. Thom grabbed a lid and hopped back in the SUV. While they drove, he poked a couple holes in the lid with his pocketknife and strung some rope through them from his backpack.

"Voila! A sled. This will come in handy," Thom said proudly, but they were unimpressed. 'They will be,' he reassured himself, 'they will be.' The adrenalin from the standoff was still affecting him, and his headache was pounding. Having this little project to focus on really helped his situation, but the headache and random changing thoughts were working against him. It was a constant struggle.

Father Michael followed the man's directions, and fresh footprints could be spotted along the road for most of the trip. A couple of times the footprints disappeared then reappeared with a probable roll into the ditch in between. The sight of the footprints was comforting, but also with each passing second, they were getting closer to the freeway. The place Thom dearly wanted to see and dreaded at the same time. The questions running through his mind fed the headache and built it to a crescendo by the time they reached the interstate.

The sight was breathtaking. Father drove across the bridge, displaying abandoned cars for as far as could be seen in both directions. Some with doors still open, some in the ditch, all with snow piled high and wind drifted at the corners.

"Where are all these people?" Thom said under his breath. There were lots of old footprints in the snow, most drifted over. There was a group of people in the distant south, and they appeared to be continuing south. That was it, no other life to be seen. Father parked the SUV on the bridge, and they followed the man's footprints down the hillside to the freeway. The man was right; it would be tough getting a wheelchair up that steep hill. A more gradual slope was defined on the north side of the overpass that might be better when they returned.

"Guys, we may need to put her on this sled and pull her up the hill, when the time comes. Does that make sense?" Thom said, receiving nodding agreement from both. The eerie silence of the freeway brought everyone to speaking in a whisper or not at all. The absence of sound reminded Thom of the food run at the abandoned house; the quiet didn't feel right, but disturbing the quiet didn't feel right either. Nothing felt right about this place.

The truck was a little bit to the south of the overpass, so they quickly headed that way. Several fresh footprints in the snow made Thom very uneasy, but he also figured they must be the group he saw from the bridge heading south. He felt very vulnerable on that interstate; there were lots of places for people to hide. Taking on the role of the group's sentry, Thom pulled his gun to have it on the ready. A sideways look from Father fell upon Thom soon after, and he put the weapon back in his waistband.

The black SUV was found deep in the ditch, proving that the wild-eyed man knew how to wreck a vehicle, along with wrecking everything else. The SUV appeared empty with no sound or movement. Thom noticed that the fresh pack of footprints continued past the SUV, going south. The man quickly opened the door, almost as frantically as he opened the church doors earlier. His wife was petrified inside, mascara streaming down her face. It was hardly definable what she said while she cried. It seems that a pack of men had just gone through and were loudly talking about killing anyone they found and taking their food. They even talked about eating the people they found too, which put her into a complete tailspin.

Both the man and Father were concerned about calming her down and making her feel better before they could make any moves. Thom walked around to the tailgate and opened it up.

"How much of this stuff needs to go? We need to get moving guys," he said, trying to speed things along.

"All of it, of course," said the man, as if there couldn't be any other answer.

Father Michael had opened the back door and was talking to the daughter, helping her to be comfortable with the situation. She was scared also, but you could see the cold was affecting her more than fear. Thom began pulling out the luggage in the back, and was happy to see a cardboard box of canned goods on the bottom. *At least he was thinking a little bit,* he thought.

Four pieces of luggage, a box of canned goods, and a wheelchair. He unfolded it up at the berm of the highway and scaled the hill back to where Father was holding the daughter's hand.

"My name is Thom," he said after stealing a glance at Father. "I think we'll be carrying you out of this ditch to your chair up there."

"Cynthia," she said, taking his hand. An expression of confidence came to her face as she unbuckled her seatbelt and positioned herself to be carried. Thom was suddenly glad he was dealing with Cynthia instead of her hysterical mother with mascara trails.

The process of getting her into the chair took everyone's attention. It's not surprising that they were caught off guard when the group of men to the south returned right at that moment.

"Awww, ain't that nice," their leader said in an irritating baby voice. There were three of them, and they walked right up on the group. Thom was too busy with the luggage and helping with the wheelchair to perform his sentry role. He was kicking himself as he turned around, blaming his lack of focus at this inopportune time. The leader was pointing his gun at the group and his smile was so big that he giggled while he talked. The other two, one in a blue jacket, and the other in brown, had their handguns at their side. Looking at the group, they knew more guns weren't needed. A kid in a wheelchair, and a priest? Come on.

"I got me some people! And some food, I see! I told you guys this was where to come!" He couldn't keep his feet still, doing a bit of a gallop as he waved his gun around, pointing at each one in turn. Thom stood there trying to look relaxed with his hands to his side. He rebelled against raising them, to see how the bad guy would take it. The two henchmen flanked him on each side, watching, and letting the leader have the floor. And boy did he like having the floor.

"Is that an Escalade up there on the bridge? That's what I want! I want the keys right here on the ground. Right here! I always wanted an

Escalade!" The words were almost coming out in song he was so giddy with himself.

Thom was kicking himself again for letting them park on the bridge. It was like putting meat out for the wolves. He didn't realize how stupid they were for parking it in plain view.

"It's just a Suburban," Father Michael said as he reached in his pocket and pulled out the keys. He threw them on the ground with a clank.

"Yee-haw! We got us a pony to ride now! I'm going to call it an Escalade anyway. It's mine now, I can call it what I want! Yee-haw!!" His feet couldn't stop moving, and the adrenalin of the moment surely wasn't helping any either as he continued.

"I know somebody has a gun. Who's got the gun? Who's got the gun? I want it on the ground right here with the keys," he said, pointing his gun at the ground. He looked at Thom and his poker face revealed nothing. Then he looked at the husband and all was lost. The husband just stared directly at Thom, no eye contact to the gunman, just Thom.

"Not much of a poker player, are you?" Thom said across to him, glaring.

"Give us the gun or the kid in the wheelchair gets it," he said in a quirky voice.

Thom twisted his face on his unnecessary comment and reached into his waistband. The Glock came out and he held it completely in his hand, not doing the two-finger style hold, and showed it to them. Then he tossed it to the ground with a thud.

"Woo hoo! I am the Humongous! The king of the wasteland!" he screamed, as he continued to dance around. He still had his weapon leveled on the group, waiving back and forth while he kicked around. Thom noticeably sulked and put his hands into his coat pockets. The leader didn't give it much notice, as he performed his dance routine around his trophies on the ground.

"We are going to rise out of this darkness, and we will RULE the wasteland because we are the Road Warriors! We will take what we want, and rape and pillage and kill and eat! We will rise above the rest! I am the Humongous!"

He picked up Thom's gun and used it in his dance now. He continued to move about with both guns leveled but not really aimed at anything. His henchmen were standing with their hands on their hips; the guy in brown was rolling his eyes at the performance. Thom continued to sulk, waiting. Waiting with his short barrel auto in his coat pocket, following the man doing a dance, careful not to push it forward so that it would be noticed outside. Thom had practiced this technique a couple years ago at a backyard firing range with a junk coat. His aim wasn't great in this stance, the moment needed to be right. Hopefully he wouldn't have to wait too long.

"But you. I don't like you," he said, pointing his gun at Thom's chest. "I just don't like you. After I kill you, and cook you, and eat you, I'm going to take out your wallet and find out where you live."

His dancing was moving from his legs to his arms now, doing a gallop with one hand circling around over his head. Eventually the other arm rose too and waved around.

"And I'm going to go to your house, and find your family, and…" Poof. Poof… silence.

The bullets pushed out clumps of down feathers from the lining of Thom's coat as they travelled out. The sound was muffled in his pocket, and although he certainly heard the shots, it didn't appear that anyone else did. The floating feathers seemed to hypnotize everyone in the radius. The crazy guy just stared at them, and so did the henchmen. Thom slowly pulled the short-barrel Glock out of his pocket and when the henchmen saw it, they dropped theirs.

When the leader finally fell to the ground, the hypnotic trance was broken. Thom looked to the side, and his companions seemed to start breathing again, as if they had been holding their breath all this time.

154

No one knew he had the extra weapon. They were dazed by the event, and although their expressions didn't show it, they were happy to see the madman fall. Only Cynthia smiled, and a precious smile it was. The feathers were still floating, and Thom noticed some smoke drifting out of the holes in his coat. It seemed so surreal. If things had gone differently, Thom could have had bullets coming *into* his coat just as easily as the ones that came out. The smoke and the feathers would have probably been the same.

Father stepped forward and made sure everyone in the group was okay, and then checked the vitals of the gunman. He stayed hunched over the man for a couple minutes, but Thom moved his attention away from what Father was doing. His concern was more for the two bad guys that were still alive, not the soul of the lunatic on the ground.

"Don't move guys, don't move at all." He looked at the henchmen sternly.

"Not moving," Brown Jacket said.

"What the hell was he on? Was he high?" Thom's mood was exasperated, and he was not about to tone it down.

"Meth," Brown Jacket replied in a matter-of-fact way.

"Crystal Meth? What, you guys got a lab or something?"

"Yes, we do. We're running out of food though and needed to get some."

"So, you got high and came out to get food? Are you crazy?" Thom sternly replied.

"He's always high, but he is really high today. At least he was," Blue Jacket jumped in on the conversation.

"Well, I'll bet you're glad to be rid of him then." Thom tried to justify his action to them.

"He's my brother-in-law," Brown Jacket said, "and he had a plan to use this lab to make us rich. We would have something no one else

155

had, and we could charge anything we wanted. 'The lab is making gold,' he would say. We would rise out of this shit-storm and come out smelling like a rose."

"There are some issues with your logic there, especially if you are consuming all your gold. But that's stoned-logic for you, I guess," Thom said, trying to make some reason out of the situation.

"You called him your brother-in-law," Father Michael stepped away from the dead man and into the conversation. "Are there women and children at this drug lab?"

"No, no, no," said Blue Jacket, shaking his head.

"You wouldn't lie to a priest, would you?" he said, in his most guilt-ridden voice. Once again flexing his superpowers.

Brown Jacket gave in to the guilt. "My sister and her two kids are there in the house. But man, you might as well kill us, because this is what we have to do. We are all set up."

Thom looked at Father Michael and shook his head. "Well? Should I?" rattling his gun around.

Father Michael just smiled at the joke. "It might save the kids, but you can't."

"What if I came up with a plan to get you all the food you needed right here where we stand? Could you let go of your plan?" Thom ventured.

"Maybe, that would get us some food, but it doesn't get us paid." Brown Jacket wasn't letting go of the dream that easy.

"We'll work on that too. But first, I would say that twenty percent of the people who left their house packed up a box of food like this family did. They thought ahead a little bit and threw some food in the trunk. You follow? Then, when the traffic stopped moving and they were put to walking, they had to make a choice. Either they could carry their luggage or their food. The luggage was easier to carry, and

156

their clothes cost more than some cans of soup, so the choice was a no-brainer, and they left the food behind. So, right now, two out of every ten cars here have food in the trunk. All you got to do is start pulling trunk latches, or grab a crowbar out of a trunk and start popping them the easy way. Got it?"

Brown Jacket started nodding first, at about halfway through, and Blue Jacket got it at the end. They made some comments to each other while Thom retrieved his Glock from the crazy guy and took the dead man's gun as well. Thom then searched his coat pockets and found an extra clip. The heat coming out of the holes in his body created an eerie steam that he caught himself warming his hands in. He pulled them back when he realized what he was subconsciously doing.

"Did you have to take his gun?" Brown Jacket said. "We only have so many weapons to defend ourselves."

"In keeping with *The Road Warrior* tradition, I'm able to keep what I kill," he said, even though it sounded harsher as it came out than he wanted.

"That was *The Chronicles of Riddick* that they did that," Brown Jacket corrected sternly.

"Right you are, but it was still a wasteland," Thom nodded his head in agreement. "Look, I'll let you guys keep your weapons, but I need you to move over here." Thom's gun motioned them to a parked car away from their guns on the ground.

"Wait a minute," Thom said as he walked over to their guns, pointing at them in the snow. "That is a Colt 1911 nickel-plated with a walnut handle. It is an elite weapon, an expensive weapon. I've always wanted one."

"Remember your promise; you heard it right, Father?" Brown Jacket called back.

"Sorry, Thom, but you did say it," Father said to him with a smile, putting his hand on Thom's shoulder.

157

"Look, you guys go ahead, and I'll catch up," Thom said to the rest of the clan. "You'll have to move slowly with the chair, and I'll be there to help on the hill. Leave a piece of luggage for me to carry; I need to take care of these guys."

"Take care of them? You're not going to kill them, are you?" Father whispered in his ear.

"I'd like to, I really want that Colt," he whispered back with a smile. "Go on, I'll catch up."

The clan obediently began moving. Everyone just wanted to get away from the dead body, and maybe forget this whole thing ever happened. Father Michael picked up his keys and grabbed a couple of bags. They did leave one large bag behind for Thom.

"Okay guys, what we are going to do here is build some trust," Thom said, as he turned to the henchmen. "I want to make sure that you don't try to follow us or hurt us as we get away. You probably wouldn't, but I'm going to make sure. So, I want you to brush off the snow, and climb up on the roof of this car. Just sit up there where I can see you until we get to the bridge and then you can have your beautiful gun back. I'll keep my promise and you keep yours. Okay?"

"Alright man, we can do that." They began sweeping the snow off with the arm of their coats. They weren't happy, and still didn't seem excited about popping trunks. "I wish you guys well, I hope the handicapped kid is okay," Brown Jacket said, striking Thom with his sentiment.

"I wish you the same, but you know that Father was right about closing down the lab. You are putting your sister's kids in real danger."

"I know, I know," he said as he started climbing the car. "But I'm also trying to provide for them too."

158

"How about if I gave you an idea that could get you ahead, not just get you food? Would you promise to shut down the lab if you used it?" he said, the short barrel pointed away from them, but still in his hand.

"Maybe. What's the idea?"

"No. I'm serious here. If you use my idea, you must shut down the lab. Don't make me bring Father Michael back here." This time he pointed the weapon at them for emphasis.

They looked at each other, arms suddenly raised, "Okay we promise. What is it?"

"Well, do the crowbar on the trunk deal and take home the food you find. Then at home pick up some wire cutters and come back. There are a lot of cars with dead bodies in them, and most have wedding rings on their fingers. You get the picture?"

"Damn, that's a great idea! If we weren't high all the time, we could have thought of that!" Suddenly Brown Jacket's face was beaming, and he was looking around at all the cars as if they were chunks of gold, deciding which one to pick up first.

Thom let his statement fade in silence and then he began to speak in earnest. "We are trading one despicable act for another, but at least this act won't put those children's lives in danger. My only concern here is helping those children, and it should be yours as well. It will be despicable, what you do. But other people will have this same idea, and if you are not the one doing it, someone else will. Sad to say. The silver lining of saving a child's life will be the only redeeming thing about it."

"We'll keep our promise. Now get going, this metal roof is freezing my ass off!" Brown Jacket said with a laugh. "Hey, what's your name, if we ever cross paths again?"

"No, it's probably best we don't do that," he said, picking up the luggage. "If we cross paths again, then we'll decide. Adios!"

159

They stayed on the roof the entire time, and Thom could only imagine the conversation they had. Every time he looked back, there were arm movements and back-slapping going on. He was just glad they weren't vengefully attached to the guy lying on the ground. Maybe they assumed it would happen sooner or later with him anyway.

By the time Thom rejoined his crew, they had gotten Cynthia to the top of the hill on their own — Father Michael pushing and her father pulling. Thom waved to the guys on the hood as they loaded into the SUV and headed down the road. The ride was very quiet, and Thom just stared out the window at the snow-covered trees as they passed them. Cynthia sat in the middle, and sensing the solitude, she put her hand on Thom's. They merely looked at each other for what seemed an eternity. She wanted to say thank you, he could see that, but neither spoke. They didn't really need to; the private look was all they needed to communicate.

"Father, does anyone at your home want to travel south? I can give them a ride, and help them along the way," Thom called out from the backseat as they neared the church.

"I don't think so, but I will check."

When they got back to the minister's residence behind the church, it was all hands on deck to unload everything and everyone inside his home. Food was waiting for them at the residence, and Father pulled Thom aside while he was eating some chili.

"There was nothing you could do about that wild man. You did what you had to do, Thom. I just wanted to say that to you."

"Thank you, Father. I hope it's the only time I need to do it." Thom looked at the floor. It had not fully hit him yet that he had taken a life.

"I will do some work on your idea about the safe houses, though. Is it okay for me to come to your home in two days?" he asked.

"Is it okay? It would be great. Could we have Mass?"

"I would love to. I will try to arrive early so that we have time to fit everything in," he said.

"So two days, that's New Year's Day, right?" Thom said, counting on his fingers.

"Yes, that would be New Year's, I had forgotten," he said with a smile. "Christmas is the only important holiday at the end of the year in my book."

"Is there anything you need? Do you have enough firewood?" Thom asked, looking at the wood stove in the middle of the room.

"I am a little low on firewood," he said a little humorously. "This thing was mainly for decoration, left over from the previous pastor. My supply of wood was for ambiance, not for heating the house, so it's going fast."

"Well, bring the Suburban, and we'll set you up. Anything else?"

"No, I don't think so, the Lord has provided. How about you?" he turned it back to Thom.

"I would have to say that the Lord has provided us in marvelous ways. We need nothing, except maybe some electricity… I don't know how you feel about weapons, but you are welcome to the crazy man's pistol, if you need it." There was a silence. Thom was afraid he'd asked the wrong question to this man of the cloth.

"I fear that I may need to say yes to that, Thom," he finally said. "I have religious relics here that some people would have no problem killing us all, for the metal they are made of. Taking another's life is not what I was put here for, but saving lives is. I was shown today that there are situations when a gun can be useful. When all the reason and talk in the world won't work, it's good to have one in the house. But don't give it to me."

Thom looked around the room and took in all the clusters of families in the living room and the family room of the house. The families were separated from each other to take care of their children, and he

161

picked two middle-aged families situated close together. One of the men had a full beard. Thom walked over between them and began to talk discretely. The Father had introduced him to everyone when they came in, so introductions were not necessary.

"Hey, do either of you gentlemen know how to handle a gun?" Thom blurted right out. He was met with blank looks from the men, partially because they were in a priest's home. It's something one doesn't expect to be asked. "I don't mean to profile here, but I was hoping I might be talking to the right guys," he smiled.

"I've been to the firing range a few times with my brother-in-law," said the non-bearded one. The one with the beard was not proficient with a weapon either but had also fired a gun at a range.

"Father wanted me to give this to you to protect the house." Thom produced the wild man's pistol and the extra magazine. "This is for you guys in case things get ugly around here."

The bearded one handled the weapon well. He chambered a bullet then ejected it and removed the magazine to check the ammo count.

"Come with me," Thom said. "We need to come up with a protection plan. Guard posts need to be defined, and you need to know what to look for. Father can't be expected to help with this, but it needs to be done. You have been in a safe zone behind the church for a long while. Only people in desperate need would approach the door. The aggressive people could start coming any time, though."

A game plan was worked out, and the guardsmen who were up for the assignments were defined. The house was brick, so they had an advantage there. The vehicles needed to be moved, to give a clear line of sight. They found an antique pair of binoculars in the china cabinet that served their purpose, and more people stepped up than Thom expected. Once the plan was worked out, he knew it was time to go.

Before the exit, Father joined hands with all the people in the house for a prayer. He asked Thom to speak of any prayer requests, and he mentioned Candice struggling with cancer and for his family to not have anxiety about his return; he trusted the Lord would deliver him home. He finished the prayer, and the group all said a Hail Mary in unison. It was beautiful.

Thom gave a kiss on the cheek to Cynthia, as she thoughtfully met him at the door to say goodbye. Then she did something completely unexpected. Her arms made a violent jerk, and a loud noise came from her hands. Startled, Thom looked down at her hands to see a roll of duct tape pulled out and extended toward him. It was the pulling of the tape that made the loud noise.

"So you don't lose any more feathers," she said, putting a piece of duct tape over the holes in his coat.

He laughed and held out his jacket to her hands. "Can I take you home with me?"

"Only if we go right now… Or any time later. I'm all booked up other than that," she said without missing a beat.

Thom was taken aback by her answer—maturity beyond her years. He then stooped down to one knee, at her level, and reached behind his neck. Out of his shirt came a sterling chain with a crucifix made of alabaster.

"I got this necklace in the Dominican Republic. That's the first island Christopher Columbus landed on, and it is considered the first island of the Americas. Christopher Columbus later retired there, lived out his days, and was buried on the island. The oldest Catholic church in the Americas is there, and that is where this crucifix is from. I want you to hold onto this for me and take good care of it because I'm going to want it back someday. Can you do that for me?"

She nodded her head, not sure what to say, sitting forward to let him put it on. They had a moment in silence afterward, as he held her hand and looked at the crucifix around her neck and into her eyes.

Thom walked out the door into the bitter cold with a smile on his face. The sun was getting ready to set, and there was no doubt about that in

163

the temperature. He started a slow jog to the place where he left the truck, a couple hundred yards away. He took a couple of moments at the fresh gravesites again and took note of the number of fresh tire tracks on Route 36. There were a lot, it seemed, that had passed around this accident today. The road was still being used, and people were still attempting to travel on the unplowed state route. The infrastructure has completely broken down, and the people of the area were undoubtedly on their own. The thought that people were dying ran through his mind as he stood before the gravesites. He was a testament to that fact.

Sitting in the truck while it warmed up, Thom realized that he would have to regurgitate this story for the people in his home. It would not be pleasant. But they needed a wakeup call like this; no one really believed that bad stuff was going to happen. They were watching out windows, and kind of playing Cowboys and Indians in the back yard. They didn't treat it like a war or think that people could die right in front of them … by their own hand. This was real, and they needed a level of alertness that matched this reality. Thom waited for the perfect moment to fire his weapon on the freeway, and it could have cost someone their life. That mistake couldn't be afforded again. Hesitation kills.

Chapter 11: The human animal.

The next day Thom was on duty in the three-season room, watching the back yard. It was about noon, and he was playing chess with David in the guard bunker. Nothing was happening outside, and David had just pulled a major coup by taking his queen. A triumphant "Check" was stated when his rook took the queen's square. But somehow, Thom would be rescued from his lack of focus by another child entering the room.

"Refugees!" JP's daughter was the runner this shift, and she had news of people spotted. A minute later, Brad came in to do the forward guard post of the room and Carl took the point position at the door. Thom and David kept their sight out the back windows, looking for any surprises.

The couple, with a young child about ten years old, walked up to the house, completely empty-handed. It was curious; most people carried something, even if it was completely worthless in the new cold reality. Their expressions and actions told a story as they walked up to the porch. They were very protective of their daughter, and she was always between them, one guarding each side. They looked tired and scared, but they also had an angry look, like they were willing to fight if they had to. The complexities of their appearance gave Thom concern, and he announced to the room to take nothing for granted.

Carl asked the standard questions of the travelers from the point spot. The husband complied with the need for safety and dropped his kitchen knife in the plastic bin. They had no food. They had nothing else. They were destitute and desperate. When they came inside, Carl continued being the point man on Thom's request. He had enough excitement the day before.

Carl made introductions around the room, and they found that their names were Joel and Sara. The little one was eight, and her name was Megan.

"Where are you folks from?" Carl asked in a polite voice.

165

"Reynoldsburg," the man said. "We're trying to get up north to Mansfield; we have family up there but have had some issues." The woman had yet to really look Carl in the eye since entering the room. Something definitely didn't feel right. Thom continued to watch from the corner.

"Where did you sleep last night, or is that part of your issue?" Carl asked, trying to keep it light.

Joel glanced over at Sara, looking for an answer, or maybe how much of an answer to give. "We stayed at a house on Reynoldsburg Road for the last several days. It was bad," he finally said.

"It was an abuse of people in need," Sara interrupted him. She finally looked Carl in the eye, and it was a look of anger he hadn't seen since his divorce.

"Let me say right now that our help is free, our food is free," Carl put in. "But what are we talking about here, really?"

Both let out a sigh of relief, and Joel even gave Sara a little hug. He gathered himself, saying to her, "I told you that not all people would be like him." Turning his attention to Carl, he continued; "I am so glad to find some good people like you! He really had us believing that everyone outside of the city would be wanting a payback from the city folks. He called it the 'big equalizer,' this storm."

"Can Megan go inside, please?" Sara said to Carl. "We can speak a little more freely then."

David reluctantly left the chess board, with his distinct lead in the game, and took Megan to the fireplace to warm her up. As he got up, he reminded his father that the game would be finished when this was over.

As soon as the door closed behind the kids, Joel began talking; "We came to his door with our luggage, the car was in the ditch. The first two houses we stopped at wouldn't even talk to us; one shot a rifle in the air to get us moving. He took us in, but he talked about payment

166

for food and shelter the next day when we woke up. He held us hostage for five days until we escaped yesterday."

"We stayed in an abandoned house last night," Sara added; "Because we didn't want to deal with people anymore, but it was a very cold night. We don't want to put Megan through that again."

"So, you paid him with your luggage? I see you no longer have it," Carl pressed.

"No, we left the luggage in our getaway," Joel responded but was quickly interrupted by Sara.

"I had to pay him. I paid him."

"What?" Carl recoiled in surprise. He looked over at Thom and then began to point at him. "I'm never being point man again, if this is the kind of shit that happens."

It was becoming clear, the conflict in their expressions. Their trauma had created a storm of emotions that Carl and Thom couldn't begin to grasp.

"He described it like a business deal. He asked permission. With a gun in his hand," Joel responded to the questioning looks. The real deal came out with the rest of it, however. "Oh, he never pointed it directly at me, but he made threats. He politely asked. Then he mentioned that Megan didn't interest him, he'd leave her alone if we agreed."

Joel looked over at his wife who was biting her finger so she wouldn't cry. She was done crying.

"Yesterday afternoon we saw our chance," She broke out. "There was a distraction out front, someone wanting in, or wanting food, and we made our break out the back. Joel grabbed a knife in the kitchen, and we lit out. He had tried to brainwash us to think that everybody would treat us just like he did. They would demand payment or leave us to the coyotes. He said that country folks have been waiting for this day for generations. He said that we should show up with food at a house, or we would *be* the food. We had five days of this torment."

167

"He started getting crazier after I asked about a woman's picture on the mantle," Joel added. "It was his wife, and he would always say that she was 'long gone' with this weird smile. I think he killed her when this emergency happened. He would talk about people dying during this thing and leaving no trace. No way to find out what happened to them, or who did it. I think he used the blackout as his chance to kill her and get away with it. I did not doubt that we would be next, once he was done having his fun."

There was an odd silence after Joel stopped talking. Finding something to say was difficult considering the subject matter. Brad decided to throw his hat in the conversation ring, and it didn't work out so well.

"I read a news story about two men convicted of murder connected to the twin-towers bombing back on Nine-Eleven. They both claimed their wives were in the towers when they fell down, but instead, they were simply murdered by their husbands. What you are talking about has certainly happened before."

"You guys look hungry," Carl decided to break up the next uncomfortable silence with something that would get a better response. He threw a sideways look at Brad also, but it didn't register that he had said anything wrong.

Thom got up from his spot in the corner and gave Carl a break; the weirdness of the conversation was getting to him, and it showed.

Thom's detox-ravaged brain suddenly had some clear thoughts due to the emotions of this moment. He always knew that there were people who would commit horrible crimes during this emergency with survival as their excuse. He now saw that some saw the emergency as an opportunity. A window in time to do all the things that they had only fantasized about but didn't have the guts to do in normal society. The Storm was a 'free for all' for them, like a kid in a candy store.

"Look, we need to get you inside and put all of this behind you," Thom said. "I just want to ask you to raise your jackets to prove you

168

don't have any more weapons. I know you don't, but I need to treat you like every other traveler through this home. For everyone's safety."

"We must look so horrible for allowing this to happen," Joel nervously said while raising his coat. "It's difficult for me to face you men now, knowing what you know about me, and us." Sara was staring sadly at the floor, raising her coat as well.

"Look, folks," Thom solemnly spoke, "there is only one man in this universe that can really judge us for our actions, and I'm certainly not him. Boy, am I not him." He suddenly got lightheaded at this statement, and the room began to spin. The detox was crunching again. He felt concerned about having a gun in his hand and put it on the cupboard shelf behind him. He steadied himself against the wall and wearily looked at the new travelers.

"We all have our demons. Please come inside where it is warm. We'll fight them together."

Sara started to walk in, but then she stopped. With her face still flush from the discourse, she looked at Carl with sudden urgency and said, "I'm gonna get sick." She then ran out into the yard beside the porch. The look of concern swept her husband's face as he accompanied her for comfort.

Thom could see her on all fours through the porch spindles as she heaved. The events of the last few days must have been horrendous to push her to this point. He lowered his head and put in a request to the guy upstairs. She needed it.

Thom started to walk inside, but Carl stopped him with a look. It was the rapper Ice Cube's snarl that he had on his face, and it wasn't pretty. "What was that about? And don't play dumb."

Erich respectfully left the three-season room; he had probably seen that snarl directed at him enough times to not want to be around it. As he walked out, Thom saw Toni walking in. He knew this was going to be bad. Thom slid open the back door and walked out onto the deck.

169

A path had been shoveled on the deck to the garage in the foot-deep snow. He hoped that the colder air would clear his jumbled mind. It didn't work.

"What happened out here?" Toni asked Carl.

"Your man is falling over out here like he's on something," Carl replied. Attention then turned to Thom.

"No. I'm not *on* something. I'm *off* something. I'm off my meds," Thom said, looking directly at Toni.

Toni paused; her head seemed to jerk back like it had been punched. Carl looked at her questioningly, and she responded with one word: "antidepressants."

"That's depressing," Carl gave the half-joking knee-jerk comment.

Thom smiled and pointed at him; "That's what I said." He wandered off the shoveled path into the virgin snow of the deck, making a production of it to buy time. He needed to get to a wall of the house, falling over right now in front of Toni would not have been good. The stress of the moment was not helping though. The dizziness and the headache were punching in the nitro canister right about now and going for maximum torque.

"How long?" Toni finally queried.

"Since day one. I had one pill and I cut it in half as my step-down." The wall felt like it was going to fall down anyway. It seemed to be wavering behind him like might not hold his weight.

"What? The step-down is supposed to be a gradual three or four weeks. Cold turkey can really do damage. People have died."

"Yeah, I know." Thom could have sworn the wall behind him was moving.

"And you didn't tell me? This is bullshit!"

170

"We had enough going on; I didn't want to add to it. Besides, I thought I could handle it."

"Handle it? People don't just *handle* stuff like this!" She paused, looking at the path, and his new footprints in the snow. Gears shifted. She was calming down and switching into Mother Hen mode. "Well, there's not much we can really do in these conditions, but I needed to know damn it! That stuff is a brain function drug, and seafood is brain food. You are now on a tuna diet, and I'm going to look for all the fish oil pills we might have gotten from other houses. It may not make a hill of beans difference, but it's all we can do. When you are done holding up the house, get in the kitchen for some pills."

With that, she spun on her heel and walked inside.

"And I thought Deloris was bad…" Carl said with a chuckle. Carl didn't realize the severity of this detox, but he saw the reaction from Toni. He watched Thom's silent shuffle through the snow to the door where he stood. Thom looked him in the eye and tried to say something. Nothing came out though, so he just shrugged and walked inside.

"Is it really that bad?" Carl said, disbelieving. "It's just a medication."

"Yes, it is, friend. Yes, it is. And just imagine how much of the population is on some sort of mind-altering medication, and how many are coming off cold turkey right now. We could have those people coming up to our door, psychotic, delusional, homicidal, who knows what. I'm feeling it, and they will too."

"No shit?" Carl still didn't get what Thom was going through but was concerned about crazed refugees coming to this door — that idea hit home.

That night around the wood stove a county map was pulled out and Joel defined the couple's travels. The approximate location of the house in question was marked on the map for later reference. It was certainly a house to warn people about, but also a place to visit when the lights came back on.

171

The couple had a shower; it was remarkable that the house still had water and natural gas. Thom noticed that they spent an awfully long time in there, but he imagined it was not to be frisky as others had done. They were probably trying to scrub away something grimy that would take more than a shower.

Thom took the pills that Toni found, along with the browbeating that accompanied them. She put together a dish of macaroni and cheese with tuna and some canned vegetables. It was tasteless. But dressed with some Tabasco, it was palatable. It was going to get old quick, though.

That night was New Year's Eve. David had the job of making sure the radio battery was charged, and he did a great job. All of the adults thanked him for his work a few times through the night, as the radio kept playing. He beamed with pride over the radio and his chess victory when he finished the game with Thom. Many congrats about the chess game flew around the wood stove to poke at Thom's pride.

A couple of wine bottles came out of the cellar, and everyone partook, even those on watch, only less. It was a good night, and they rang in the New Year together. The previous had been a crazy year, the presidential race does that, for sure, but the mudslinging was beyond normal. The new element in that election was that the broadcasters were much more active in the attacks on the candidates. The runners hardly needed to attack each other; the news guided the public to the obvious choice and destroyed the rest. It seemed like they were on a mission to protect the public from making a bad decision.
Inauguration day in three weeks would be quite interesting. The group might need to drink then too.

"So, the 800-pound elephant in the room is wondering what this New Year would bring," spoke up Carl. "We're not talking about that much."

"Oh, Carl. You're not that heavy. You've lost some weight this week." Thom lightened up the room to some laughter and refilled his glass of wine.

172

He then pulled out a tablet of paper and decided to make a project out of his question.

"Ok guys, I've got my Central Ohio iPad out. What do you guys think the year is going to be like?" Thom was still trying to keep this light, if it got too serious, it could turn into a sob-fest.

"We are certainly going to war. We do know that much, but with who is anyone's guess," JP spoke up, and all in the room agreed.

"And with war, comes a spark in the economy," Brad added.

"Let's not forget the people going to fight; I've got a brother in the Air Force," Brad's wife Amy spoke up. And around the room, they found that everyone had a relative in the service. All this concern at home is one thing, but those serving abroad have a different and more pressing set of concerns.

"Things should get back to normal pretty quickly when the power comes back on though." Carl tried to tide the negativity of the room.

"I can see that," Thom chimed in, helping to right the tide. "Once the businesses can begin work, we will spend a lot of time doing clean-up in our jobs, but normalcy will come back around. There will be plenty of work, that's for sure. The high unemployment rate that molded everything, including the election this year, will disappear."

"Because so many have died." Amy brought the room down again. "We will be filling their jobs."

"I guess so. I guess that is true. But also, the construction industry should go wild with repairs to homes from this event. There should be lots of work there." Thom tried to shine a light.

"Lots of time will be spent getting businesses back on track, putting everything back together," Brad added. "It will be an exciting time, and people with the right attitude could move up in society."

"Yes, that may be true, but to what end? Society is changing as we speak." JP finally put his conspiracy theory hat on. "This event is

173

changing society; and its values and we have no idea where they will end up. You might as well put away the notepad because we have no idea how this year will work out. It might seem like this event is a haphazard mixture of random weather and warlike attacks, but it is not. Someone is manning the switchboard, and they have much more control than anyone realizes. There is a master plan, and I bet that everything has gone according to that plan so far. But mark my words; they have much more in mind than creating a new housing boom. Much more."

The room quieted, waiting for a comment, a rebuttal. But they all had the same fear. The fear that maybe he was right: maybe this wasn't random.

Thom ripped out the notebook page, crumpled it up, and tossed it into the fire. It was a much-exaggerated move and got some giggles out of the room.

"But the weather, they can't control the weather, right?" Amy kept the talk alive.

"Many say they can," JP responded. "The theorists talk about a project called HAARP that started in Alaska but has locations now all over the world. It is a huge array of electrical towers that shoot waves into the sky; they bounce off the atmosphere and maybe cause earthquakes, or intensify a storm. It can't create a storm, but it can take an existing storm and change it. Some even say that Katrina and Sandy both were made more intense using HAARP."

"That's just conspiracy theory stuff," Amy shot back.

"HAARP exists, I've seen several videos of it, and the government has no reasonable explanation for creating all these facilities. Is this a product of HAARP? Who knows? But it's amazing how the standard answer for anything relating to the government is that it's a conspiracy theory. And with that statement alone, it's pushed to the side and given no credibility. If it's a conspiracy theory, it's in the same category as UFOs, not even worth investigating. Anything labeled a

174

conspiracy theory is pigeonholed and cast aside. I think the mass media has gone a long way to push that attitude on the public. My answer is that we have a right to know what our billions of tax dollars are being spent on, like HAARP, but they won't let people in on the secret."

"So let me put this together," Thom said to JP, "So our own government, or a shadow division of our government, sees this storm coming and zaps it with the HAARP to turn it into a blizzard. Then they send a computer virus to the power station so that it self-destructs. Then they plant whatever evidence is needed to point to one of our enemies. Then they sit back and watch. Is that what we are talking about here?"

"That is a really good synopsis, Thom," JP said while refilling his wine. "Only I don't think they are just sitting back. I think there are more moves to the game yet to be played." Looking over at David, he smiled and continued his thought. "I think we have just lost our queen and we have a rook breathing down our neck, but the game is far from over."

"You had to bring it in again, didn't you? Just had to rub it in one more time. So you are saying that we are going to lose? There's no way to win?"

"Survival is winning. How many survive is up in the air, but I think the body count is going to get a lot higher."

"It's already pretty high, JP. I was on that freeway, and I saw it. Just imagine how many miles of freeway there is in this state alone, and add Pennsylvania and New York," Thom argued. "Haven't we been hit with enough?"

"I think so, but have *they* thought so? I just see more. We are on the ropes, and we will be kept there. Mark my words."

"So what do we have to look forward to? What do you think is next?" Amy asked, trying hard to hold back her skepticism.

"I don't know, I really don't. I think illness will be the next logical progression. Maybe even an epidemic of some sort. With limited travel, and the medical system crippled, we would be a prime target."

The room got quiet on that statement. He was right. Planned or not, an illness that was easily passed along would be devastating. Thom looked around the room at all the eyes, and finally stopped on the newest couple to the clan, Joel and Sara. They had been quiet the entire time, unmoving. Thom forgot they were even in the room. Their eyes were wide as saucers.

"I'm so sorry guys; you were probably not expecting such a conversation from us," he said.

"No, it's fine," Joel said. "The farmer had mentioned HAARP too, but he went off the deep end after that. He talked about a minute-man militia of civilians banding together to create a new government and fight the next civil war. Yeah, a civil war that is primitive like Gettysburg, but with guerilla warfare."

Thom ripped out another page of the notebook and threw it in the fire. "I think we are done with this 'feel-good' discussion." A chorus of uncomfortable giggles went around.

They listened to the radio of the countdown to midnight from whoever that guy from American Idol was. They played some music, and it was entertaining. It was broadcast from Houston; the best short-notice location they could work out since Manhattan was out of the question. The state of Texas has its own power grid, and they were having the most consistent power stream in the country. They stopped every so often to talk about the people caught in the outage and wish them well. They would say best wishes, Godspeed, and such. There was only one point in the broadcast that an actual prayer was said, and it had to be completely unscripted. It came from the most unlikely person, and they were probably ready to pull the plug on Kanye West, even though he was so popular. But before his performance, he asked everyone to bow their heads and pray for those struggling to survive in the Christmas Blizzard and pray for their power to be restored soon.

176

The group around the wood stove prayed with him and applauded his strength for doing it. They clapped more for the prayer than the song, that was certain. The only occurrence of a prayer was not lost on the group, and the double whammy of using the title of Christmas Blizzard added to the surprise. Some news affiliates used that title early in the storm, but they suddenly stopped. It was never publicly explained why the term wasn't spoken anymore.

The ball finally dropped, and they had an excuse to go to bed. The conversations of the evening had not painted a rosy picture of the near future. And a few were afraid of having some nasty nightmares about truly possible demons. Thom's only salvation was that Father Michael was visiting in the morning.

Chapter 12: The railroad gets wheels.

Someone got it in their head that it was bath day for all the kids. The fact that water and natural gas were still flowing into the house ten days into the emergency created amazement and urgency. It couldn't last much longer. Little Gloria enjoyed her bath, and all the women of the house tried to squeeze into the bathroom to watch and help. Thom needed to get away from all the commotion and commandeered Erich to help him stage some firewood for Father Michael to take home with him.

"So, you were a prepper, huh?" Erich flippantly said to pass the time.

"Yeah, but that was a while ago."

"What were you prepping for? On that prepper TV show, they prepped for a certain situation to happen."

"That's kind of true, but most try to cast a wide net in case their scenario doesn't happen. I was concerned about an EMP happening mostly."

"A what?"

"Electromagnetic Pulse." Thom said while staking the firewood. "It's caused by detonating a nuclear weapon in the upper atmosphere — even a small one. That explosion would cause an electrical pulse that would short out every electrical machine for thousands of miles. Every automobile with an electrical starter would not run, and anything running on electricity would be useless."

Erich started to laugh but was stopped by Thom's focused look. "This is science fiction stuff, right? I thought this kind of thing was made up for movies."

"No, it's the real deal and our government has tested the effects of it since the sixties. One explosion could have whipped out the same amount of acreage as this blackout we are dealing with, only the effects would have been a hundred times worse. Nothing would run, no cars, no radios, maybe not flashlights, who knows. We would have all been dead in the water right where we were when the bomb detonated."

"I would have had to walk home from school that first day. Dad would have had a cow trying to find us."

"Now you are getting the picture," Thom pointed at Erich with the statement. "And that would only be the beginning because every electrical transfer box on every pole would have to be repaired to get power flowing again someday. We are hopeful that the transistors in that transfer box over there will handle the load when the power is turned on again. There is a reasonable chance that this system of ours can be restored without replacing everything. But with an EMP explosion, it's pretty much expected that we would be replacing all the components. We would be turned back to plowing our fields with animals."

Erich continued loading the wood, letting the words sink in. "This is the scenario you were preparing for?"

"Yeah. All my radios and electrical equipment were stored in old microwave ovens in the garage. Their structure is designed to keep the microwaves contained inside and would also create a shield to keep the damage of an EMP outside … supposedly. But who knows for sure. There's a lot of misinformation out there on the internet."

"But this was the thing you were prepping for, and thinking about twenty-four seven? No wonder you had to go on drugs to cope."

Thom unconsciously stepped back in response to the statement and Erich sheepishly looked at the ground for his overstep. He wasn't supposed to know, his dad made him promise not to tell anyone. The word 'anyone' certainly included Thom himself. Luckily for Erich, Father Michael broke up the uncomfortable moment.

The black Suburban pulled in while they stood there looking at each other. Father Michael stepped out with one of the families Thom had met at his home. There wasn't room for Cynthia to make it this time, which disappointed Thom greatly. His family wanted to meet her, after the harrowing story was told around the wood stove.

Thom greeted Father Michael with a warm man-hug, and he pulled Erich in for a hug as well. Erich was noticeably surprised by his actions, thinking he would be standoffish and proper, not to mention his young age. There was a magnetic pull between them from the beginning, and Thom was glad to see it. He walked Father and the family to the door and introduced them to everyone. After the greetings were done, Thom hit Father with the question he loved asking people when there was still hot water in the house.

"You are kidding me!" Father Michael exclaimed. "Saints be praised! Clear me a path, I'd hate to knock somebody over in my rush to the shower!"

"I thought I'd tell you as soon as you got here, so you could get comfortable before we get into our day. Toni will show you in while we load up your firewood into the Suburban." He also directed the family accompanying him that they were welcome to become human again in the other shower.

The house finally settled in about an hour and a half later, and everyone in the house had a smile on his or her face that couldn't have been removed with a jackhammer. It's amazing how in the past, people took something as simple as a shower for granted.

"Thom," Father Michael began, "the Johnstons here are traveling to Pataskala. They want to check on some relatives that are not in good health."

"Okay," Thom responded, gathering the group's attention with a map on the kitchen table. "There's a barn along this county road with several motor homes inside being used as a place of refuge. My friend Jonathan is there. I will write his full name on your map here and mine as well. You can use them as a pass code of sorts to show you are on the level. Hopefully between the six or seven families in that barn they will know of another stopping point in your journey. You

180

should only need four or five days of walking to make your destination."

"You are welcome to stay the night here," Toni jumped in, "and get a fresh start in the morning."

After the invitation was accepted, Father Michael broke out a map of eight safe houses volunteered by his parishioners. "Here's my map," he said. "It looks really good that your homes, Thom, are mainly to the south and east, while mine are north and to the east. We have the area of concern pretty much covered. Going directly south, or to the southwest, would take a person into the heart of Columbus. Believe me; you don't want to go there unless you have a 100 percent positive destination. I have been to the hospital twice and it's not a place you want to go unless you must. So I would imagine anyone wanting to travel will be going in a direction that we have covered for the first night or two."

"Let's get someone who can write better than me to trace some copies of this map with the important roads defined," JP brought the good idea to the table. "If we have some luck, a duplicate copy of the map may find its way back here with some additional safe houses written in. We might create ourselves a Refugee Railroad if we are not careful."

"That would be pretty cool, JP, I like that name," Father Michael congratulated him. The title had been kicked around the Vesper house a little, but this was the first time he had heard it. "Communication is the key with this situation, and the maps solve some issues, but we need more. The roads are not being cleared, and travel is going to become more limited than it already is."

"I have to imagine that road crews are just not showing up to work," JP jumped in, "they have families too, you know. And if they did, the truck depots have limited fuel supplies for them to work with, and abandoned cars littering the roads. How about snowmobiles or quad runners?"

"I could ask the parishioners. It would be a good tool if they can get the fuel."

"I have a five-gallon can," Thom volunteered. "Once the freezer is emptied, my generator isn't as necessary. The fuel could be better used elsewhere. Cross country skis could also be useful, but not very practical."

Carl looked at each of the faces around the table and said, "how about Daimon Hellstrom?"

"Who in Saint Peter is that?" Father Michael was a little freaked by the name.

"A ham radio operator that likes to hang out around the 94 frequency on the FM dial," Carl continued. "He's a bit of a conspiracy leaner with a flair, you could guess that by his name. But he has a way of putting out helpful advice to the stranded motorists, and he gives his own spin on the news announcements. How right he is, is anybody's guess."

"So we have a ham radio guy in the neighborhood," Father Michael calmed a bit. "He could be useful if we find him, but I'm not sure how useful just yet. If he were to announce our safe houses on the air, it could help a lot of people, but might overload them also."

"It could send a bad element of people to those locations too," Thom added. "Giving the address of locations with supplies could be too tempting for folks who are only looking out for themselves."

"It's still the best use of 20th-century technology we have right now," Father Michael was still looking for the positive side of this news. "I will ask my contacts to the north if they know any ham radio operators, especially any with a handle as odd as that."

It was at this time that Toni put her makeshift guest book in front of the new travelers, right beside the map to the motor home barn. "This is the guest book of all the travelers so far through our household," she announced. "I want your contact information here next to your names. Maybe someday after the lights come on, we will have a reunion and bring together all our new family members."

Thom looked at his wife and saw the woman full of the positive spirit that he fell in love with twenty years ago. Her naive plan to have a picnic someday brought a feeling of normalcy to a moment in time that was far from normal. It shielded everyone from the danger and uncertainty that hung over them like the snow clouds outside. The clouds of doom and gloom that never left, ever present in Thom's mind. He continued to smile as he watched her put the guest book away on a shelf for safekeeping. *Plan your reunion, honey; more power to you,* he thought.

After plans for the railroad were completed, it was time for mass. Brad and Lisa were also Catholic, so they were able to participate in the Eucharist, along with the Vesper family. This is the ceremony in which the priest converts the bread and wine into the flesh and blood of Christ to be ingested. Only Catholics are permitted to participate, and it was one of the true joys of Thom's life upon conversion to be included in this ceremony. Blessed are those who are called to the supper, as Father said.

Christopher Columbus held mass and had communion as soon as he landed on the New World. Buzz Aldrin carried the blessed sacrament of communion to the moon for the first landing. He held a small ceremony on the lander before stepping out and walking on the moon. The very first food eaten on the moon, the first liquid drank there, were communion elements. It was something that was not publicized, and just got lost in our politically correct world. It might offend someone.

After the communion was ended, he handed around sheets of paper with the words to *Amazing Grace*, which everyone sang around the stove. Father Michael gave special attention to David with his communion and spoke to him afterward for a few minutes. The events lately had been quite difficult for David to grasp. Thom and Toni were glad that Father was available for him to reach out to.

183

Toni also discussed with Father the idea of baptizing Gloria, the new addition. The mother was gone, and the Vespers were the closest thing to family that the child had. But baptism and naming of godparents hadn't been determined. It was a rushed idea without much forethought, and he asked them to pray on it for a while. It was a happy thought, nonetheless. The child had begun to grow on Thom he had to admit.

When things began to settle down, Joel and Sara pulled Father away to talk privately. There was no question what they were talking about, and it would be the first conversation of many in their recovery. If anyone could ease their pain though, he was their man.

The time soon came for Father Michael to travel back home. The snow had accumulated a couple of inches during his stay, and it was certainly time to go. A prayer was spoken around the wood stove before he left, and he made a statement about hating long goodbyes. He left quickly, in the swirling snow, looking back only once to wave.

Everyone recounted his visit around the wood stove later that night and marveled at the Father's amiability. For the non-Catholics in the room, it was the first priest they had spoken with. He certainly was not the priest they were expecting.

"You know, Carl," Thom said. "Profiling is not a good thing to do."

****

The sails cracked in the wind as the catamaran came about the island. Large Ospreys were spooked by their approach and flapped their four-foot wingspan desperately taking flight. Thom released the lazy jack lines and turned the sails to give them a forty-degree change of direction. He looked back at Randal to see his nodding approval of Thom's captainship. His left leg came up to point a toe at one of the slipknots coming loose on the tie down. He then relaxed back and took another sip from his tea.

"All of the time around New Year's down here was another chance for people to pull their crazy shit," Randal lazily commented. "There were some break-ins and fires, but not to the point of riots. I just pushed off and got out to sea where it was safe. I wish I had packed more food, but the fishing pole did provide."

"I'll bet it did. That's one of the great things about being out here. Food can be found, with some work of course. Being on the water to escape their craziness must have been comforting. But I must say that Father's visit gave me peace. It gave so much comfort to know he would be part of the team."

"So the Father got things going and got more travelers through your house?"

"It didn't happen right away. We sent his family on to the barn, and Brad, Lisa, and Little Brad moved to another house in the village. But we didn't have as many refugees until almost a week later. That's when Ohio started to feel like it had a bulls-eye painted on it. We couldn't catch a break. I don't want to think about that right now, though. Let me just take in this sun, and my full sails being pushed across the sea by God's hand…"

Chapter 13: Glowing Mudhens

"No water," Toni said quietly.

She put her hand on Thom's shoulder as he sat at the post in the front of the house. The clouds outside the window were so thick with snow and ice that the sun was barely noticeable. The natural gas was lost soon after Father left, so sponge baths were the only route for cleanliness anyway. It was just the finality of it all. All of the resources were lost now — they were completely adrift.

Thom looked over at the wood stove and saw the saucepan simmering. Baked beans for breakfast. The differences in meals because of the time of day had disappeared. They had what they had. The meal was for nutrition, not for flavor. The only exception was when Carl got in a cooking mood and took over. He hadn't been in the mood lately though; the gloom was settling in for everyone in the household. Thom took Toni to his chest and looked out the window. The snow was piled high, and more was coming down. The roads were impassable, and now there was no water. He closed his eyes and rocked back and forth with her in the chair. It was all he could do.

David brought the radio into the room and announced it was all cranked and ready to go. Maybe there would be some good news, something positive, Thom thought. Good news would turn things around and make it a sunny day, even if the sun wasn't cooperating. But it wasn't happening that day. Nothing good was going to happen that day, and no one was ready for what that radio had to say.

"We have just received a report from Oak Harbor, near Toledo, and we are still gathering information on it. Please excuse the holes in our report, but we will share the tidbits of information we have received so far. An attack has been made on the Davis-Besse Nuclear Power Station up by Lake Erie. It seems that a band of local minutemen militia have hijacked a semi tanker that was refilling the diesel generator tanks at the power plant. Three employees of the plant were shot and killed in the hijacking, and the refilling equipment was

186

damaged. Even if another tanker is brought in, refilling the underground tanks would be impossible because of the damage."

"The generators were performing the duties of cooling down the uranium stacks in a controlled manner after the power went out. The power-down process takes a total of forty days and was only half completed. With the loss of the generators, the uranium rods are now out of control, and a meltdown is imminent. Residents within a seventy-mile radius of the Toledo Metro area should make preparations to move out of the vicinity. The purpose of the attack has not been determined, but it has been reported that two large jewelry depositories have been attacked while authorities were focused on the power plant. The president has condemned the actions of the local militia group and has vowed to bring all the power of Homeland Security and the National Guard on these cowards as they attempt to take the lives of helpless Americans in this time of dire need. All local militias will be considered hostile until peace and security is restored to the area."

Thom sat back quietly and looked at Toni. Her forehead was wrinkling up in anger. "Why can't this just stop? Can't they let go of us, and just be done? When will they be done?"

He pulled her close as she pounded her fists into his back. "They are far from done with us, honey. Not by a long shot."

"What do you think it means?" JP pulled up a chair to say. "Reading between the lines, like we try to do, what do you think it means?"

"Do you think the government did this too?" Thom said in a surprised tone.

Reading his body language, JP knew he needed to tread lightly. At least at first. "That's one option. Having a big deal like this would justify all their actions against militia groups in general. What else do you think? Could it really be a militia group?" JP was playing professor, but Thom kind of liked it.

"You mean to steal the diamonds? I guess so. Maybe to fund their militia, or because they are greedy bastards," he responded.

"Something else you may not know is that there is an old military camp in Perrysburg, a Toledo suburb, called Ft. Meigs that is rumored to have been converted to a FEMA camp. It was also rumored to be the location that northern Ohio residents would be herded to in an emergency."

"An emergency like now," Thom completed his statement.

"Exactly. Maybe the group wanted to make sure the camp couldn't be used by FEMA. Maybe the diamond heist is not even true, even though we love hearing those stories, and secretly hope it is."

"So, they stopped the generators to mess up FEMA's plans, and now Homeland Security is pissed. I don't know man, that's reaching a little."

"Could be, but the bottom line is that the radio's story isn't the whole truth. It can't be. There is something more going on here, and I'm not getting it."

Carl came into range and sat down to hear the report repeated on the radio. He sat in amazement and had no interest in the theories. "What does this mean to us? That's what I want to know. What does this mean for us, right here, right now, sitting in this house?"

He looked around at the group, waiting for answers, but they had none.

"They said seventy miles; we have to be over 100, as the crow flies even. We're safe," Thom said.

"Are we? There will be no cloud that comes this way, and drops some acid rain on us? Maybe contaminates our firewood so that when we burn it, we get asphyxiated? What does this mean to us?" Carl was getting flamboyant with this devil's advocate approach, waving his arms and pacing a bit. "Whoever really did this had their agenda, and

188

we can't do anything about that. My agenda is to keep my little girls alive."

"Thanks, Dad," Erich said to being left out.

"You can take care of yourself," Carl flippantly said, turning to the group for an answer.

They sat in silence. JP had no answers, and they had just proved to themselves that the radio was not telling the whole truth. That statement of seventy miles may have been a lie as well.

"We have no internet, no way to research and find out the truth. We have no way of verifying that seventy miles is the line of safety," Thom spoke out.

"But they couldn't put it out on the airwaves in that report if it weren't true," JP rationalized. "Others in the southern states have the internet; they would debunk it right away. They would have to fix the story. Right?"

"Maybe so, but maybe after it was too late," Thom said. "We haven't proven anything with this kangaroo court."

"Alright guys, hold on. What did people do before the internet?" Toni was wagging her finger around the whole room. She was coming to the rescue, and Thom knew that finger was going to finish with pointing at him. "Remember that garage sale purchase I made ten years ago, that you said was so stupid? That you had to lug around in the basement, and hated?"

"Those damn Encyclopedia Britannicas. I threw my back out on those things."

"Best two dollars I ever spent. It will be the first time we ever cracked them," she said in a congratulatory tone.

"But what do you look up in a thirty-year-old encyclopedia about the range of a nuclear meltdown?" Carl was almost there but not quite.

189

As Thom got up from the chair and headed to the basement stairs, he called back: "Three Mile Island!"

They had some fun with the research, looking up different references such as "nuclear meltdown" and cross-referencing the results. In the end, though, they came to the conclusion that the news report was partially right with the seventy-mile number. The report didn't consider wind, though. When wind was considered, which blows east usually, Cleveland, Akron, Youngstown, and maybe even Pittsburgh had reason to fear, even though they were more than seventy miles away. The jet stream would move everything in their direction, and Columbus, directly to the south, should be safe. A change in wind direction could spell disaster for all of them though. It was rare for wind direction to travel north to south in this region, but it did happen. If fallout did blow towards the southern direction, staying indoors was the best solution. It was also found that lightly contaminated individuals would lose much of their radiation simply by removing their clothing.

They came up with a plan that if they did have a Toledo-ite arrive at their door: they would be forced to come in the house naked, leaving their outerwear in the yard. Would that help? They really didn't know. The book said it might. Thom did not pack a Geiger counter in his emergency supplies crates; that part he knew for sure.

One point became crystal clear from all this research — there would certainly be an influx of northerners leaving their homes and heading south. Many would travel west. That would be the smartest move, but those trying to escape by traveling east would unknowingly have danger following them. It was also noted that the lake effect snow probably gave them twice the accumulation that was currently in the Columbus area. Travel by vehicle would be impossible, especially if they were without road crews. They would be traveling by foot, so how soon they would be seen was anyone's guess, but it wouldn't be tomorrow.

Thom closed his encyclopedia and put it back in the wooden crate. Carl noticed the finality of the research and took the situation into his own hands. He put his book down as well and held out his hands to his neighbors.

"All we can do is pray," he said.

And Carl was right. There was nothing they could physically do for these people in danger. They gave it to God.

The radio continued to report on the problems of Toledo, but the focus of the report did change over the hours. Condemning the local militia group became the meat of the report as the day continued. Militia group names and even some leader's names started coming through on the reports. They reported about other small attacks that had happened in recent days in upstate New York and Pennsylvania, adding to the fervor.

"It's time to hear Daimon's spin," JP called out as he switched the radio dial. There were no objections, but Carl winced at the idea of what he might hear.

"It's now open season on any organized and weaponized group of people in the government's eyes. You all know that, friends, right? The government has shown some weakness in this attack, so some confidence has been given to the looters and pillagers out there. The government will need to give a showing of strength soon, in an attempt to get things back under control. When that will happen is anyone's guess, but it's my thought that the chaos lovers out there are going to have a nothing-to-lose mentality until it does."

This rhetoric was going nowhere, and JP began to reach for the radio dial until Mr. Hellstrom changed direction.

"But let's take a deeper look at what happened near Toledo today. My group of ham radio operators out there have given their ideas and information to me, and two or three scenarios seem to rise to the surface in all of it. The idea that the attackers wanted to stop Ft. Meigs from being an internment camp has a nice sound to it. It works on many levels, especially since there must be a hidden agenda to this attack, and that's a positive one in my mind."

JP was pointing around the room at Daimon's statement, giving himself an *I told you so* pat on the back. But Daimon was not done.

"But more information has come across my desk — information of another agenda. The rumor is that the Davis Besse computer system was the entry point of our cyber attackers. They entered the network at this plant through the internet, and wiggled and wormed their way through the entire northeastern grid and brought it all down from there. An interesting twist happens with that tidbit of information. The on-site investigation of who did this and how they did it will be closing up shop very soon as they evacuate the plant. And the fingerprints of what happened will be erased by nuclear fallout, so all proof of how the attack occurred will be lost."

Aghast expressions circled the wood-burning stove. Everyone leaned forward in their seats, listening for more.

"Well, friends, this is a lot to digest, but there it is. And it makes us question: who really were the militants that attacked this nuclear power plant near Toledo? Were they civilians with a grudge, or the original attackers still working on their agenda? Was this plant a loose end that needed cleaned up, much like Building 7 with the World Trade Center? It's a scary thought, friends, that the attackers might still be operating here, or who the attackers might actually be. Could this be an inside job? And then if you follow that line of thought further, blaming the attack on civilian militia might be the second bird they are hitting with the same stone. Now, as I said, it is open season for any organized civilian militia. Something that seems to be undesirable to our government and the media. Friends, my concern is growing, but I don't have an answer for you yet. Stay safe out there."

Everyone sat dazed around the wood-burning stove, not sure what to say or do. Thom pointed at Erich and reminded him of his earlier dramatic statements: "The locusts are coming."

Chapter 14: Boring Insects

A few days later, it's day twenty. Thom is pulling the night guard watch at the front window, and he's taking note how difficult the job is. The cloud cover blocks out the moonlight and details are difficult to see. It was almost totally black. For the prep kit, Thom had a chance to buy some night vision binoculars but didn't want to spend the cash. He regretted that now. The comfort level of night vision would have made such a difference.

It was about 3 a.m. when David wandered into the room. No one else was awake, except Erich out in the three-season room post. Chloe had kept him company for a couple hours, but she had already gone to bed. JP's wife, Lisa, decided to keep Thom company at the front post.

"Hi, Dad," he simply said, walking in slowly. He stopped at the stove and warmed his hands. Thom stepped over to him and put a small throw blanket around his shoulders over his bathrobe.

"You OK, buddy?" Thom said, rubbing his arms to warm them up.

"I'm good," he said, and without much expression, he walked into the kitchen.

Thom could see his back, as he stood in the entranceway, unmoving. He stood there for what seemed like a long time, looking into the kitchen. Between looks outside, Thom sneaked looks in his direction, and he still hadn't moved. Thom had sleepwalked a few times when he was a kid and was beginning to think this was happening with David. He motioned for Lisa to cover the window and whispered that David might be sleepwalking. Concerned about his safety, Thom knew David needed to get back to bed.

Thom crept up behind him and heard him saying words to something in the kitchen. Thom got around the weight-bearing wall enough to look into the dark room, seeing nothing out of the ordinary. It sounded like he said, "Okay, I'll try," as he looked towards the top of the refrigerator. Thom knelt down behind his shoulder and looked in the same direction he was. His forehead wrinkled as he looked at the fridge. Just a fridge is all he saw.

David then bowed his head and clasped his hands in front of him. He stood immobile like that for another minute or two, as Thom looked around the room. Nothing. Everything was the way he left it at bedtime. Looking back at David, he began to waver. Thom's hands came up just as David's knees gave out. He fell back into his father's arms and looked directly into his eyes as he fell. Before his head hit Thom's arm, he began to speak excitedly.

"Did you see her? Wasn't she beautiful? Did you see?" He spoke so fast, and so clearly, Thom was put aback by those facts alone. He had so much trouble speaking, and a tougher time pulling his thoughts into words; Thom was completely at a loss.

"No, son. What did she look like?"

"She was the most beautiful lady I've ever seen." He paused for a second then added, "Besides Mom."

Thom caught himself and smiled. Of course, he would say that, even when his mother was not around. "What did she say?"

He stopped to think, he was concentrating on his words. "She said to think of her when I'm confused. She said 'Think of me, and I'll help.'"

He smiled wide, and a tear ran down his cheek during the smile. One ran down Thom's face at the sight of it.

"Did she say anything else?"

"It was weird. She looked up kind of, at another light coming down. Did you see the other light? It was over there," he interrupted himself, pointing at the cupboards.

"No, son, I didn't."

"She looked up to the light, and she said, 'This is the one I was telling you about.' Do you know what that means?"

194

"No, David, I don't. But it sounds very special. A very special message just for you."

Thom awoke at sunrise curled around his son on the couch by the stove. He wasn't sure what happened after his conversation with David in the kitchen. He drew a complete blank. He thought it might have all been a dream until David repeated the story to Toni. He had the same excitement, but the words were not coming out as easily this time. Thom reminded him to use what she taught him, and after closing his eyes to concentrate, like snapping one's fingers, he was gathered. The story came out smoothly and became its own proof as he said it.

When Toni began to cry, David thought that something was wrong and became gravely concerned. He didn't buy Thom's statements that she was fine until she pulled herself together enough to smile through the tears. She beamed and it couldn't be denied. She asked him what he'd like for breakfast and wanted to make something special for him. When he requested eggs, she was so disappointed. The eggs had been gone for quite some time, with no way to get more. They compromised on the last of the venison sausage in the freezer.

Thom sat back on the couch, drank some nasty coffee and just watched the two of them interact. It was almost like a normal, happy morning for those few moments.

There had been several new travelers through the house that week — nothing exciting, mainly tired, cold, and hungry people. Two new couples were in the house, and everyone started milling around the living room. The wood stove doubled as the cooking surface now, and it became quite crowded around it most times. The freezer was being shut down today with the last portions going on the stove. Canned chicken, tuna, and beef were still being held on reserve; the protein needed to be rationed for the long term.

Thom took his coffee and an extra cup into the three-season room to Carl at his post. He thanked Thom for the coffee and talked about the latest news reports. It seems that Iran had become pinpointed as the

195

target of aggression from the attack. There was also talk warming up about the inauguration of the newly elected president. The current president was handing over the reins in two days.

"You know something, Carl, I feel like we are living in one of those glass snow globes." He met Thom's statement with a smile, waiting for the reason why. "Every now and then our world gets shook up, and just when all the little plastic snowflakes settled on the bottom, and we think we are fine, our world gets shook up again."

"Somebody needs to smack the kid's hand that's doing the shaking. That's what I think. He might even need a whoopin' by now even!" he replied with a laugh.

Just then, Toni sounded the alarm. "Refugees!"

JP joined her at the window looking south, towards the square. "There're three of them. Did you see that? Did you see that Toni? He made an arm motion to someone we can't see!"

"I saw it. There was only three when I spotted them. They must have split before I could see," she said.

"Okay guys," Thom called out loudly, entering the front room. "We need to consider these guys as hostile from the start. Carl, you are up front. JP is rear corner with the 30/30, and Erich you are with me at the point. Kids to the basement, and Toni, cover the back family room window. This is not a drill."

"You've always wanted to say that haven't you," Carl said to Thom, trying to lighten the moment.

"I have," he said with a smile.

The two new family men stepped forward, wanting to help. They did not want to be herded to the basement with the women and children. There were still some weapons left, so one was posted with Carl up front and one with Toni in the back.

196

The walkers came up the steps, two women and one man. This led Thom to believe there was at least one more man trying to come up from behind, making two couples. Placing JP at the backyard cover position with the 30/30 was not an accident. He had practiced with it down at the river a couple times, and he was a crack shot. JP had high ground to the backyard, and Thom had confidence it was all the advantage he would need.

The walkers faced the front door, the women in front with the man in back. They didn't even look towards the sunroom, assuming the focus was the front door. The man blatantly had his gun out in his left hand down at his leg, thinking it couldn't be seen behind the women. And what a monster gun it was. It had to be a .44 magnum, a Dirty Harry gun. It looked like a hand-cannon, hanging down past his knee.

"Drop your weapon," Thom called out from behind the wooden slats covering the sliding door.

The man was visibly startled, not expecting a voice from that direction. His immediate reaction was to begin raising his cannon at Thom.

"Keep that gun down, or I'll drop you where you stand. Drop it now!" Thom was getting loud and forceful, but all it accomplished was the gun going back to his side.

"I'm not giving this gun to you; I paid too much for it," was his only response, and they just continued to stand there. They were stalling, waiting for their flanker to get in position. The moment was getting very intense, and it was going according to their plan so far. Something needed to change.

"Move along then. Get off my porch, right now! You've got five seconds!"

"Five!"

They stubbornly didn't move.

"Four!"

They looked at each other trying to read expressions.

"Three!"

One woman made a step towards the street, and the man snuck a peek to the corner of the back yard. Thom caught a glimmer of recognition as he turned away.

"Eyes peeled JP! Okay two!" Thom said without daring to look anywhere but at his targets. The man turned with the women and began to take one step towards the street. That's when that damn cannon came up and leveled right at Thom!

Thom got off one shot that caught him in the stomach, he was certain. The other one missed, but may have hit one of the women. They were pulling out weapons as well, as Carl let some fly right through the beautiful glass French front doors. That scene was about all Thom saw, because when that cannon went off, his world soon went black. The magnum bullet hit the double two-by-eight plank and knocked it right off its mounting bracket. Maybe it hadn't been hung back correctly, or maybe the gun was that powerful, but it didn't matter. The plank came crashing down on Thom's right shoulder as he crouched behind it. The weight of it spread him out across the tile floor, banging his head soundly as he went down.

The man then turned his attention to Erich at the corner of the glass room. Erich was shooting, but nothing was bringing this animal down. Erich was a horrible shot, but the guy was only twenty feet away! All it took was one shot in Erich's direction to swat the nuisance. The cannon shot sent glass and firewood splinters and chunks enough to put Erich out of commission, whether the bullet hit him or not.

Thom woke from his blackout to see the guy stepping up to the doorway with his weapon moving up to target him. Thom's gun was close to his right hand, but he could not move his right arm. It was not responding to his brain's impulses. His left arm obeyed commands however, and he tried to move it across his body to the gun. He knew it would take too long though; he would never make it. The hand-

198

cannon was leveled on him now, and this animal, this terminator who had survived at least one hit from Thom, was going to take him out. He grinned a nasty smile that hadn't seen a toothbrush in over a month and two loud shots rang out.

The shots came from over Thom's left shoulder and were the familiar sound of Toni's .38 Ruger 5-shot revolver. The slugs caught him square in the chest, and he took one step back before falling to the porch. Thom quickly sat up, grabbed the Glock with his left hand, and looked back at Toni. The astonished look on her face said it all. He wanted to say something, considering that his life was almost snatched from his body, but nothing came out. Of all the cool lines in the movies, he had nothing. He simply turned his attention back to the porch outside.

One of the women was still running away in the yard across the street, and in the adrenalin of the moment, Thom simply raised his weapon and shot. A shot was heard from the front of the house at about the same time, and the woman fell. Whose bullet brought her down, neither knew, and they didn't want to know. Thom related it to firing squads always having one blank bullet, so the shooters never know if they actually killed the person or not. There's always a doubt, and that's enough to let them sleep at night.

Thom was contemplating that thought when he saw the Terminator's hand move. Then it moved again. His head started to turn and rise. That's when it occurred to him, a vest. *He's wearing a vest! That's why he didn't fall!*

Thom stood, raising his weapon. He wanted to do one of those pretty forehead shots you see in the movies. But he was using his left — at least that was his excuse. He put it right in the bridge of his nose, making an ugly shot — a nasty splatter of red sprayed out behind his raised head onto the porch floor. It really wasn't that cool.

He looked over his left shoulder to Toni, still standing there with her revolver in both hands, lowered to the floor. The classic patrolman's stance and eyes that were surveying the yard outside. Her trance-like

199

stare gave the strong appearance that she was ready to fire again if called upon. Thom turned his attention towards JP at the back window, unaware of anything JP had been doing. He didn't even hear any shots from back there but looking straight out to the corner of the neighbor's yard, there was a body lying in the snow. "Got him," was all he had to say with a thumbs up.

"Erich!" Toni was out of her perimeter survey trance and was sprinting across the room. He was lying on the floor with debris scattered on and around him. His eyes were peacefully closed, and it didn't look good.

"I'll get Carl, and check the front," Thom called out, shuffling wearily to the front of the house, as she checked on Erich. Thom's injuries could wait, and he would just get in the way.

Thom lumbered into the front to see the wind blowing in the front doors. Glass and wood shards were all over. One of the women was lying in the street, a red splatter in stark contrast to the white snow. He stopped to take in that visual, not sure why it gripped him so tightly. He had seen pictures of much worse in movies and even on TV, but those were not in front of his house.

"Is everyone okay?" Thom asked, evaluating both men standing before him. They were standing, looking dazed but fine. They didn't answer.

"What's wrong with you?" Carl said, noticing Thom's sagging shoulder.

"I don't know. I landed on it. I can't move my arm," he said as Carl came close to check it out.

"Your shoulder is dislocated. It used to happen to me all the time in Rugby," he said while feeling under Thom's two flannel shirts. "Here, I can fix it right now, don't you worry."

"Wait!" Thom tried to say, but it was too late. Carl made a sudden jerking movement with his shoulder, and a piercing pain shot through

200

Thom's upper body. "Oh shit!" he screamed out, not even aware he said it.

"You feel better?" Carl said as helped Thom sit down on the bunker wall.

"No, I don't. That really hurt, man!" he said while flexing his right fist. Movement was coming back, for the price paid. "Oh, hey, sorry Carl, my head is swimming. But Erich is hurt back there, Toni is working on him."

"What is it, Thom?" he said, as he began moving in that direction.

"I don't know... I just got out of her way... to let her work. Sorry, I didn't say something sooner." But he was already around the corner. Thom's words turned into mumbles, and he began to feel light-headed. He turned to Steve, the new refugee in the house, and tried to say something, but then fell off the bunker wall. Luckily, he was there to catch Thom, and he was moved over to the couch. Thom awoke with a cold compress on his forehead, his wife's smiling face in front of him, and David sitting on the floor watching intently.

"How long have I been out?" Thom wearily said, annoyed by the thought of more things going wrong with his body once again.

"Less than an hour, are you feeling better?" Toni tried to console him.

"I'm not sure," he said while slowly trying to move his right arm. "How's Erich?"

"He has a concussion, and he has several fragments of glass and wood splinters in his chest. No bullet wounds though. He managed to walk to a bed in the living room by the fireplace. A couple of his impalements are large and deep though."

"Will you be able to get them out? Infection will be the enemy here," Thom said thoughtfully. "There's no way we can get him to a hospital with this snow."

201

"I can get some of them out, but we really need a trained hand and some antibiotics. I think he needs to see your new doctor friend at Tall Timbers," she said.

"Dr. Cliff. I'll go with your opinion, but I doubt he'll have any antibiotics at his home. Check my prep-box in the sunroom. On the advice of a friend, I bought some pet-store antibiotics."

"Animal antibiotics?" her tone started to get loud.

"No, not really. Supposedly the same antibiotics used by humans are also used to disinfect a fish tank. I got two types, one with penicillin, and one without. He will probably need something stronger, but it's all I could get without a prescription," Thom said while sitting up on the couch.

She came back into the room with a couple of pill bottles, reading them incredulously. "Fish Flex? Is that right? And Fish Flox? You've got to be kidding me."

"Hey, one is Cipro, and the other is Keflex. It's the same stuff that you would get at a pharmacy. We could have asked one of your doctor friends for a script, but back when I was serious about this stuff, you were ready to put me in a psych ward." Thom had a good argument, but there was no way she would give him the win on this one.

"I can't believe I'm going to give Erich some aquarium pills. This is insane, that's for sure." Her tone was accusatory, and nothing would change about it, even if this worked.

"If he starts growing gills, let me know," Thom groaned while rubbing his shoulder.

Thom stood up and tried to take inventory of his faculties. His legs were holding his weight and his right arm hurt a lot but was okay. He looked at his watch and said: "We only have another hour of light left; it's too late to travel now. What's going on with the bodies?" He pointed to the woman still lying in the street.

202

"We pulled their weapons," Steve spoke up on this subject. "While you guys were being tended to, the rest of us covered the French doors and checked on them."

"We'll need to get those bodies out of here. Take them down to the cemetery or something. We can't leave them here," Thom said, and then another thought came to mind. "I call dibs on that bulletproof vest!"

JP spoke up in agreement to moving the bodies before dark. They may draw coyotes. So the men got to work getting dressed for the cold, and the ladies to preparing a meal for them when they returned.

Outside, as they searched the pockets for valuables, JP struck up some interesting topics of conversation.

"These people were not carrying anything, right? If they were looters, they should be dragging their loot," he said.

"Makes sense," Thom speculated. "Maybe they didn't want to be bothered with it during the attack and left it behind somewhere. They planned enough to split up before we could see them, maybe they were organized enough to stash their booty too?"

"You are starting to think like I do, and that scares me," JP replied.

As they mounted two of the bodies on trashcan lids fitted with rope pulls, Thom called Steve over. He was instructed to follow the looters tracks back about 200 yards at the most and see if they left any bundles behind. He went off on his mission while Carl and the other new refugee, Jim, mounted the other two bodies.

The bulletproof vest was a nice one, and still had Toni's slugs in the chest. Thom's first shot was in the stomach too, and there was one extra in the stomach, so Erich must have scored a hit. Thom pulled Toni's slugs and put them in his pocket. An odd trinket of love and devotion, but there it was, just the same.

JP and Thom had their sliders ready first and headed out towards the cemetery. The snow had accumulated to a daunting amount. It was past their knees now and higher in some snowdrifts, as they drudged down the street. At this point it became obvious that driving to Tall Timbers was not an option; foot power was it. While pulling, JP brought the next subject up.

"What if the police or the National Guard or whoever try to come in here and say that we murdered these people and jail us? There's no proof that we didn't. It's just our word."

"They couldn't do that to us," Thom replied. "What's their motivation?"

"Just to put us away — to have control. Some reason to bust us apart, maybe define us as a militia group." He dropped the new buzzword that meant nothing a week ago.

Thom prodded along in silence, pulling the dead body of the man who almost killed him. He stopped to catch his breath and noticed the grooves in the snow made by the man's dragging feet.

"Let's assume you are right. What can we do? We can't hide the bodies. They will certainly find them. I guess we could deny that it ever happened. Just say the bodies appeared at the cemetery, and cover each other's butts," Thom said, trying to step through the logic of the theory.

"But there is still proof that we did it. Physical proof."

"What are you talking about?"

"The bullets. They can be traced back to our weapons. The bullets are the proof that we did it," he explained, and the light bulb came on for Thom.

"You are saying that we need to dig the bullets out of these bodies? Is that what you are saying?" Thom asked incredulously.

"Yes. If we want to play it safe, and play by their rules, then that's what we must do," he replied confidently.

204

"No, that's what *you* must do. Count me out. My bullet went all the way through on this joker, I'm not digging anything. You know, a couple months ago I was working on my golf swing at the driving range, and now you got me digging bullets out of dead bodies. No thank you!"

JP replied with a chuckle, obviously entertained by the comments. He advised Thom to dig the bullet out of the porch floor or wherever it ended up. He also advised a house meeting to instruct everyone to keep this event to ourselves, at least until it was known if it could be used against them. It was realistic advice, and Thom was glad to have different points of view of this situation to consider, and not just his own.

They laid the bodies by the groundskeepers shed, and a thought came to Thom as he straightened the man's legs on the ground. He checked his boots, and found a sweet hunting knife. He had forgotten to check there. "Thanks, buddy," Thom said to him, tapping the blade on his leg.

"Shouldn't we say more? We are putting them to rest," JP said to Thom with a hint of sarcasm.

Thom made an expression of agreement and stepped over to where the bodies lay. He took off his hat and noticed that JP respectfully followed suit. Thom did not know these people, and they attempted to kill him and his family. What does a person say in that situation? But just as blank as his mind was, suddenly the most appropriate few words appeared to him out of the blue.

"Forgive them, Lord, for they know not what they do. May they rest in peace," he said in a solemn, heartfelt tone. He crossed his chest and turned to see the face of JP crushed by the words. The simple statement struck him and caught him off guard.

"If you tell anyone, I'll shoot you," he said as he brushed his eye.

Carl and Jim were entering the cemetery at about that time, and everyone helped to unload their freight. On the way back to the house,

205

Jim mentioned that the house was essentially unguarded while they were doing this work. The alarm was calmed though as JP pointed out that anyone would be completely stupid to attack our house now with all the proof of carnage around it. "Would you attack a house with red snow all over the place?" he asked.

"Oh yeah, let's attack here, they obviously are unarmed!" Jim said, bringing awkward laughter to the group.

At the house, Steve was standing there with four large pieces of luggage at his feet. "These things are heavy. I don't think its clothing."

They carried in the luggage, being oddly excited and a little concerned about what was inside. Thom let the guys go ahead of him on the porch and stopped where the Terminator fell. He checked the plastic porch flooring and found a slug embedded in it. Using his newly found knife he dug it out and put it in his pocket along with Toni's slugs.

The hungry crew returning from their work enjoyed the beef stew, but the odd silence was noticed by everyone in the house. The death, destruction, and uncertainty about Erich's condition created thoughts that went in every direction. Thom was learning to eat with his left hand and feeling a knot throbbing on the back of his head, then noticed Toni with a faraway look on her face. He took her hand and asked what was wrong.

"I just killed a man today. It finally hit me. I killed a man," she said to no one in particular, just staring.

"No, you didn't. You didn't kill him. He had a bulletproof vest on, so you didn't kill him. But you did stop him from killing me. That's what you did. You didn't take a life, you saved one."

She snuggled close, under his good arm. It was a good moment, an opportunity for them to put the antibiotics fury behind them, but it was eventually interrupted by the opening of the luggage Steve found.

206

The luggage was filled with cash and silver and other valuables. It was quite a haul, actually. In dollars, it had to be tens of thousands worth of other people's stuff. What to do with the loot was the real question. No one in the house stole it, but it *was* stolen. Getting it back to the rightful owner, even after the lights come on would be difficult. It would probably languish in a police stolen-property room forever. The issue was for another day; they put the luggage away in the basement.

The useful finds of the attackers were their weapons, a total of five, including the hand cannon. There was quite a bit of ammo and a couple more hunting knives as well. There were a few homes in the village that were woefully under-gunned, and these would be welcome additions. It was left to JP to divvy them out; Thom couldn't keep his eyes open anymore. He put some Ben Gay on the shoulder and took something for the headache. Toni caught him as he was getting into bed and said that Erich is starting to run a fever. The antibiotics still needed time to work their magic, but he needed to see the doctor soon.

"I'll take him. I know the way, and the doctor," Thom said wearily.

"But your arm," she argued.

"I've got another one, don't worry about it. Make me a sling. I'll be okay. Who else should go?"

"Carl. It's his son!" she said flatly.

"Sorry. I can't think. Wake me at dawn." And he was asleep before she left the room.

The next morning Thom bounced back incredibly. The coffee even tasted good. He looked out the window looking at the snow flurries, preparing himself for the day.

****

The sun came in across the palm trees as Thom brought the boat back into the harbor. Steering the boat for dockage is the hardest part, and can be the most damaging to the vessel, not to mention damage to the captain's pride. Randal guided him the entire way, with the patients of a mother hen.

"So, do you still have the slugs that you saved? Or did you lose them along the way?" Randal asked when the docking was complete.

From underneath his shirt Thom pulled up a crucifix on a sterling chain. The crucifix was noticeably darker than the silver chain, but very well crafted.

"The cross is made from her slugs, and Jesus is from my bullet. Someone could argue that it's sacrilege in some way, using a bullet that killed a man in the creation of a crucifix. And I might even agree to a point. But I'm over it. I did it to remind me that somebody loves me. Somebody loves me very much. And that is what a crucifix is all about," he said in a very final tone.

"So, you took Erich to the doctor?" The sight of the crucifix concerned him a little, and Thom's mood on the subject made it easy to push on for more fun stuff.

"Yes, but the exciting thing was the inauguration. That happened while we were with the doctor. What was that like here? You were able to see it on TV," Thom threw at him.

"Yeah, man, it was crazy. The riots were something. I think people were just looking for a reason to loot again, thinking they had missed out on their other chances when the power first went out. They just saw a chance to do something while everyone was stirred up. It was crazy."

"Am I doing well with the boat? Do you think I'm getting ready for a long trip? I want to take a week here soon and go somewhere far … maybe a trip to Key West or across the gulf to Cancun. What do you think?"

"Key West is a good trip, and we can see land for a good part of the run. Unless you would like to swing wide out into the gulf and take the open sea route from Naples to the Keys."

"I would like to do the open sea route, maybe we could skirt the islands a little on the return trip," Thom thoughtfully said. "Being out to sea with no land in sight is what I want."

"Would you like to get your wife down here for this trip? I bet she would like it, and I'd like to meet her," Randal said, waiting for a reaction.

Thom's reaction was slow, but he finally got it out there: "I'll make some calls, but I want to do it soon regardless." There wasn't much eye contact, and Randal noticed.

Chapter 15: Doctor Dictator.

The group tried to get out early, but the provisions packing took longer than expected. They kept on thinking of more to bring just in case and it got out of hand. The stay was expected to be several days until Erich was strong enough to walk the four miles back. Enough food for six days was packed, along with the Tequila, and an antibiotic skin cream found in the medicine cabinet. It wouldn't be strong enough, but it was all they had.

A thought also came up at this time to put together an already-packed travel kit for emergencies. It was realized that if they needed to take Erich to the doctor immediately yesterday, it would have taken forever to pack. Having a kit ready to go on a moment's notice could be the difference between life and death in the future.

The two-person plastic sled was connected to one of the trashcan lids so that Erich could lie down and be pulled comfortably. Some of the food provisions were packed in the trashcan lid around Eric's feet. Both Carl and Thom carried backpacks full of supplies as well. Thom had one good backpack and gave it to Carl to use. The only other good-sized backpack in the house was David's Spider-Man backpack for school. "It matches my red coat," he told David as he put it on, adjusting the straps.

Thom could see the concern in David's eyes, and he must have looked pathetic with the kid's backpack and his right arm in a homemade sling. David reached out and held Thom's hand in the sling and said that he would pray for his father to return home safely.

"That's wonderful, son, that's exactly what I'd like for you to do for me. But let's go a little farther than just praying for me to get home," Thom said as he knelt down to look him in the eye. They had a little space from the rest of the people milling around, and Thom took this moment to elaborate on his thoughts: "Remember when we were on vacation last year, and we went snorkeling in the ocean? Remember how fun that was to be out on the sea, and doing something that we all love together as a family? That's what I want you to think about also, and maybe when you pray too. Think about us all doing that again soon, as a family in the sun and the warmth. Because that's what I'll be thinking about out there in the cold. I'll be thinking about being on the sea sometime soon, and if we are on the sea together someday, then I'll have made it home safely by default!"

"So, I'm praying for us to go snorkeling so that you get home safe?" he said, kind of getting it.

"Think warm thoughts for me, that's what I need." Thom smiled widely as if he was handing down the keys to his kingdom. "I'm sharing something special with you. Thinking about the sea kept me very warm while I was traveling to the church the other day. With your help, I'll be able to keep warm and safe."

David acted like he understood, but he couldn't be expected to be in tune with Thom's off-kilter brain. The tangent was very flawed, but David shook it off by producing something from his pocket.

"I want you to take this with you for protection," David proudly said, handing him a small superhero action figure.

"Daredevil. I don't know, David, he's your favorite."

"No, dad. Ironman is my favorite. But this is the one I want you to have."

"Thanks, son, I'll take good care of it." Thom put the figure in an inside pocket and zipped it closed for safekeeping.

They set out with Erich in tow: Carl and Thom as the Alaskan sled dogs pulling the sled. The household watched them leave from the front porch, and Toni put up a good front for the children. She was crying inside but wouldn't let it show. The temperature was warmer than it had been the last two weeks. The news report was saying that a high-pressure system was coming up from the south, bringing some warmer air. It would still bring lots of snow, but it would be warmer at least. The jet stream was still moving any fallout to the east, but still, being outside was a concern they just had to deal with.

211

They pulled through the square and across the bridge over the Big Walnut River. The bridge was due for replacement in the summer, and the load limit had been reduced last year. Thom looked at the rusting handrails and wondered how long it would take to get this project back on any sort of work list now that the blackout had happened. Several years, he decided. The river below was frozen solid, and probably had three or four feet thick of ice on the surface. It moved slowly, so the ice had lots of opportunity to form in these frigid temperatures. The snow piled on top of the ice looked to be turning solid as well. The river had a look that he'd never seen before and was drawn to look at it in amazement.

They finally got comfortable with the dog-sled process, one taking the lead and breaking the snow with the other walking behind and guiding the sled. They learned that keeping the sled to the side, in the virgin snow, made for a much smoother ride for Erich. The men switched jobs every so often, because the lead guy had some hard work, getting through drifts above the waist most of the way. Thom preferred being the lead dog though because it was a better job for one arm.

"Did you have one of the dead bodies in this sled?" Erich broke the silence with an awkward question.

"Not in the sled, we use that for firewood," Thom replied. "But the lid that your feet are on, well, I can't be sure," he hemmed and hawed, trying to make light of the subject.

"I'm a little uncomfortable with that you know..." Erich said.

"Well, I should let you know that your shooting is not that horrible. You did catch that maniac once in his vest during the craziness yesterday," Thom said, trying to change the subject, but realizing it wasn't much better.

"That's good to know, but I'm afraid I'll never live down the terrified feeling I had — the feeling of helplessness, because nothing was working on that freak. I don't think I'm cut out for this stuff man." He sounded very final in his statement.

212

"Nobody is cut out for that stuff, Erich," Carl responded in a consoling tone, and it brought a silence to the hike for a bit.

Carl looked at the road ahead and let out a little whistle. They were coming out of the river valley and had a massive hill ahead of them. It was drifted over because of the trees to one side and made them both sigh to look at it. They switched places and Thom took the lead for the first leg. The road was slick and difficult to keep traction with all the weight being carried by his two feet. It was found that the berm was the better track, even though the drift was higher there. About midway, they switched lead dogs, and Thom was back closer to Eric. The rider took this time to break the awkward silence with a new awkward subject.

"I would like to ask you a serious question, Thom, and I'm not sure how to ask it, so I'll just say it." Erich rambled about nervously.

"Spit it out, Erich. We're all men here. Don't make us freeze to death waiting though," Thom joked, and caught a smile from Carl as he pulled along.

"When this is all over, Thom, I'd like to know if I could ask your daughter out on a date," he blurted out, and said it so fast, Thom wasn't sure he heard him correctly.

"My sixteen-year-old daughter," he said flatly. Carl looked back at Thom, who wasn't smiling now. It was obvious that this was news to him as well. "You know Erich, the apocalypse is not the best time to start a relationship … your timing isn't the best. This is all under my roof too. No romance starting in my house, I'll tell you that right now!"

Erich tried to explain and calm Thom's concerns, but he was on a daddy-rant by that point. He had a few things to say about this being like the Old West, and we make our own laws in our households now, and our own punishments for breaking those laws. He ranted for quite a bit, with Erich trying to get a word in, but it was no use.

213

"Why are you talking about this now, Erich? Couldn't you find a better time than now?" Thom said, looking up at the dark clouds, and the snow beginning to turn to sleet.

"Because if this doctor can't save me, then she'd never know," he said with his voice cracking a little.

"You're saying that she doesn't know you have this crush going on?" Thom said in a surprised tone.

"She has no clue. We have spoken a few times, but I have too much respect for you sir, to let her know," he said.

Thom took a deep breath. He was relieved to find that it was just a crush that hadn't progressed any further, and Carl's smile had returned also. "And she's not going to find out for a long time either. Let's just get you healthy so she doesn't need to find out," Thom said, smiling back at Carl.

"Or we could just let him go right now," Carl added in. "If we let him go, he'd slide all the way to the river from here, and we wouldn't have to worry about any of it."

"You know, that's not a bad idea," Thom said while grabbing Carl's elbow, and he already knew what Thom had in mind. They gave a little slack in the rope and let him slide a little before jerking him to a stop.

"That ain't funny man! That ain't funny at all!" Erich yelled out.

Carl and Thom joked to each other the rest of the way up the hill, and it made the work much easier. The sleet and the warmer temperature had made a thin layer of ice on the top of the snow. Sliding Erich along became easier, and they were grateful for it. At the top of the hill, the sled dogs took a break and had a power bar. The rest would be mostly level ground, which they had both been looking forward to.

They reached the gate to the development a couple of hours later. Thom and Carl both noted that no fresh footprints were going in from this entrance. The freshest looked to be a couple of days old, but that

214

didn't mean much. All it could take is one set of prints to create havoc.

They worked their way through the winding road of the Tall Timbers until the doctor's house stood before them. They could see and smell the smoke coming out of the chimney; it was a good sign. They proceeded to the house but saw no signs of recognition. Here they were, on the other side of the coin. Approaching a house, needing help, and Thom's friends may not even be in the house anymore. They might have gotten evicted or worse, by a group more aggressive than they were. If the friends had been evicted, then they were in real danger, walking up on some nasty people. It was a scary feeling, and it helped Carl and Thom to respect those who were brave enough to walk up to their door.

When they were close enough, Thom took off his hat and yelled for Ed and Kara. Hoping the name recognition would get them somewhere. They couldn't stand and wait though — they had to keep pulling. Erich had fallen asleep and was unresponsive for the last half hour. He needed to be inside and go under the knife real soon. As they turned the corner to the back of the house, Ed came out to greet them.

"How bad is he?" Ed didn't even say hello. His concern for others trumped the need for pleasantries. There was an injured person that needed immediate attention.

"He has splinters in his chest. The doctor needs to see him right away." Thom was to the point.

They carried in Erich and laid him on the couch. Explanations were given to Dr. Cliff, and he pulled open Erich's shirt to appraise the situation. Thom looked around the room to see about fifteen people, including a few children, standing around. The house was not kept very warm with the fireplace; all wore layers, and most had hats on. Their faces looked tired and frazzled, but all were willing to help the injured traveler.

215

The doctor set to work preparing for surgery. The kitchen table had the best natural light, and a lantern was hung from the chandelier, creating the operating table. The liquor turned out to be a good idea, and luckily the doctor had some tools such as a scalpel and retractors at home. Sadly, Thom was correct about the antibiotics; he had none. Cliff was intrigued by the fish tank antibiotics, and was fine with using them even though he had not heard of such a thing. It was the best solution they had, and it was worth the risk. The alcohol was good for cleaning the wounds, and the antibiotic lotion would only be useful to a minor degree.

Erich had become awake and aware, so he was fed some of the Tequila as a painkiller. Cliff jokingly told Erich it was the best painkiller that he personally knew of, and it should work well for him. Thom did not assist the operation, others were better suited for the job, and he let them have it. He found other jobs to fill his time, such as carrying in firewood, and a lot of praying.

Ed, Carl, and Thom took some time to stand in the front room away from everyone to exchange status reports. The front window had a great view of four of the houses in the development and had a huge setback from the road. They had lots of warning from any possible intruder, and so far, there had been no attacks. The natural gas stopped flowing in the development about the same time as the village, and Ed's house merged with Dr. Cliff's house. They did decide to raid the neighbor's pantries and were thankful for doing so. There were two other occupied houses in the thirty-house development, and the others had multiple families as well.

As a warning to looters, Ed proudly produced a sign he posted on the vacant homes. It read: "All food has been removed. Looters will be Violated." It had a little twist from normal warning signs, and he thought it would get a looter's attention.

"It didn't work though," Ed said. "We had a couple groups wander through that broke into some of the empty houses. One group was ballsy enough to try coming up Dr. Cliff's driveway after breaking into that house across the way. They had to have known we had people here because of the smoke, but they came up anyway. After we saw what they did, I gave a warning shot out the window to show they were unwelcome, and they changed their minds."

"Probably would have been different if they had broken into your house, huh?" Thom ventured.

"Heh, maybe I would have taken a little more aim." Ed's devilish smile brought question to where his moral line might actually be drawn.

"I wonder what would have happened if we did a warning shot with our crazies," Carl put into the air. "Maybe they would have gone elsewhere, but I bet they would've tried to turn the house into Swiss cheese. That hand cannon would have made some new windows."

"Speaking of which," Thom broke in. "I brought that .44 magnum with us. Ed, do you think you could make use of this?"

The weapon was produced from Thom's backpack and Ed held it in his large linebacker hands. "At the beginning of all this, I would have waved off such a thing," Ed said with a sullen look on his face. A comfort level began to creep in the more he held it, though, and a smile began to appear. "Weapons have become an obvious necessity. Yeah, I think I could make use of this."

"It fits you, Ed, I have to agree." Thom liked the look of this soft-spoken giant holding the giant revolver, and the smile continued to grow. "Here's the extra ammo we found on the original owner."

"In the future, Ed," Carl proposed, "warning shots should now come from this weapon. If people still come after that, they'll deserve whatever they get."

The three men turned to see Dr. Cliff walking into the front room with his left hand extended in front of him. In his gloved palm were four large splinters of wood and two pieces of glass. In an exhausted voice, he began to speak; "I did the best I could, considering what we have to

217

work with. I don't think there is any internal bleeding, but we can't be certain. We just have to go forward from here."

"Thanks, Doctor." It was all that Carl could muster. He knew it was a crapshoot from the beginning.

"He's all stitched up and should be moved to a more comfortable bed. I have to imagine that he will wake up with a massive headache from that Tequila," he said as all the men smiled agreement. "When he does wake up, give him another dose of aquarium pills. I'm going to take a nap for a bit."

"Thanks again, Doc," Thom said as the doctor shuffled to a mattress lying in the corner.

The men laid Erich near the fireplace, and everyone watched him sleep. At about the same time Ed began a prayer, Thom felt a wave of nausea and dizziness hit like a freight train. He had been feeling rough the entire trip, with his joints aching more than normal, added to the ever-present dull headache. The aches and pains were expected with all the exercise, but the nausea was new. Clutching his stomach, he excused himself from the prayer and stepped quickly to the garage. Leaning on the firewood pile, he dry-heaved for a solid ten minutes before finally catching his breath.

The nausea slowly passed, and Thom sat on the edge of the woodpile. Looking out the window at the frozen trees, he began to speak to himself: "I can't handle it if he dies, I just can't. How can I go home to face everyone if he dies? I'd rather just check out of the game and call it quits right now. What's left for me? Nothing. That's what's left." The frozen trees outside continued to sway in the wind as he stared at them.

"Who you talking to in here, man?" Carl stood at the door of the garage, checking on him.

"To the palm trees, of course," Thom quickly replied, pointing out the window. He joined his friend at the doorway and put his arm around Carl's wide shoulders. "Maybe I should eat something."

"That sounds like a great idea." Carl practically lifted Thom off the floor with a sudden burst of energy.

Thom knew what was going on; Carl needed something to take his mind away from Erich. It was the best solution possible, Thom thought. Everyone will benefit from Carl in a cooking mood, regardless of what raw materials he had to work with. Thom helped him get situated in the kitchen with a couple other cooks and then got out of the way. He had another issue to address with the household for his own peace of mind.

"Ed, I'd like to talk to you about something we are calling the Refugee Railroad." Thom gathered the attention of the adults in the living room. "You folks are not seeing the amount of foot traffic that we are in Galena. There have been a bunch of people put to walking from the traffic jam at the freeway. We have received several families into our home from those freeways. One family told us that they had walked to the exit about twelve miles from us and lived in a Cracker Barrel restaurant for several days."

"I think I know which exit you are talking about," a man named William said.

"Well, you wouldn't recognize it now," Thom continued. "The McDonalds and every other building have been taken over by stranded travelers trying to seek shelter. Whatever food that was found went quickly, but the Cracker Barrel had the added benefit of a fireplace. When the firewood ran out, and all the rocking chairs out front were burnt, they started throwing in anything that would burn. Whatever food the family came across was given to their children, because what parent could eat while their children were still hungry? But the really bad stuff started when some help arrived."

"What are you talking about? Help coming was the bad part?" William continued to banter.

"Yeah. The mob mentality kicked in when a truck showed up with food and supplies. Even though they had a National Guardsman with a

219

rifle to try to keep order, it just didn't matter. I mean, just from the size of the truck they could tell there wasn't enough for everybody at the exit. People were fighting to get closer to the truck before it was empty. The people who did get something had to fight off others to keep it for their own families. The riot caused by 'help' put this family to walking and taking their chances away from the exit. And I'm so glad they did, because they found us, and we were able to help them."

"But you can't help everybody. From what you're saying, that exit must have hundreds of people stranded there." William's wife chimed in with a softer tone than her excitable husband.

"That's true. The village of Galena could only house a small fraction. But housing them is not our ultimate goal. We are trying to turn Galena into a way station of sorts, to find other homes further out from the freeway. Maybe help people to a destination with homes to stop off at along the way where they are welcome and won't get shot for knocking on the door."

"And if they have nowhere to go?" William's pointed question earned him an elbow in the ribs from his pleasant wife.

"Well, spreading out the stranded travelers as far as possible from the freeway is certainly best. The homes close to the freeway are hostile to anyone showing up at their door. Maybe they've taken in the few they can support, and the nastiness of the ones turned away has forced them to be hostile to the rest. As you say, there's only so much one family and one home can do for so many. But if we can feed and house them for a couple of days, then move them on further away from the freeway, more lives can be saved."

Silence fell on the room as the words sunk in. Saving lives. The people in this room might have been concerned about family members caught in this storm and, of course, saving their own skin, but saving strangers hadn't made it into their mindset yet.

"What can we do?" Ed finally spoke, bringing a smile to Thom's face. If he could get Ed on board, every occupied house in the development would follow.

"I have a map of about eight homes that will take in travelers so far. I'm looking for more."

"So, the travelers would get there using the map, I get that. But how would they get in the door? Even in the outskirts away from the freeway, people will be leery of strangers."

"We've worked through that," Thom said while putting some wood in the fireplace. "We would give the traveler the name of who lives there, and a reference name of who sent them, that the household would recognize. It should build enough trust for the person to get in the door."

"It sounds like a good plan, a good way to help several families."

"Yeah, that's what Father Michael said. He supplied half the homes on the map."

"You should have led with that, Thom. Show me the map." Ed tossed a piece of firewood to Thom with a little more velocity than he expected with his words. "Father Michael is doing well, I suppose?"

"He is doing well."

Work on the map occupied the house for quite some time and the meal that came later became the reward for their hard work. Carl proudly watched everyone eat for several minutes before stepping away to check on Erich. Eventually, the radio was turned on, and it was suddenly realized that it was inauguration night. The craziness of the day had caused everyone to forget. The local news preceded the event, with the headliner being the weather. The front was warming things up more than expected, and rain instead of snow was heading towards central Ohio tomorrow. Everyone's faces began to brighten at that news. The rain would melt the snow, and any temperature above freezing would certainly be appreciated.

221

"Wait a minute. Let's think this through," Ed spoke up to all the smiling faces. "We've been melting snow from the backyard to use as drinking water and bathing. If the rain washes it away, we could be in a bad spot. We will need to fill every bucket we can find with rainwater tomorrow. A dry spell could follow this rain, and we need to be prepared."

"Have you used bathtubs to retain the water in?" Thom asked.

"No, we haven't thought about that. We haven't needed to hold that much water aside. There was always so much snow; we'd just go to the yard each day for what we needed. I guess we'll need to do something along those lines now."

"I would advise taking the time to clean the tubs, duct tape the drain, and only use it for bathing. Use your other containers for drinking." Thom detailed the process before any questions got him into trouble like the last time.

"I bet we could cut into a roofing downspout to get a bucket-full quickly and create a system to get the tubs filled. The water should be relatively clean," Ed chimed in. "We have Brita filters we run it through for drinking too."

"I guess it helps to be a roofer for ideas like that. I would have never come up with using a downspout."

"I'll let the other houses know about the plan; they will need to do the same," Ed said.

"Won't we be able to travel again with the snow melted? We should have the option to leave without the snow keeping us here, right?" William's pleasant wife spoke up, trying to shed light on something overlooked.

"That does make sense," Thom replied. "But there are some other things to consider. First, there still aren't any road crews coming around with salt. This rain will eventually freeze at night, and the roads will be treacherous to travel on. Also, I don't know if anyone has seen a freeway recently, but they are completely gridlocked. They are impassible with all the abandoned vehicles on the roads. You may be able to travel on the back roads — there are fewer abandoned cars — but those would also be the most slick. I would have to say that the safest mode of travel is still shoe-leather right now, even after the rain."

The smiles were pretty much gone by then. Whatever brightening thought the warmth and the rain brought, Ed and Thom effectively squashed it. Then came the inauguration. The warm-ups to the ceremony had already begun during the discussion, and a speech by the president-elect was just getting going.

The first female president had won by a landslide, and by the time Election Day had rolled around, it was pretty much expected. All the competition was soundly knocked off their soapbox either by her, or by the media. Everyone seemed to welcome this moment when she took the podium. She said plenty of pleasantries at the beginning of her speech, but you could tell that the events of the last month were weighing heavy on her. Midway through her speech, she even acknowledged it.

"At this moment, Americans are facing troubling times on many fronts. We are considering war with more than one country, and even considering Nuclear War. We are battling against a militia within our own borders, and we are desperately trying to restore power and services to twenty-five percent of the nation. I must admit, this is a lot to walk into on the first day on the job. As a matter of fact, I do not believe that I am the best person for this job just coming in. I think the best person to handle these issues, has been handling them for the last eight years, and is standing here beside me." Applause was coming from the radio, but not around this fireplace. Odd looks were going around, not applause.

"What's going on?" Ed spoke out loud to no one in particular. It was a very unsettling feeling. They had just seen this person elected, but the old president retained the role. Did America just become a dictatorship?

The president-elect went on to explain that she would be involved in every decision that came across the president's desk. She would have a role in everything but felt that a change in stewardship of the nation would not serve the public in the best fashion. She stated that she would be inaugurated at a later date, and until then, the current president would remain. The speech went on, but it seemed to rehash the same points and the room realized that they had gotten all the information they were going to get.

"I think I have whiplash," Carl finally said. The surprised faces looking back at him may have felt the same way. "I have been through so much in the last month, that I feel like I'm in a car that's been pushed off a cliff. I've been bouncing off the cliff walls for twenty-eight days now, and I'm still waiting on the big crash at the bottom."

The statement did not change the dazed look everyone had, still staring at the radio in amazement. It took Ed, the voice of reason, to really get to the bottom of things.

"I don't know whether I agree with her decision or not, and it really doesn't matter. What is becoming completely apparent is that the American voters, the people sitting in this room, are no longer in control of their country. The rules are being rewritten, and we are not in the mix."

Just then, Dr. Cliff walked into the room from his nap. "Did I miss anything?"

The stoic William broke out in laughter so loud and lengthy that his wife slapped his back several times to prevent hyperventilation. With perfect timing Thom spoke up with just the right answer.

"Is there any of that Tequila left?"

Chapter 16: Bridge to Oblivion.

The next couple days were spent helping the houses of the development save the water coming down from the sky. The group also worked on the safe house map, utilizing the information of the two other occupied homes. An additional nine locations were added to the map, and it was really taking shape. A county map was found in a car and a complete master map was made with accurate county and township road names. Everyone was happy to work on this project, and it gave them hope. Hope that they will actually survive this mess, and hope that they would not have to push others away to make that survival possible. Hope that they could bring others along with them, as they trudged on through the unknown.

Erich recovered slowly, and his body fought the infection they knew would come. The antibiotics worked to a degree but were not knocking out everything. The skin cream seemed to help more than expected, and drew out some of the infection, in the form of a greenish-yellow pus.

After two days, Erich was up and about, getting his feet underneath him. He was ready to go, or so he said. They decided to wait another day and let him get stronger for the trip. It was one of the best decisions they made. He needed to be stronger than anyone knew.

It wasn't until that second night that the radio shared the turmoil caused by the presidential inauguration that wasn't. The riots and unrest caused by her decision were quite extensive but weren't broadcast in the outage areas until that time. There must have been concern about triggering more militia events based on this news. The death and destruction in areas that had power was very alarming to the folks listening in the living room. The riots and looting in these areas seemed to be still feeding into a larger master plan. As they spoke around the fireplace later that night, discussions of martial law and Homeland Security in all major cities became the focus. All this activity by the public, and media coverage of it, certainly led to that conclusion. Martial law in the outage areas had already been in place for quite some time and was kind of expected. But in other parts of the country? It seemed that the riots forced that decision, and the decisions of the government created the riots. It seemed kind of circular when they looked at it from a distance.

Carl, Erich, and Thom set out the next morning on their trip home. The roads were a sheet of ice, but the snow on the ground was much less. It had rained for two days straight, and either melted or compacted much of the snow. Slush coated the roads, with an ice base. Travel by vehicle would be insane in the current conditions. They walked on the berm of the road or the grass, to keep a better footing, but travel was quite slow. They tried an experiment of putting their backpacks of the remaining supplies on the sled and pulling them, but the plan didn't work. The sled kept on getting away from them and sliding into the ditch. The backpacks were finally put back on, and the sleds tucked under an arm. It just worked better.

"Why did she turn down the presidency?" Carl asked, trying to pass the time.

"Man, that's tough. You got a theory?" Thom replied.

"I think she was just covering her butt. I think whoever is in charge during all this blackout is going to be blamed for everything and just can't win. She's letting the previous president get thrown under the bus and take all the dirt for these decisions. Then she can step in after he has taken all the hits, and she becomes a hero. That's what I think," he said flatly.

"So, he's the fall guy? The scapegoat?" Thom said. "I could see that. Do you think it's by his choice?"

"Hard to tell. It's hard to believe this is happening without his approval somehow. But I think she is just looking out for herself, and making sure she gets elected to the second term."

"Carl, we need to have another discussion about your distrust of women sometime real soon," Thom said in a condescending voice, while Erich chuckled in the background.

They trudged along, bickering amongst themselves until they reached the crest of the hill, down into the river valley.

"Damn, you guys pulled me up that thing?" Erich said with a whistle.

"Reluctantly," Carl said, and the tone of his voice recalled the conversation on the hill also.

"Hey guys, let's just forget the things I said here, okay? I was delirious with fever," Erich said.

"Fever," Carl simply repeated. "Got it."

"The track to the right of the road looks the safest," Thom said, pointing down the hill, and desperately trying to change the subject. "Let's walk single file, with a good amount of space in between us. If someone falls, maybe he won't wipe out the rest of us if we have some space."

"Okay, let's make this move. We're almost home," Carl said, trying to rally the troops.

The hill was treacherous, and the berm was not wide at all. A guardrail began about halfway down, protecting a larger ditch at the bottom. Carl took the lead with Erich in the middle and Thom last. Thom's balance was not working well with the narrow berm, and a steep, painful looking ditch to the side. Large boulders were at the bottom of the ditch to stop erosion during rainfall. Every time Thom looked into the ditch, he pictured himself sprawled across it, in a heap. The third time Thom's foot slipped towards the ditch, he let out a defiant "screw it," and launched himself at the road. In a semi-athletic move, the sled was pulled from under his arm and positioned underneath his torso to land on.

Thom's landing was much like a drunk partier doing a belly flop in the pool: messy and much more painful than expected. But the ride was the adrenalin rush that he did expect. The slush of the road made a great sledding surface, and he built a speed that seemed crazy to someone with their face six inches from the asphalt pavement. When he passed Erich and Carl, comments like "cheater" and "you're flippin' nuts" were tossed at him, but he didn't hear. At the bottom, he used the momentum to round the corner towards the bridge and rolled off the sled when it slowed to a halt.

Thom stood to look back at the father and son working along the guardrail. The guardrail took even more of the berm, but at least it gave them something to hold onto. They reached the bottom without a single fall, and they looked to each other in amazement of their success. Erich's upper body was still very weak and the use of his arms on the guardrail took its toll. Carl noticed this in his son's stance and put his arm around him to help him the last short distance.

At this point, Thom noticed the sound of the raging river behind him. It was expected that two days of solid rain would create a rushing river, but this sounded like a freight train. It was louder than Thom had ever heard, in his twenty years of living by the river. The sound was crushing down upon him, and he crouched down a little as he turned in the direction of the river. When Carl and Erich approached, Carl called out to the "crazy bobsledder," but got no response. Thom simply stood with his back to them, looking towards the river. When they were beside him, they saw why.

It looked like an illusion from a distance, as if the sun was playing tricks on them. Much like how water appears to be on a hot road, but it's just a heat reflection. The illusion in this instance was that the bridge wasn't there at all. They hoped it was an illusion. They prayed it was an illusion. But that was a prayer unanswered.

The river got even louder as they approached the edge. The rushing water over the debris made a forceful sound. Chunks of ice the size of small cars were strewn about the wreckage of the bridge. It was a massive sight.

"An ice dam," Thom said solemnly. "All the water coming downstream lifted the huge chunks of ice and carried them like a wave hitting the center post. That's all I can think of that happened, it's still hard to imagine though."

"Well, it happened." Carl tried to get past the disbelief. "What do we do now? How do we get across this river? I mean, the house is right there!" he said, pointing through the trees.

"Let me think," Thom said, looking at Erich to try to evaluate how he was holding up. "There is a bicycle path bridge about a quarter mile upstream. We could get across on that."

"Is it made of large wooden posts?" Carl said, watching the river.

"Yeah, steel frame with wood posts on top."

"Like those down there?" Carl said, pointing down at the tangle of debris.

"Yep. Exactly like those down there," Thom's said. "Now it makes a little more sense. The bicycle bridge went first. It was lifted off its mountings and carried by the ice dam and used as a battering ram. I can see it now."

"I don't care if you figured out how it happened. It happened! How are we going to get my boy home?" He was tired ... they were all tired.

"We have a much longer walk now. It's seven or eight miles either upstream or downstream to another bridge. In my estimation though, it would be easier to go upstream. We could use some of the bike trail to skirt along the river, and short cut a little bit."

"Sounds good to me, let's get to it," Carl said, turning from the bridge. Erich was getting weaker by the minute and Carl didn't want to spend any more time looking at the depressing wreckage in the river.

"Wait a minute," Thom said, as he pulled out one of the protein bars from a pocket. It had a matte brown wrapper, in an attempt to have the all-natural look. Then he pulled out an ink pen and scribbled on the wrapper, "Be home soon. T, C, + E."

"Think you can get this to the other side? My arm is not in shape yet," Thom said, handing the bar to Carl.

229

He swung back and gave it a heave, well overshooting the mark.

"I guess I don't know my own strength," he said. "Thanks for thinking of my baby girls. I'm sure they are worried about us." The expression on Thom's face gave away that he was being completely selfish here. His family was his only thought when he pulled out the protein bar. Luckily, Carl didn't see it.

Chapter 17: Son of Satan.

They turned and headed away from the bridge, digging deep for new strength that they didn't expect to need for this trip. The trip should have been over by this point. Now they needed to go eight miles out of their way to a bridge and eight more back to get home.

Back at the curve, the road forked, and a side road headed upstream. The side road also had to climb out of the river valley, and it was just as unforgiving. Their footing kept sure though, and they made it to the top without incident. At the top, they sat on a guardrail to rest. Carl handed around bottles of water, as they looked back on their accomplishment. They prodded along in silence most of the way, trying to reserve strength for the journey.

Eventually they turned off the road to another small road that followed the river more closely. The sign at the turn told them that this was a dead-end road. Thom explained to his companions that the road stopped at a huge farm, but then they could pick up the bicycle path, and take it to another dead-end road on the other side of the farm. They agreed that this route sounded much safer than anything else. Running into looters wouldn't be expected on a dead-end road.

The road eventually ended, and the bicycle path was found through the slush to continue. A large part of the farm had been purchased by American Electric Power, and a huge substation had been built there about four years prior. Part of the payback to the community was the creation of the bike path. The mounding and trees tried to hide the towering structures but did a poor job. The pine trees on the top of the mound of ground needed many more years of growth and still they would be inadequate.

"These things are huge," Erich commented when the path veered exceptionally close to the site.

"I half expected to see them smoldering or discolored," Carl commented. "They look fine. All the wires are still connected, nothing broken from what I can see."

231

"It's so quiet," Thom said. "Normally there was a loud hum from this station. The silence is what makes this so eerie. Now they are just huge and silent." They stared up in awe as if they were in a redwood forest that sprouted up in central Ohio, creating huge, quiet, leafless trees.

"Do you think they can get this station up and running again soon?" Carl asked the question that got no answer.

It was above their knowledge base, and they knew it. Getting the high voltage electricity to this substation and converting it into lower voltage to be sent, and transformed again close to their homes was like shooting a rocket to the moon to them. They had no idea how any of this junk worked, and they were completely at the mercy of those who did. The massive towers served to drive home the point of just how helpless and dependent they really were.

"Do you smell that?" Thom awkwardly changed the subject.

"It's sulfur or something. I can't be sure. Is something wrong with the power station?" Carl was always looking out for danger, especially with his son in a weak state.

"This power station can't do any more damage to us than it already has," Thom replied. "No, that smell is coal. Somebody is burning coal, and I think I know who it is."

"Sounds like a plan to me." Carl had already grabbed up his son's shoulder and started walking faster down the path.

"Don't be getting all excited yet, Carl," Thom quickstepped up beside him. "First, we will be going probably two miles out of our way to get to this hillbilly, and well, he's a little nutso too. You might not like him."

"When do we need to decide about going his direction or the bridge?" Carl had his mission parameters, and number one was under his arm.

"Soon. The guy's name is Dominic Santori. He was my Concealed Carry Permit instructor, when Toni and I took the class two years ago.

He held the class at his property a couple miles from here. There was a big stash of coal in his barn, and he said that he heated his house with it."

"Sounds good so far. How about nutso? Why wouldn't I like him?"

"He's a prepper, big time for one thing. I would have to say that he was the catalyst for me jumping headlong into the prepper pool — in the deep end. After the twelve hours on a Saturday of hearing his stories during our CCW class, he invited Toni and me over the next day to spend the day with his wife and him. I haven't spoken to him since, but I think he'll remember me."

"I guess that is a concern. If we go two miles out of our way, we need to get in the door." Mission Priorities again.

"I think we will be okay. The man's heart is in the right place, even though I wonder about the rest of him."

They reached the spot where the bike path crossed the county road, and Thom looked to his friend. "It's time. This way is the bridge, the other is…"

"Dominic huh? Alright, let's go." Carl measured his steps a little to pace himself now. "Tell me more."

"He had this crazy idea of converting a truck to hydrogen power so he wouldn't have to rely on gasoline. I wonder if he ever figured it out."

"Sounds like he's smart anyway."

"He was a helicopter pilot for a while with the National Guard. He was there during Katrina, flying a chopper. The stories he had to tell. You can understand why I became a prepper, right?" Thom was realizing that this impending meeting was going to be a venture down memory lane, and he was uncertain if he was ready for it. Things were starting to hit close to home. Doors in his mind were being opened that he had bolted a year ago.

233

"Hey man, you don't need to explain nothin' to me. As far as I'm concerned, you picked the right horse in this race. And I'm glad to be the guy beside you when it happened. The guy beside the ticket holder always benefits!"

"Yeah, it's always easy to congratulate the winner after the race is run. But what about before? If they were congratulating him before, everybody would win. No, everybody has their own picks, their own choices for where they think the world will end up and they bet on them. Maybe the preppers didn't know this scenario was going to happen, but they knew something was going to happen. While others were placing bets in their life that expected the world would stay the same or better, the preppers were betting that the world would change."

"I guess I did too. I believed everything I was told. That we all lived in this protective cocoon called the U-S of A. No Worries for us folks." Carl smirked and looked sideways over to Thom. "But the world is the way it is. The three of us walking down a snowy road out here in the sticks ain't gonna change none of that. Tell me more about this Dominic. What happened in New Orleans?"

"Yeah, well, the pictures you saw on the news were after the troops were in there on the ground, which was about day three. He was in there on day one with the chopper. He flew supplies right into the Superdome area. He saw what it was like when a huge number of people were in one place without any law and order. He could only get within twenty feet of the ground and drop his pallets of supplies from there, destroying half of them when they hit the ground. It wasn't safe to land the copter. People would attempt to crowd onboard and overload the craft. And at that point, his life is in danger. He even said that pilots have been taken hostage in other emergencies by the refugees they are trying to help. All to receive more supplies as ransom for the pilot."

"You've got to be kidding me, man," Carl said. Thom could see that Erich was walking a little better and looking Thom's way. If the stories would keep Erich's mind off the pain, and give him drive to walk, Thom was in on the game. He'd channel the conversations just as he heard them from Dominic, and he'd give 'em the drama they wanted.

"First off, he said there was a lot of death happening around the Superdome and inside. The official number of bodies taken from inside the Superdome is so far off it's laughable. They say it's haunted now too. The people died from murder, starvation, and drinking bad water. Now, murder is expected. We are human animals. But the other two stem from a lack of supplies, and there was a shit-ton of supplies dropped on that zone. The thing is, the supplies were captured by the strong as soon as they were dropped. The strong did not bring the supplies back and give them to the weak. The weak had to pay. Or they got none. Jewelry on their person was the first to go. If a weak person didn't have any, they found a weaker person to take it from. The strong set themselves up in gangs within the Superdome with their storehouses of supplies and marketed them to those who had something of value to trade.

"When the troops did arrive, the gangs eventually gave up their supplies, but not the booty. Because well, the booty is the booty. The first troops found so many dead bodies that they had to clear them away before the film crews got there. The scene was R-rated and needed to be PG-13 before it was piped into everyone's living rooms. It was the work Dominic did in New Orleans and what he saw there that changed his life direction forever. He came back to the family farm in Ohio and worked towards a minimalist prepper lifestyle. Because he knew it would happen again. The head-scratcher is that he talked about his bug-out location near the Ohio River. I just wonder why he is still here. He should have bugged out to Steubenville already."

"Steubenville, huh?" Carl continued to press. "Are you sure it's his coal we are smelling?"

235

"Oh yeah, it's getting stronger, and he's right over this ridge. I can see a little of the smoke now." Thom's expression became a little more serious as he continued. "He spoke a lot about conspiracy theories to us on that Sunday we came back to chat. He detailed to us how the Twin Towers had to be an inside job. Building Seven was the key, and it all made sense when he said it. Actually, I think it still does. He talked about setting up Claymores around his yard in an event, and civilian militias. Yeah man, he even talked about civil war."

"Funny how you tell me this when his driveway is just down the road," Carl moaned.

"I told you that you may not like him."

"There's a difference between not liking him and finding out he might be a white supremacist. I have an aversion to being lynched and shit."

"I never heard him say a racial slur or anything like that. I think all his hate was directed at the government. Civil war has a different meaning now than just white supremacy. But to be safe, make sure you mention that you're not Muslim." Thom smiled at him for the joke that he feared might be the truth.

The driveway was bordered by trees on both sides, making a tunnel effect even in winter with no leaves. Forty feet inside was a steel gate blocking the driveway. The group walked up and stood at the gate, not sure what to do. Thom looked at the keypad and voice box for the gate and pushed the button as if something might actually happen.

"Quit touching that." A voice from the tree next to the gate said. A speaker was noticed about twenty feet up and a small camera.

"I'm Thom Vesper. I was in your CCW class..."

"I can't hear a damn thing you say. There's no microphone down there. Look. The rest of the driveway is mined. If you guys try to jump the gate, you'll be dragging somebody out of here screaming in agony. And that's if you're lucky. So just turn and find somewhere else to go."

Thom was downhearted for a minute, looking at Carl who had walked an extra two miles. Erich needed a warm bed tonight. "Hey, let's take a stance of shooting at a firing range. Maybe he'll get the point that I have been to the firing range at his house."

"We are playing pantomime now?" Carl stomped his foot on the ground with the statement. "Okay Thom, but let's point away from the man's house. Hate for him to get the idea from the pantomime that we are threatening him of attack!"

The stage was set, and Thom made his case to the camera for even longer, trying to give the impression that he was not leaving until he was heard.

"What? You haven't left yet? Stop your acrobatics down there. Look. I'll turn on the gate box microphone. But you've only got two minutes. That thing sucks the volts out of my batteries. I think it's got a short in it."

The red light on the keypad came on, and Thom immediately punched the talk button. "I'm Thom Vesper; I took a CCW class from you two years ago."

"I did a lot of classes, buddy." Thom's heart sank. He was foolish to think the guy would remember him and that he would get inside. But just as instantly, his heart rose.

"I attended the class with my wife, Toni. She's a short brunette and busty. She wore a low-cut camouflage tank top to class to put her in the mindset for CCW. She got lots of attention in class and you invited us back the next day."

"The Ruger 5-shot revolver. I remember her. I regret that she is not with you. Yeah, maybe I remember you."

"She shot someone recently with that 5-shot Ruger."

"Tough lady. I knew she had it in her."

"Look Dominic, I've got an injured man here. All we want is one night sleeping in a warm building. We've even got our own food; we won't need any of your supplies." Thom went for the kill. His two minutes were almost up.

"Food?" The voice sounded a little higher pitched. "You've got food? What do you have?"

Carl stepped to the voice box and Thom pushed the button. "Got enough for a mess of soup beans and a kick-ass chili, that's for sure."

A few seconds passed and the gate clicked open. Thom noticed that the light on the keypad box had turned off. "Please latch my gate closed behind you. Stay to the left side of the driveway until you get to the edge of the trees. At that point, follow the red laser beam to the house."

Quizzical looks went between the men, including Erich. Even he wasn't too tired to see the weirdness of what just happened. "He's a prepper from the word go," Carl pointedly said to Thom. "He certainly has food."

Thom silently took the point position and walked in front of his team, weapon out.

"And here I am walking on the left side of the driveway," Carl continued his tirade. "Am I actually walking through a damn minefield? What if we walked on the other side? Would I explode? Are you kidding me?"

"Carl," Thom said in a stern voice from the lead. "At this point, all we know is that he's a chili lover. My question is, how much do we have?"

"Four men max."

"It will be soup beans for us if there are more chili fans in there. I can go without food if I must. It's all about getting Erich home."

"Affirmative." Carl was back in the groove. Mission Priorities.

Thom abruptly stopped when the trees ended. A red laser light greeted them in the snow. In single file, the men followed the laser through the yard to the front door. It was a two-story saltbox home, probably built in about 1880. Several outbuildings could be spotted peeking out from behind the house and a couple of trucks parked in front of the garage. It was unnerving for the men to walk through the front yard instead of the driveway to the sidewalk. In the yard, the appearance of walking in a minefield was being drilled into everyone's brain.

"Gentlemen!" Dominic greeted them at the door holding the laser pen. He stood tall and very Italian, with a broad smile on his face. "Please come on in and warm yourselves by the stove."

Quizzical looks still abounded, but Thom stepped forward and shook the man's hand. "Thanks for inviting us in Dominic. I expect that we should leave our firearms at the door, correct?"

"Yes, just leave them with your coats. Not a big deal, you will be able to see them all the time by the front door. I won't mess with your weapons, but I also expect that you won't either." His words were stern on that point but then lightened. "Step over here to the stove. Yeah, Thom, I recognize you more now in person and with your hat off. But I must admit, Louise would probably recognize you more quickly. She was sweet on you."

It brought to Thom's mind what he thought two years ago about the special invite after the CCW class. Thom had an inkling it was a warm-up for some swinger lifestyle invitation, but he got so interested in the prepper talk that he derailed it that day, if it was the case.

The large potbelly stove sat in the living room, and the furniture around it was sturdy but probably hand-me-downs from his family and well-used. It appeared that only a few rooms were being used now, and some were blocked off by packing blankets nailed over the doorways. Introductions went around and areas gone numb from the cold were finally regaining feeling again.

"I take it that you are the injured one," he spoke to Erich directly. "This couch here is calling to you. Get warm and comfortable. I'll take on the injury in a minute."

Turning to Carl, he abruptly changed the subject. "So, what kind of chili do you have? Hormel?"

"Yeah, I think it is," Carl answered kind of slowly. "Hey man, from what Thom told us, you are the king of the preppers. Don't tell me you don't have some chili."

"Heh, I guess that is kind of funny." Dominic rubbed his hands together over the stove. "I've got my Steubenville spot prepped out with all the stuff. You know, all my good stuff is there, along with my wife and friends who are eating great. Here, I thought I'd be fine with a pallet of MREs till I bugged out. They last forever, you know? But hell, a month straight of that junk for breakfast, lunch, and dinner will drive you to shoot somebody. Maybe that's why they give it to the Marines."

Carl looked around the room nodding his head to the answer. He was satisfied with what Dominic had to say and more so, he was relieved. He was dealing with a real person who made a bad decision, not a loony tune. It was time to treat him as such. "How many men am I cooking for sir?"

"Me and my sentry Kirksey. He's sleeping and will take his shift in a couple of hours. It would be great to wake him to the smell of some good food."

"Is this my cooking surface?" Carl said nudging to the potbelly stove. "If so, I only see a small, flat spot on top."

Dominic grabbed some gloves and set to work. Two arm brackets were hanging on the back of the stove, and he mounted them into the proper holes in front. The cooking surface was hanging there also; he laid it on top of the arms, fitting them into holes in the surface. This stove was easily one hundred years old, and it probably served as a main cooking surface back in its day. Carl reached out and gave the

240

surface a shake, and found it to be rock solid. He turned to Thom and smiled a wide grin, saying, "I like this guy."

"Let me show you the kitchen, you'll need a saucepan." Dominic was on the move. With a lantern to light the way, he pointed out the pan's cabinet and the utensils drawer.

"Got a spice drawer?" Carl asked while pulling out some canned tomatoes from his backpack. Dominic pointed, and Carl followed up with, "How hot do you guys like it?"

"Medium Well."

Carl took a second to make sure he understood the mismatch of cooking terms and verified he needed no further direction. He simply gave a thumbs-up and got to work. In crisp, military fashion, Dominic switched projects and turned to Thom. "Tell me about your injured man."

Thom took a second to absorb everything that had just happened and catch up to the moment. But once he got some words flowing, he came up to speed. "He had some splinters of wood and glass in his chest from a near miss of a .44 magnum."

They were walking back to the stove. "Was the .44 magnum the man Toni brought down?"

Thom took a second to register the question and determine the best short answer. "Yeah, yeah it was. She brought him down. We took Erich to a doctor over in Tall Timbers and he removed the splinters. Now, we are mainly dealing with infection."

"A doctor at Tall Timbers huh? That's good to know." Dominic placed a wooden chair next to Erich on the couch. "Okay friend, let's see the damage."

Erich lowered the blanket and unbuttoned his shirt. The bandages came off with a little pain, but luckily the tape was old and didn't stick well. Erich kept his eyes on the ceiling throughout the process. He was afraid to look and verify that the puss was back.

241

Thom produced the aquarium pills from his backpack. "This is what we've been giving him, and this hydrocortisone cream."

"I've heard of these pills. I mean, it's not the greatest, but it's better than nothing. And that cream should help to draw out the pus. When the pus comes, try to pull it with your fingers like string cheese." Dominic demonstrated the motion with one of the wounds.

"Really? What does that do?" Thom leaned over his shoulder to see.

"Well, sometimes the pus will encapsulate a fragment that was left behind and draw it to the surface. You may have to tug on it to get it out of there, but it's got to get out." Of the four open wounds, one had a puss capsule that he described.

"Hang tough." Dominic put his hand on Erich's forehead to check for fever and didn't look happy. "Let's get him some medicine."

Thom obediently followed him into a large laundry room that also had a door to the back yard. Plastic bins were neatly arranged on stainless steel shelves along one wall and cryptically marked with what was inside. A large, shallow bin was selected and placed on the washing machine for inspection. A few bottles were pulled and dropped back into the bin before he found what he was looking for.

"This is Amoxicillin. It's some strong stuff, and he'll need to eat something with each dose, or it will turn his stomach upside down. Now we need something for pain." The bottle was handed to Thom. It said fifty doses and felt full.

Thom stood there bewildered. The plastic bottle he held in his hand could very well be the difference between life and death for Erich. Equally amazing was that the large, shallow bin was full of similar bottles. Dominic continued to pull up bottles and read the label then drop them back in systematic fashion, not finding what he wanted.

Then something happened that scared Thom. A bottle was pulled and read, but nothing happened. Dominic just stood there clutching the bottle. Thom had been watching his hands methodically pull and drop,

242

but now his vision traveled up the arm to Dominic's frozen face. He stared at the bottle as if in a trance. The hand holding the bottle began to quiver.

"Take this. Take this out of here. It shouldn't be here. Take it now." Dominic's motion was not smooth, more robotic. "Don't tell anyone you have those. Nobody. People will kill for that."

Thom looked at the bottle. Percocet. Another fifty count. Dominic began breathing better when the bottle left his hands and more so when it was secured in a backpack pocket. "It could also save a life too, right?"

"Only in extreme situations. Never use them for anything else, and don't tell anybody you have them," he repeated. "If word gets around, even a little bit, Hell will come knocking."

Thom wasn't going to bridge the conversation to what happened with Dominic and these Opioids. He didn't dare. Addiction had swept through rural and suburban Ohio like a plague the last few years. Almost everyone was touched in some way, to some degree. It appeared that Dominic had been touched and it might have been more deeply than Thom wanted to know.

"Here we go. Ibuprofen. 600 milligrams. Every four hours." Another full pill bottle was handed to Thom.

The medicine bin was replaced and an MRE box was pulled from the next shelving unit. The two men returned to Erich at the couch. Carl also stood there, stirring the pot on the stove.

"That's what I like to see!" Dominic stepped a little faster to the stove. "Let me have a smell! Oh boy! I think my stomach wants to jump out of my body and give you a hug, Carl!"

After a quick smell Dominic left the food to sit in his chair by Erich and went to work. "Let me pull something out of these MRE boxes for you to eat before you take this pill." Erich sat up and got some food down but wasn't looking very good. "Get this nasty stuff down, friend; you'll get the good food later. Now, we'll take two of these antibiotic pills for the first time to jumpstart this thing. But after that it's just one. And here's something for the pain. We'll get you going again soon."

Dominic then turned in his wooden chair and was startled to find Carl kneeling on the floor beside him. Carl's hands were clasped and eyes tearing over as he prayed with the intensity of a man pleading for his son's life. "Could be better medicine than mine," Dominic said as he moved the chair and got down on his knees. Thom joined them on the floor to pray, but after a short while was interrupted.

"What do I smell?" Kirksey stood in the doorway, lifting a blanket to come into the room. "Sorry guys, is he OK?"

"He will be tomorrow," Dominic answered, rising to his feet. "This is a CCW student Thom, and Carl and his son Erich on the couch. Friends, this is Kirksey."

Kirksey was big, burly, and unshaven. Over his un-tucked flannel shirt, he wore an old west gun belt with a revolver on the ready. "What's cookin'?"

"It's chili!" Dominic excitedly said. "Come here and give it a smell!"

Kirksey was almost as excited about the meal as Dominic, Thom noticed. But Thom also gave him credit that he just woke up; he might reach Dominic's level yet. He turned to look at Carl, who was just now stirring from his prayer. Thom extended a strong hand to help him from the floor.

"Give it a taste, gentlemen. I'll modify it to how you like." Carl was back on the job. In his mind, it was all about giving thanks. He may not have much, but he'd give it all. "And hey guys, Thom and I are happy to have an MRE tonight. Maybe there will be enough in the pan for you to have leftovers tomorrow."

Thom turned to him with some mock disappointment. "You could have asked me first. That stuff is smelling pretty doggone good."

244

The food was served and the two could not stop talking about it. They ranted and raved as if they hadn't eaten food in a month, because well, they hadn't. Carl and Thom were fine with the MREs. They were not horrible. Thom even mentioned that he liked it but agreed that it would get old after a while.

"So, you said that Louise is in Steubenville?" Thom went for some small talk as the meal finished up.

"Yes, she is, and she's doing fine. I talk to her just about every night." The room got quiet, waiting for the punch line.

"But probably not tonight, huh?" Kirksey kept it going, knowing the newbies were in the dark.

"No, too much cloud cover to get that far. But I do feel like taking the air." Dominic sat back in his chair, smiling at Kirksey. "Nothing like a good meal to make a man feel like going to work."

He stood and waved to Thom and Carl to follow. After checking the temperature of Erich's forehead while he peacefully slept, they walked into another small room with a blanket over the door. With the blanket removed and a lantern in hand, Thom saw an extensive ham radio system sprawled across three desktops in the room. Above the desks were re-purposed kitchen cabinets with the doors removed for storage.

"Holy cow," Carl finally found his voice. "You're... You're Hellstrom, ain't you!"

"Yeah. You've heard me huh? Glad that somebody is listening." Dominic sat down and started flipping switches and dials.

"And the name?" Thom was still coming up to speed.

"Well Daimon is pretty close to Dominic, but I didn't make up the name, I stole it." He reached up to the top of the kitchen cabinets and retrieved a knick-knack of sorts. It was a figurine of a muscular man with a cape riding an old roman chariot being pulled by three white horses with flames coming out of their nostrils. "This is Daimon Hellstrom. Marvel comics invented him as the Son of Satan with a

245

human mother. He has magical powers from his father, but he chose to follow his human side and protect humanity. Even though humanity hadn't done much for him. Kind of what I did here with this radio. I could have left when the storm hit, but I decided to stick it out and use this radio to help humanity."

Kirksey stuck his head in the doorway with a jeering comment. "And those folks in their Benz's you helped would probably spit on you, just as soon as look at you, before this blackout."

"Come on Kirk, I can clean up if I want to." Dominic continued his jovial attitude while he got his system up and running. Carl and Thom sat on an empty desktop beside him to watch him work.

"Hello friends, Daimon Hellstrom on the air again. This broadcast will be a short one; my batteries look a little low. The cloud cover didn't let my solar panels do their job, and some visitors helped me tap them out a little this afternoon." After a look over his shoulder for the inside joke, he continued: "Let's take another look at this inauguration, or the lack thereof, friends. From what I'm hearing, the current president almost *had* to stay. Some of the new cabinet appointees were at a meeting in Philadelphia when the blackout occurred, including the ones circled in controversy by the media. It is uncertain that any of the missing appointees are even alive at this point. Nothing has been confirmed about their condition or location. With most of the lady president's team out of commission, the hand was forced to keep the old administration. Was this by design? Did the terrorists know that much of her cabinet was meeting in Philadelphia at the time of the attack? I'll leave that one for each of you to contemplate, but the gist is this: the same administration is in place now that was in power when the lights went out. Take it for what it is.

"The last bit of news I have for you friends is about the Powered States. As you all know, the Powered States all went bat-shit crazy when the inauguration went sour. Maybe they wanted to take out some frustrations, or maybe they wanted to bust into Best Buy and grab a new TV. Whatever their motivations were, the repercussions

246

are now being laid down. Almost a thousand people were shot in various riots across the country and now most major cities are in a state of martial law. Gun control is becoming a major focus of the riots as expected. Guns are not being taken from people's homes, as many feared would happen. The local governments have promised openly that a person should be allowed to protect their homes, so guns are allowed there. However, if a gun is found in a person's car or carried outside the home, it will be confiscated. And having a CCW permit doesn't matter either. No ifs, ands, or buts, the gun will be taken and not returned. Sounds like bad news to the folks south of the Ohio River, but what does that mean to us up here in the frozen tundra? Well, friends, don't expect some civic organization out of Memphis or wherever to try to bring a truckload of food and medical supplies up here to help us out. They would be crazy to enter the Non-Powered Zone without some form of protection, right? So, they won't be coming. We're on our own, folks. Just like in the beginning when the reporters told us we were carved off the grid. We've been carved from more and more as this goes on. Just like a Christmas turkey on the dinner table, and we're almost down to the bonezzzzz. Be safe, friends."

Dominic powered down his system and looked at his watch. Spinning around in his office chair, he addressed Thom and Carl: "Okay, gentlemen. I've got ten minutes before my check-in call. Tell me more about this doctor at Tall Timbers."

An information dump was given to Dominic, enough that he took some notes on a pad. The ten minutes passed quickly, and he crisply turned to power up the radio system again. New frequency settings were made, and he picked up the microphone.

"Red Robin, Red Robin, this is Fly Boy. Have you got your ears on? Over."

"Fly Boy, this is Red Robin. Low batteries but power is on. Over."

"I have some new visitors with food and news that's noteworthy. Over."

"Food. I bet you're happy, over."

"Yessir. Fat and happy. First news: There is a doctor in the Tall Timbers Development. Address 442 Timbers Drive. He has limited abilities and very limited supplies. I may try to help that situation, but it is what it is. Over."

"Good news. 442 Timber noted. Over."

"Next news: The bridge to Galena from the East is gone … taken out by an ice dam and completely impassible at this time. When the water flow goes down it might be crossable by hopscotch on the debris. Over"

"Not good news. Any injuries? Over."

"Unknown. Poachers attacked a home on the square in Galena five days ago. One home occupant was injured and is lying on my couch. The four poachers met their maker. Over."

"Score one for the good guys. Prayers sent to the injured, he's in good hands. More good news? Over."

"My travelers have a list of safe homes for travelers. Some may be in your direction, but we do not want to overload them. I will compile the list and get it to you at the noon call. Over."

"It's about time these calls had more good news. I've recently become overloaded myself. I look forward to the noon call. My batteries are pooped, with some sunshine tomorrow morning I should be ready for a longer call. Anything else? Over."

"Nothing else. Over and out."

"Over and out."

Carl and Thom looked at each other in quiet amazement. Dominic powered down and left the room to check with his sentry. The two men continued to sit and let what just happened sink in. After the initial excitement passed, they realized how tired they were.

Erich was stirring on the couch and Carl took the opportunity to give him another dose of pain meds. Allowing him to lapse on pain meds right now would not be a fun way for him to wake up. Carl made himself a bed on the floor next to the couch and Thom took over a side chair. It was not a comfortable night's sleep for either of them, but their thoughts were with Erich. As long as he slept well and healed some, it would be considered a good night for all.

"I dreamed that I was Evil Knievel jumping twenty busses," Erich told his father in the morning.

"Did you make it?" Carl was draining the pus.

"Not quite. I went over the handlebars and rolled on the ground forever. My body feels like it actually happened."

"Let the meds kick in. We may have gone too long between pain pills."

"I feel better than yesterday, I must admit. Maybe we are rounding the corner?" Erich's words were hopeful.

In the radio room, Dominic set down his microphone and powered down the radio system. "That was exhausting." He looked over to Thom who seemed to echo the sentiment. The two had been busy for the last two hours compiling data and then making the noon call. A tired euphoria was setting in now that the task was completed.

"Red Robin was not prepared for all this information," Dominic continued his thought. Before him was a detailed list of names, addresses and pass code names to get a traveler in the door. He picked up the map drawing and continued to review it.

"You know what this is, don't you?" Dominic held the map and directed the question to Thom in his office chair. "This is two more weeks at least. That's what this is. Kirksey and I were planning to bug out of here a few days ago. But we keep on finding an excuse to stay. To get this map up and running will push us back two weeks for sure."

"We'll feed you."

"Damn right you will." The defeated tone was still there, but it was brightening.

"Seriously, I'll lead a team back with some food as soon as we get Erich home. It's the least we can do."

Dominic sat quietly soaking it in. "Maybe I could donate some of the medical supplies to your doctor. Your team could head to his place after you drop the food."

"Sounds like a plan. A good use of manpower and resources."

"Is there anything in particular that is needed beyond antibiotics?"

"I can't think of anything, besides something on a personal note."

"What's that?" Dominic saw that the conversation was taking a turn.

"Something to help a cold turkey detox from Prozac. It has not been a fun ride."

"How long?" Dominic's concern was immediate.

"Since about day one, so almost a month."

"That stuff is rough. And it hangs on. You could still have a while to go. It really messes with your mind. Do you fight it with a Happy Place?"

"It's the only thing that's saved me. I go there a ton."

"I'll bet. How do you sleep?"

"Horrible. I toss and turn all night. I can't turn off my head."

"What you need is sleep. Let your brain reboot. I'm going to give you some sleeping pills and I want you to just zonk out. Take my bed and sleep. You have no responsibilities here. Carl has Erich, and we have the house under control. I want you to sleep for at least twelve hours. If you have some alcohol in that backpack, maybe a shot with the pills will help knock you out to slumberland."

"I really appreciate your help with this; the comedown has been difficult with all this stuff going on. Yeah, I think we have some booze left in the backpack."

"I have a pretty good idea of what you are going through. Speaking of your backpack, Carl doesn't know what's in it, does he?"

"No. I have not shared that with him, and I won't. The only one I'll tell is my wife. It will be safe with her."

Dominic sat back and reflected on the amount of concern he had for that bottle of pills. Just mentioning the backpack forced him to talk about them. Maybe a little more talk would be good. "That eight months of my life. I'd like to have that back."

"Eight months, huh?" If Dominic wanted to share, Thom was compassionate enough to help him do it. Again, it was the least he could do.

"Eight months. I was lucky really, to only be hooked that long. They say that everyone must hit bottom before they get out, but each person has their own bottom. Mine is higher than most I figure. I didn't have to find myself crawling in a ditch before my eyes were opened. But really, I just started listening to the voice in my head that spoke of warnings. It told me where the road was leading and I listened to it, even though the other voice was much louder. The other voice was there, boy was it there. And I fell victim to it a few times before I learned to focus on the better voice. The whispering voice, I called it. It showed me where I was going, and how it was going to end. So I listened. And I believed. That's all I had to do, listen and believe."

"The detox I'm going through is nothing to Opioids, though. I've heard its hell."

"Oh, yeah. It's all about the highs and lows of the roller coaster. It brings a beautiful high, an amazing high, and so of course it will be coupled with an amazing low. That's a low I do not want to repeat, ever. It keeps me in check — to not chase the high again, because of the low."

251

"Did you go to a clinic? I've heard it takes medical care to get through it, and certain drugs to help."

"I made my own clinic. And I used unconventional drugs."

"This sounds interesting."

"Weed. I used weed to get through the detox." Thom sat back with an odd smile to let the story continue. "I was stoned morning, noon and night. And coming off that stuff was still hell. The weed helped to give me an appetite and take the edge off the pain. It was still there, though. Still there. I had a couple friends helping with the process and monitoring the effects. We did it at my farm in Steubenville. I guess that's another reason I'm delaying my bug-out. I don't have very many happy thoughts about that place right now. I'm not in a big hurry to see it again."

The odd smile continued on Thom's face as he looked at the ceiling. There was no response for what he just heard. He just smiled. That's when he noticed the collection on top of the kitchen cabinets that framed the room. Not only did Dominic have the figurine of Daimon Hellstrom on top of the cabinets, but he also had dozens more superheroes.

"How many of those doggone things do you have?" Thom broke the awkward silence.

"A bunch. Friends and family started picking them up for me when they found them. It made birthday buying easy, I guess. But I lost a couple to my dog a few months ago. He chewed them up pretty good. That's why they're up high now. They were a couple of my favorites too. Power Man and Daredevil."

"You're not going to believe this." Thom reached into his coat pocket and produced David's Daredevil figurine.

"Holy Smokes!"

"I was trying to get us off the subject of detox, but there you go again…"

****

Thom, Carl, and Erich stood at the doorway getting geared up to leave. Thom had slept like a rock and felt like a new man. Erich's recovery gave him the confidence to travel, and Carl was just happy to see all the smiling faces. The backpacks had been emptied of food, but were now loaded with MREs. A pre-payment for the food expected to come in a couple days.

"I can't believe you are making me keep your son's toy," Dominic said to Thom. "I've got an extra Captain America. Take it to him in trade. And how are you guys on basic first-aid stuff?"

"We are okay on the basic gauze and stuff, although changing Erich's bandages all the time has put a dent in it."

"Here's an army surplus kit. I've got several; it should cover what he needs."

"Dominic, this is great. You have helped us so much."

"Just get back here with some food," he said with a smile and a hug.

The goodbyes were quick but heartfelt. The bond built over the two days had strength. Silence was the protocol for the walk home. The open excuse was to conserve energy, but each man's mind was far away. Carl was thanking the Lord that his son was walking beside him, and Erich felt like Evil Knievel after a successful jump. Thom's mind had so many thoughts that he felt like a butterfly in a field of Daffodils. He would land on one subject just long enough to spot another one and take flight.

Galena finally appeared on the horizon, and the travel had no issues. The bridge upstream was fine; the roads were slick but manageable. Toni ran out and greeted the men in the street before they reached the house. The homecoming was wonderful, but Thom was quick to point out that he would be leaving the next day with supplies for his new friends.

Before getting inside, Toni also dropped the bomb that Candice had finally succumbed to cancer. Her son Philip was taking it hard, and Jeffery was putting on a good front, but he was a wreck inside. In his case, the emergency was a godsend. It gave him something else to focus on and more people to care for. The caregiver role was so ingrained in him, he would have been lost with it suddenly taken away. The intensity of the story caused Thom to embrace his wife as the tears began to swell. The couple sat on the front porch steps, still entwined with each other, and let their emotions flow. The happiness of being home and Erich's recovery, mixed with this sad news made climbing the stairs too much to bear.

****

The waves lapped up on the boat while Thom and Randal were anchored at the deserted mangrove island.

"It must have been tough to go through all those emotional ups and downs," Randal tried to console.

"It was tough, yes it was. I was so tired of the roller coaster. I just wanted to make it stop. To be able to just turn it all off and just watch old movies for a couple days would have meant the world to me. But everything just kept coming. It wouldn't stop, and it just continued to get worse," Thom said, looking up at the warm, blue sky. It was so warm, so very warm.

"It must have been nice to finally get home though, and see your family," Randal continued.

"Yes, it was. David was waiting at the door with my scribbled-on protein bar wrapper. Toni told me that he never doubted my safe return. When I told him that I gave away his superhero, it didn't bother him at all. He said that he expected me to lose it anyway. But he was pretty happy with the Captain America. I guess it was a collector's edition with more detail and features. He was happy. What a kid."

"I look forward to meeting him. Will he and your wife be meeting us for the trip to Key West? We have most of our provisions and we're ready to go anytime."

"Maybe, we are still working that out, it will be a last-minute decision," Thom replied.

Randal gave a little sideways look as he got up from the chair; he wasn't very satisfied with the answer. "I'll get the rest together tomorrow, and we can push off any time after that. Come on, let's pull the anchor and get back to port. I've got a big day tomorrow."

"Okay, but let me enjoy this sky just a little bit more," Thom said, not wanting to let go of the moment.

Chapter 18: Wolf Pack.

"Thom, the real question is how can so many things go wrong in this one event?" JP had his conspiracy theory hat on. It helped him pass the time of walking to Dominic's. They hadn't even left the city limits of Galena yet and he had climbed on his soapbox already.

"I'm really afraid of getting you and Dominic in the same room together," Thom joked along, adjusting his backpack full of canned goods. "And you too, Brad. I didn't realize you were an Alex Jones fan."

"Now really, listen to me." JP would not be derailed. He began counting off things on his fingers in front of the three of them. "The cyber-attack, the storm and the nuclear power plant attack, the inauguration, then there's the cabinet in Philadelphia. Either someone has been pulling puppet strings through all this, or we've had a load of random events turning out really badly."

"If somebody pulled the puppet strings on that bridge back there, I'd like to un-pull them," Thom chimed in. "Our trip would be a lot shorter if the bridge was still there."

"He's got a point, Thom," Brad jumped into the fray. "And we don't even know what's going on with the stock market or the financial markets. That kind of stuff isn't even mentioned on the radio."

"I'd hate to see what my 401k looks like now," Thom shook his head.

"The stock market has taken a dive, I'm sure," JP continued on his soapbox in the new direction. "But I think it will only be temporary. There is no way the economy is going to tank and our U.S. dollars become worthless. I can't see it. The Fed is owed thirty or whatever trillion right now, and if we know one thing for sure, they are going to collect. They will not allow us to hit bottom so hard that we are plowing our fields with a mule again. One of those puppet strings is being pulled by them, I'd *bank* on it."

"That's funny JP, I'd bank on it too." Brad then jumped in with some insight that surprised the other two. "It's funny how back in the

Middle Ages, and Victorian times, and even Colonial times, the common folk always knew who to blame. They knew who was pulling the strings. It was that guy over there, in the castle, who likes to wear metal hats with jewels on them. The Royalty, they liked to be called. When it came time to say enough is enough, you always knew who to put in the guillotine. In current times, you don't. They have learned from the mistakes of those before them. The men really pulling the strings are hidden behind corporations and shell companies and bank chairmen. I think if we really knew whose castle to storm, the castle wouldn't be standing long."

Thom opened his mouth to agree, but out of the corner of his eye he saw them. Three of them. Or was it four?

JP spotted them also and froze. Two of them carried long guns; one appeared to be an assault rifle. The backpacks of food suddenly felt very heavy, and the disadvantages of their situation came crushing down upon them. The men were caught flatfooted in the middle of the street. The recent calmness had lulled them into being less aware of their surroundings, the first mistake of the day — the first mistake of many.

Thom glanced to JP for guidance and when he turned back to the walkers, they were gone. Fear and shock hit immediately. They had taken to the backyards to get the first jump. The shock was that they made the decision to advance so quickly. Thom's crew appeared to be walkers themselves with limited firepower; only JP carried a rifle, the 30/30 from the abandoned house. They appeared to be easy prey out in the open, a tempting quarry for a pack of wolves with superior firepower.

"Let's move!" JP said grabbing Brad's coat sleeve because he was standing there stunned. The best plan was to get back to the protection of the house, and there was no time to waste. The backpacks were slowing them down, but cutting them loose wasn't even considered. It probably would've slowed them down too much to try. JP led the way, being the most athletic of the group, with Thom giving directions

257

from the middle of the trio. Cutting between some houses for the shortest route bought them some time, but it wasn't enough. The pack of wolves had a head start and was closing. It became apparent that Thom's house was not the answer. It was too far.

"Allen Lansbury's!" Thom called out. "They are armed. It will be a good place to make a stand!"

A couple more backyards were cut through and then the house came into view. A white two story with a detached garage, a couple large trees and a neighbor's shed at the property line closest to them. Not much as far as cover, but the extra firepower in the house might make the wolves give up and go away.

"Allen!" Thom called out as they ran. "Linda! We got company!"

The window in the top gable slid down with more of a bang than probably intended. "Got you Thom!" Linda's shrill voice came from the window. A rifle immediately emerged, sliding across the window frame to take aim at the company following them.

Three shots rang out from the gable, but the quick aim did not wound any of the wolves. The misses were close enough, however, to force them to cover. She continued to fire upon on the two in her sight, and kept them pinned down.

"I'll take the shed!" Thom staked his claim of cover options. The shed was the closest cover and Thom wanted a spot that he could turn and shoot. He didn't realize that Brad wanted it just because he was flat-out winded.

"Me too," was all he could get out, trying to catch his breath. "Till I find a better spot."

The wolves had closed much of the distance during the chase. The men knew that attempting to scamper the entire distance to the security of the house was too risky. They needed to take cover immediately. JP had sprinted to a good lead and reached a tree deep in the yard with a branch to rest the 30/30 on. Just as Thom and Brad

258

reached the shed, they heard the 30/30 pop and a scream sounded behind them. The wolves were focused on taking cover from Linda's attack from the high window. JP's angle on the ground opened a shot and he took it. A first-floor window also opened, and Allen pushed a rifle through the opening. He took a few shots to keep the wolves nervous, but Linda had effectively pinned them from the house's angle.

As soon as Thom reached the shed, he dropped to a knee and found a target to engage. The target found cover, but the rounds helped Brad, who was bringing up the rear, to also make the shed. The wolves began to scatter when one went down, but they were not going away.

Two shots rang out from the gable window of the house that brought another wolf down. With two verified baddies out, would the rest give up and leave? In the normal world, maybe that would happen. With every ticking second and every gunshot clap, Thom was reminded that this was no longer the normal world.

The more Thom thought about his situation and location, the more he didn't like it. The wolf pack still considered them prey. They were going nowhere, and that fact caused Thom and Brad to look at their location more closely.

The shed did not afford complete protection. It was at an angle to the bad guys and getting around the flank would not be difficult. The ideal plan was just to dig in and let JP and Linda pick them off one by one from their sniper locations. Not many things were going according to plan that day, though. Brad and Thom removed their backpacks and caught their breath while watching for anyone approaching. The wolves were not firing upon the shed much, and a couple more rifle shots from the house window gave comfort.

A large ash tree in the yard was a tempting second firing position, and Brad announced that he was going to run for it. It was a split-second decision, and he seemed confident that he could get there. The bad guys were probably not set up to exchange fire, and if he was going to go, it needed to be now. Thom didn't stop him, but while he unloaded

259

the 9mm giving covering fire, he wished he could call him back. A feeling of dread swept Thom at the first step, even though Brad got all the way to the edge of the tree before they dropped him.

Thom recognized the AR-15 sound when the first round was shot. The cover fire hit nothing; the 9mm pistol did not have the range to accurately reach the baddie 150 feet away. He looked over at Brad while loading one of his two extra magazines. Blood was coming out of his mouth, along with a horrible gurgling sound.

Thom stood behind the shed, trying to calm his breathing, but not having much success after what he saw under the Ash tree. The AR-15 knew where he was, and the flimsy aluminum shed was not feeling like good protection anymore. His own loud breaths were all that he could hear, coming in and out as he franticly looked for the next target. He knew he wouldn't be able to aim and actually hit anything with his breathing out of control. This knowledge made things worse. He began to hyperventilate. In Thom's emotional collapse, he did not notice the AR-15 moving to his left for a clear shot at him. He was unaware of the weapon being raised and focused. Then the welcome sound of JP's 30/30 was heard again. Thom turned to see the assailant as he spun and fell. The close call had the effect of a jolting scare on a person with hiccups; the breathing began to slow. It also helped that the count was now at three bad guys down. It was three, right?

Thom turned his attention to Brad, but in his peripheral vision, there was movement to the right. This was the worst spot in the world for him, and he knew it. It was out of the line of sight for both JP and Linda, to the side of the house. If someone was over there, it would be up to Thom. No help would be coming. He swung his weapon to see the man raising his rifle. The fastest would win, and the adrenalin was pumping so hard Thom thought his eyes would explode.

The rifleman was first, by a fraction of a second, and right on the mark. Thom got one good shot off as he was slammed in the chest so hard he flew. Thom fired a couple more desperation shots while he fell, but it was senseless to think they would find their target.

Miraculously his first good shot did connect and bring him down, however the baddie managed to squeeze a second shot before falling. His second shot caught Thom in the left shin while he was still lifted off the ground from the first one. The pain felt from the two hits was immense. He hit the ground flat on his back and looked down at the leg, seeing red soaking into the snow beneath him. He pulled his scarf and tried to tie a tourniquet around the leg and JP got there in time to finish the job.

"You're going to be okay," JP assured him. "Allen, go get Toni. Tell her to bring the truck, now!"

Thom could hear more voices around him, but he couldn't catch his breath to speak. The pain in his chest was overwhelming, and it felt like it was caving in. He looked up at the Ash tree branches above; they were black against the white of the clouds. The black branches began to expand, becoming thicker, and they bled into each other until there was no light left.

Chapter 19: Doctor Who.

The voices around Thom began to register again as he was being carried. He couldn't understand what they were saying — the fog of his mind was too deep. The pain in his chest became sharper as time passed, and the pain cleared the fog. Suddenly, the words being spoken around him made sense and somehow, he managed to form words.

"How do we get to Dr. Cliff now with the bridge out?" JP said, while putting the truck in gear.

"He's a butcher!" Thom exclaimed from the backseat. "All he's ever done is tonsils. Ever!"

"Calm down, honey." Toni had his head on her lap, along with a pillow. Only she would think of having a pillow in the truck for him. JP was driving, and Erich was in the passenger seat. The leg was wrapped tight, and the pain in his chest was blinding. Thom needed to talk, to drown out the pain, to take his mind off it. He needed to hear his own voice, to remind himself that he was still alive.

"I know why Erich is going with us too." He pointed a finger to the front of the bus. "Because tonsil man missed one, I heard you talking about it. It's been really bugging you, right?" Erich gave no response … it would be too easy. He absently raised a hand to his chest, to see how much it hurt at the moment.

"Toni, please. While I was there, he told me that he got his medical degree in a tiny school in Des Moines, Iowa. In the middle of nowhere! Nobody goes to Des Moines for a medical degree! And it's a limited practice degree. All he's allowed to do is tonsils. He's not trained on anything else, and my tonsils are fine! I think I had them out when I was twelve! Can anyone say hospital?"

Toni looked up to the front seat at JP. The two of them exchanged a knowing look of concern. Thom had no idea that he was creating some doubt in their general plan. He was just freaking out at the sight of his own blood, and so much of it.

262

"Calm down, honey. Here, take these two Percocets. Wash them down with this Tequila." The mixture sounded intriguing, reminiscent of some friends in college. The subject change and the taste of Tequila brought a smile to his face immediately.

"You're the best nurse I ever had... Besides Susie Norman in the second grade. She was my best nurse ever," he said after the first pill.

"Susie Norman in the second grade huh? I beat out all the rest you've played doctor with?" Thom nodded with a smile after the pills were down and hit the Tequila an extra time. "I can live with that," she smiled as she reached down to check the tourniquet on his leg. Unknowingly, her breast brushed his nose as she attended to the injury.

"Susie never did that..."

****

"I'm done talking about this stuff, Randal, is the boat ready to go?" Thom abruptly said to him.

"Wait a minute, you can't just stop there. You were wearing the vest, right?" he said, waving his arms about.

"Yeah, yeah, I was wearing the vest. I'll show you the scars later. Let's push off, Toni and David will meet us in Key West," Thom said hurriedly, as he stepped off the boat onto the dock.

"Well, let me look at the weather one more time, my reception isn't as good out on the water," Randal pleaded.

"No, no, no, let's go. I'm untying right now," Thom said while unhooking the ground line internet connection to the boat and walking to the tie-offs. Neither of them noticed on the TV screen the weather had shown a dark red blob in the middle before it went black.

The trip started out great. The water was very calm, and they even had to motor for a while even though the sound bothered them both. Thom looked up to the blue sky often and took in the fantastic views. It was

263

even better when there was no land in sight in all directions. He truly felt free and felt like he was floating in the air. He stood out on the nose of the boat, with arms outstretched, feeling the wind. He could almost hear Toni talking to him in his head, saying that everything was going to be okay. The freedom was wonderful.

Then the red blob came. They were midway to Key West, near Marathon. They saw it directly in front and set to work. Randal's first command was to bring down the sails. With the wind kicking up, all they managed was the jib sail, before realizing it was too late. The main sail would be uncontrollable coming down in this wind. They had to grind it out with the main sail up. Thom tied off the boom and asked for further instructions. Paul tried to steer out and around the storm but ended up driving into the heart of it.

Ten-foot waves were crashing, and Thom reached into the storage bin for life jackets. One was tossed to Randal, and he casually put it on, only snapping the bottom snap. He waved Thom off when he complained, saying this is a catamaran. They don't sink.

He kept a good line with the waves, trying to hit them head on. After a wave was crested, the crashing motion into the valley was overwhelming. Thom kept on looking for things to do that would help. It seemed that holding on was all he could do. The main sail was thrashing about in the wind, making insane noises that competed with all the other insane noises. The sail caught Randal's attention, and he told Thom to take the wheel.

Randal sat up at the edge of the Bimini, and tried to see what the problem with the main sail and the bottom cross member was. The cross member is called the boom. It's called a boom for a reason, and people needed to respect that. Randal was sitting next to the boom when Thom realized his tie-off was loose and slipping. He reached and grabbed hold, but was too late. The boom violently swung about one foot before he gripped it, and that was enough to send Randal flailing. He fell off the cockpit roof, landing on the handrail at about his waistline. Thom reached for his foot; to keep him from flipping over the side, but again was a half second too late.

He grabbed the Throw Ring out of the locker and clipped the tether rope end to the eyelet on the boat. Searching over the side in the ten-foot swells and darkness of rain, Thom frantically called his name. He cut the engines to make sure the boat stayed in his area, although he risked the safety of the vessel in doing so. Thom kept on calling his name, desperately searching the churning water off the side.

"Randal! Randal!" he continued to call. Fear welled up inside that all was lost, and it was all his fault.

The steering wheel was not being tended, and the boat was turning broadside to the waves, which according to the seamanship manual, makes for unsafe conditions. Thom hung on tightly with both hands, the preserver donut on one arm pushed up to the shoulder. He called and he screamed, and he prayed. He even heard Toni's voice in his head saying that everything would be okay.

"It will *not* be okay!" Thom responded to the voice in his head. "Randal! Randal!"

Suddenly, when it seemed that all hope was lost, Thom spotted Randal's life jacket. Wiping the rain from his face, Thom instinctively dove in after him. He swam to the spot, grabbed the white reflective material, and pulled. It lifted far too easily. It was empty. Randal was not in the jacket, and he would not survive in these swells. Thom called into the air until his lungs started to fill with saltwater. Then he began to weep uncontrollably and ask for forgiveness. It was all he could do.

He looked up to see the boat being destroyed by the broadside crashing waves. The sail was catching the full brunt of the wind, and something had to give. Either the sail would rip, or if it held, it could break the mast or roll the boat over. From the darkness at the water level view, Thom saw the mast give way, and a lightning strike in the

265

distance. The mast and sail came crashing down on the cockpit as he watched. The lights in the cockpit flickered then went out for good.

His world was being destroyed before his eyes, while clutching a beat-up live preserver. He reached up for the zipper of his own life vest and considered pulling it down. What's the use, he said to himself. What's left?

He floated in the crashing waves for some time contemplating his fate, still tethered to the boat. He envisioned the preserver donut's rope breaking free from the boat, putting him adrift in the storm. If it happens, it happens, he said to himself, tired of the battle. The worst of worst possibilities, it really didn't matter anymore.

Thom then heard his wife's voice again, saying something he couldn't understand, in a calming tone that helped him to regain focus. He reluctantly began pulling himself in, using the donut's rope. The boat was heaving so violently, he had to rest and regain strength before attempting to climb on board. When the time was right, he climbed the steps in one swift motion, before the next wave hit.

On deck, the debris of broken fiberglass and plastic was everywhere. Thom released the inflatable dingy, hanging on the back of the catamaran, and tethered it to the destroyed boat. There was no safe place on board, from the unpredictable broken mast. Not wasting any time, he jumped into the dingy and floated about ten feet behind. Thom felt a warmth come over his body as he lay there. "It's going to be okay" rang in his head, lying on the warm boat floor. He closed his eyes to everything, knowing he would sleep for a very long time.

****

When Thom awoke, he was in a hospital room. He knew it was a hospital room; they all look the same when you are looking at the ceiling — the curtain runners that go around the bed, the emergency lights, the eyelets in the ceiling over the bed, the drab, plain, white paint. The room was shadowy and dark even though it was daytime, but lying across his chest was Toni. She was keeping him warm in the chilly room, across his uninjured side. Thom awoke several times, feeling her there and feeling comforted, then going back to drug induced sleep.

When he did fully awake, he was completely calm, thanks to her. He tried to take in the surroundings. His vision was very foggy, but as it cleared, he saw a window. Outside the window he saw a palm tree. It looked like a glistening, shiny palm tree anyway, as he continued to focus. Details slowly became clearer as the palm tree transformed into an icicle hanging outside. Then another icicle, and another and another. Thom realized that he had dreamt of palm trees and woke to icicles. It wouldn't be his only disappointment of the day.

He looked around the room to see two other beds, one beside his so close that he could reach out and touch the other bedrail. The other bed was a hand-carried gurney propped up somehow to create a makeshift bed, stretched crossways at the foot of his own bed. In the darkness of the room, it appeared to contain Erich, but he couldn't see enough features of his skin to be certain. The room was obviously a single bedroom, crammed with three beds and hardly enough room to get between them.

"This is crazy," he quietly said to himself.

"Yes it is," Toni said, rising to be able to face him. She sat on the bed, and leaned across Thom, so that all he could see was her. She lightly kissed his lips, hugging him tightly.

"I'm on drugs, aren't I?" Thom said with the slurriness and sincerity of Otis checking himself into the Mayberry jail on a Friday night.

"Yes, you are, dear. It's nice to see you, honey," she said evenly. There was no charity in her voice; she meant every word she said. It was pure thankfulness and gratitude to see Thom alive. And he managed to capture that gratitude in those few syllables.

"Where am I?" he asked.

267

"St. Augustus. I gave in to your pleadings. It turned out to the best choice." Thom was painfully aware of her years-old evaluation of this hospital not being the best choice. In normal times, she would drive out of her way to another hospital in the case of an emergency, even though it was the closest, but not this time. Her disdain still showed in her tone even now … maybe especially now.

"How long have I been here?"

"It's been three days. You had a really rough spell there. We thought we were going to lose you for a bit," she said painfully, as she brought the memory to the surface with her words.

JP came in the room then, and immediately brightened to see Thom awake. He sat on the other side, mouthing the words 'Tell him yet?' to Toni when Thom wasn't looking. Toni shook her head in reply and her face saddened with the thought of doing so. Their communication blew right past Thom in his weary state.

"Great to see you in the land of the living," JP said with a big smile.

"The house! Who's guarding the house?" Thom realized loudly. "You've been here for three days, and the house…"

Toni placed her finger over his lips to quiet him down. "It's fine, Carl is in charge, the house is covered, I'm sure. Besides, it was good that JP was with us; it was a battle just to get in the door here." A knowing look of appreciation was given to JP with her statement.

"You wouldn't believe what it's like in the parking lot here; it's like Mad Max out there!" JP added. "And the best part was when the doctor told us that he couldn't do anything for us. He said he had no supplies, and I pulled out Dominic's stuff. His eyes went big as saucers!"

"He was finally able to help someone," Toni broke in. "We went into surgery right away."

"Surgery? Was I that bad? I had the vest on," Thom protested through the grogginess. "Why didn't you just take me to Dr. Cliff?"

"He couldn't have done anything for you," she replied. "And we felt it was the only way to save your leg."

"Leg?" Then he remembered. All the events of the shootout came flooding in: the shots, the killing, the mayhem, the trees above fading to black.

"Brad… Is he dead?" he asked the question, but already knew the answer.

"Yes, Thom. He was gone before we even left. There was nothing we could do." Tears were beginning to well in Toni's eyes.

"I should have stopped him when he ran for that tree. I knew as soon as he left the shed that it was the wrong move. I should have stopped him." Thom stared at a curtain ring hanging from the ceiling, distantly, just staring. He counted that it was the fourth from the left. He couldn't break away from it.

"Thom, I need to tell you something." Toni's eyes continued to well as she worked to get his full attention. "They did everything they could." A tear rolled out of each eye and fell to the blanket as reality began to crash down around him. "But the rifle shot shattered the bone. There wasn't anything left of it. They did all they could."

Thom pushed her aside as she spoke. He realized now why she had leaned across his body when she sat up. She was blocking the view of the bottom of the bed. Looking down at his legs, there was only one foot-lump sticking up in the blanket. He let go a gasp in astonishment at the sight. The words "one lump" echoed in his skull, bouncing around with such volume, that it made him wonder if he said them out loud.

"The doctor said that even with a full surgical operation, putting your leg together with pins and screws would have been almost impossible. There was so much bone missing, and you had lost so much blood," she tried to explain, but Thom was still in shock. He just stared at the bottom of the bed, disbelieving. *One lump, one lump.*

269

"Did you give blood for me?" he finally asked her, after a long silence. She is O-negative, the generic donor type. It had been an issue between the two of them for a few years that she felt the obligation to donate blood every three or four months because of its universal necessity. Then she would deal with the tiredness that followed for a day or two, and Thom would deal with her tiredness also. He finally came to accept her calling, it was a battle that couldn't be won and hadn't seen a real benefit until now.

"Of course I did. I gave till it hurt," she said, trying to smile.

"It's about time," he said sarcastically but tried to make up for it with a wink that didn't work.

There was an eerie silence as everything sank in. Then he finally said, "I need to see."

Toni reluctantly got up and pulled back the covers. Thom leaned forward, feeling some pain in his chest as he did so. The first shot must have bruised a couple of ribs; his left hand rose and felt the spot it hit. He looked down, and just below the knee there were bandages, then nothing. The image made him stop and shutter. It was his turn to weep. He held Toni tight but wouldn't allow himself to do it for long. He was too tired, and angry, and confused, and something else but he couldn't put his drug-induced finger on it. But JP knew.

"Are you hungry?" JP whispered when his head lifted from Toni's shoulder and his wet eyes looked around the room.

When Thom nodded, JP got up, and walked to the door of the room, and wandered out into the hallway for a minute. After making his rounds, he came back in and silently pointed to Toni. Both got to work, Toni retrieving the backpack from its hiding place in the corner, JP closing the door and placing a rolled-up towel to seal the bottom crack. Toni produced five cans from the backpack and began opening them on the bedside table. By the time the third can opened, Thom's neighbor in the next bed began to awaken. He looked over, concerned about what might happen next.

"Thom, I'd like you to meet Bill Paxton. He is one of the reasons you are still breathing." JP stood between the beds, making the introductions. "Bill is with the National Guard, and he put himself in harm's way to get you in the door."

"Just doing my job," Bill smiled and extended his left hand. Bill looked to be in his thirties, a mixture of Hispanic and black, and a smile that wouldn't quit. His right arm was in a sling, and his right shoulder was also bandaged. He looked to be in good health otherwise, as Thom shamelessly looked to see if he still had both legs.

"Bill came out of the emergency room to protect us so we could get you out of the truck. The crazies in the parking lot didn't do anything until they saw… that." JP was pointing at the backpack of food and supplies that Toni was working with. "They knew we had something then. It was so full that they probably could see the circles of the can tops in the fabric. That's when the wheels came off."

"We only had two guards out there," Bill continued the story for him. "It wasn't enough, but we used the truck for cover, and I was the only one hit."

"My truck, is it okay?" Thom said immediately. Then he closed his eyes, realizing the answer didn't really matter. It was just a truck, just a mode of transportation, a thing. "Will it get us home?"

"Well…" JP answered. "The truck bed resembles Swiss cheese, but the engine still runs. No tires were punctured either which is a miracle. It might still get us home."

Thom nodded to JP and looked back to the guardsman, pointing a thumb at his shoulder. "How bad is it?"

"Not bad at all, really," he replied. "I'm right-handed, so I'm no good at my post anymore. I'm only here because your wife pulled some strings to get us in the same room. I could probably stay in our barracks downstairs, but the food is better up here." His eyes were trained on the cans being opened across the room.

271

"MREs?" Thom said to him, getting a nodding response. "Well, I'd say that's the second time I've gotten a good shake because of the bad taste of those rations."

"Well, they are really not that bad," the National Guardsman backpedaled a little, with a wave of his good arm. "Let's just say that my stomach needs a change of pace once in a while to stay happy."

Erich sat up in his cot and held his hand to his chest from the movement. A weak greeting was sent Thom's way, and he began to wonder whose recovery was going better between the two. JP noticed the concern but decided to let the discussion wait until after the food.

Toni then dealt out the cans, handing Thom a minestrone soup. The cold soup straight from the can should have been nasty, but by all accounts, it was not. He found himself scraping the bottom for the last and turning up the can to his mouth.

"Sorry for the conditions," Toni explained while they ate. "We dare not heat anything. The people in the hallway have not eaten for days. They would be able to smell the food from quite a distance, even cold. Nobody messes with us, but if they knew for sure we had food in here and how much we would be dealing with a mob. We must protect ourselves to survive," she said sadly.

"Thank you for the food, ma'am." Bill took the opportunity to show appreciation.

"How much do we have?" Thom tentatively asked.

"Another day or so. We have eight cans left, and you need to eat more, to regain your strength. All they give the patients here is beef bouillon and sometimes more when they have it," she replied. "Would you like to have another one?"

"No, maybe later, let's see how this settles."

Everyone was done with their cans quickly, and Toni collected them quietly into a small trash bag. In the dark and shadowy room, she walked to the window and pulled it open the few inches that it allowed. She dropped the cans and closed the window in a quick motion, then returned to the bed. Thom watched with curiosity at the routine they had gotten themselves into in the past few days. They lived in constant fear, and it was obvious: They were not in Galena anymore.

"I managed to find some crutches for you Thom if you want some exercise," JP awkwardly changed the subject.

The reality of his situation came crashing upon him again, but he held strong. The fear and concern of the room meant much more than his missing leg. His wife was in danger, and he needed to pull it together. Time to man-up. "It's been a while since I've been on crutches, probably fifteen years since I sprained an ankle. I might need some practice."

Both JP and Toni's faces brightened with the interest in moving around, but Toni pointed to the chain hanging from the ceiling. JP got the message and produced a hand-pull from under the bed. It was an exercise therapy item that he found in the room's cupboard. He attached it to the chain, motioning for Thom to do some pull-ups with it. It was a good exercise for his arms, and they must have needed it. Thom fell asleep quickly after his twenty-minute workout, belly full, and blood flowing again.

He woke up a few hours later, just before dusk. Toni had fallen asleep across his chest, and it gave Thom a smile when he woke. He squeezed her close. He felt good, and his mind was clearer than before.

"It's been a while since the last Percocet dose," Toni explained. "You'll be feeling pain again soon. If you want to go for a stroll, now would be the time."

Thom agreed and JP rose from the chair that had been his bed for the last few days. Thom saw the motion of the small Glock going into his waistband as he got ready and checked the hall.

The crutches came out from under the bed, and Toni held them ready for Thom. Erich noticed the commotion and sat up in his cot to watch Thom's first steps. Thom put on his strong face and swung his legs over the side of the bed. The throbbing was there, but it was manageable so far. In a swift motion, he stood from the bed and mounted the crutches beneath him. Toni steadied his shoulder, but it wasn't needed.

"If you guys are getting some exercise, I'd like to join you," Erich announced from the cot. "I need to get out of this bed."

JP helped Erich stand while still keeping an eye on Thom's movements in the back corner of the room. Erich had been quietly listening to Thom's conversations, not wanting to interrupt, and not having the strength to do so anyway. But one subject hadn't been touched upon and he felt the need to bring it up. He just didn't realize it would spin Thom's head off his shoulders.

"Thom, I really gotta know one thing though… Who's Randal?" he asked with all the confidence of a student speaking at the front of the classroom.

"Randal?" Thom put the question back. The crutches started to become wobbly.

"Yes, Randal," JP repeated. "I bet half the people on this floor of the hospital would like to know who Randal is. You called his name for hours from that bed."

Thom could feel holes being burnt into his face by Toni's intense stare. "Do we know a Randal? I don't recall one." Her tone was soft and understanding. Thom was about to change that. He dared not look her in the eye. He was not strong enough for that yet. He crutched a few steps to Erich, the person who first asked the question.

"Randal is a friend that I go sailing with in my mind," Thom quietly said to Erich. Erich was the safest; Thom kept his eyes trained on him. There was confusion on Erich's face as he continued. "I would take a break from the stress of having your lives in my hands by imagining

274

myself sailing with Randal. I created my own little world of life after… this, buying a boat and sailing on the ocean. It kept me from going crazy. Maybe."

"It's making me crazy, I'll tell you that," Toni spoke behind him, noticeably irritated. The soft and understanding tone had left the building. "You've been daydreaming about sailing while all this…"

"Yes, while all this. And I've kept everyone alive until now." Thom finally turned to face her and paused. The silence punctuated his point.

"I have reality issues, you know that, Toni. And this detox from antidepressants has been far worse than I've let anyone know. Far worse. Going sailing was better than crawling into a bottle, or into the barrel of a gun, or some of the other options that have gone through my head. It was my medication; my happy place that escaped reality, if just for just a couple of minutes. Now I will have reality with me all the time, that I cannot escape." Thom turned and crutched his way to the door.

The smell of body odor, vomit, and urine hit Thom like a wave at the doorway. It stopped him in his tracks. JP stepped around him to lead the way.

"This is absolutely nuts," Thom said as JP guided them through the hallway of makeshift beds, and people lying on the floor. "So many people here, this can't be good. This can't be healthy. What happened?"

"Injuries from the freeways, from accidents, from frostbite, from shootings. Family members have managed to bring them here themselves, with no ambulances. I mean, the ambulances are here, but nobody can call 911 to tell them where to go. It's crazy; everyone is just showing up here. Only one family member is allowed inside with a patient, that's why so many people are in the parking lot. They have nowhere else to go. Some folks came to the parking lot because they thought it was a safe place to be. Now they are learning that's a lie. There are gangs out there controlling the area and fighting for the resources being brought here. I had to pay for the protection of our truck, so that it will still be there, and still have gas when we want to leave."

"How are all three of you in the hospital then, if only one family member is allowed?"

"Well, we have two patients including Erich, and besides, a person gets special treatment when they show up with their own medical supplies," JP said in a hushed tone and a smile. Thom crutched along, avoiding bodies on the floor, and realized that having a room at all was something to be considered special treatment.

A window at the end of the hallway gave them a view of the parking lot from their fourth-floor location. It was a tent city, with most tents attached to a vehicle in some form or another. Less than half the tents were true tents. The rest were makeshift from blankets or tarps and attached to a vehicle as a lean-to. Fires were burning in trashcans, with people standing around them. Food had to be slim at best, and illness was certainly running rampant. It was eerily reminiscent of the internet photos of Haiti after the earthquake, with the additional twist of snow and bitter cold in this disaster.

"The police do not have control of the situation down there?" Thom asked. He noticed that the sea of people extended from the hospital parking lot, across the street to an office-building parking lot. Every parking area visible from his vantage point was filled with people living in their cars or tents.

"There's no control down there. It's like a medieval battle going on around a castle," JP said in a trancelike voice, the view of the tent city beginning to hypnotize him as well.

Erich stepped forward a little and Thom noticed the reflection of his face in the window superimposed over the tent city. He looked concerned; his brow wrinkled. He looked into the reflection of Thom's eyes in the window. "Do you remember calling to Randal? Did he die?"

276

"I do, Erich. I remember it. I remember everything. And yes, I lost Randal in a storm. It was my fault. It was a horrible feeling, and I am relieved now to find that it didn't really happen."

"But it did happen," he stated back firmly.

"Yeah, I guess it did," Thom said, still locked on Erich's eyes in the window. "Randal died that day. The happy ending I created for myself died that day with him. There will be no happy ending. I must face that reality now. This will not end with us sailing off into the sunset."

Thom's focus moved from Erich's eyes back to the sprawling tent city below. "But we've got to get out of here. Now."

----END: Book One of the Cold Winter Series ----

Check out the next books:

Book 2:   The Cold Winter: Call to Arms

Book 3:   The Cold Winter: Battle on the Ohio River

Please leave a review on Amazon.com!

And check out 'Author Chris Underwood' on Facebook

###

Made in the USA
Monee, IL
24 September 2024

66512052R00163